The Final Girls Club

The Final Girls Club

To every Final Girl fighting her own battle.

Prologue

The first thing Lochlyn noticed was how much blood there was. And that it was *everywhere*. On the walls, the bed, the floor. There wasn't an inch of the room that wasn't covered in some amount of it.

The biggest pool appeared to be the spot on the bed, and given the spatter of it across the wall, it seemed the victim had been struck and landed on the sheets from the impact.

Lochlyn couldn't believe what she was looking at. It felt like she was having an out of body experience. This wasn't how this weekend was supposed to go. It was only a game. No one was *actually* supposed to get murdered.

There wasn't supposed to be a legit murderer on the loose.

"What did you do?"

Spinning on her heels, a gasp left her lips at the sudden appearance of a new arrival at the doorway she'd left open. Raising her hands, an item in her grip fell and clattered against the wooden floor.

"It wasn't me!" She exclaimed, though her bloody hands would suggest otherwise. "I didn't do this."

Chapter 1

(Three weeks earlier)

Everyone has two masks they wear. The one they show the world, and the one they only show the people they trust the most. But what if there was a third option? What if you *could* be someone else? Even only for a few hours.

Lochlyn Jones pondered that very question as her mouse curser hovered over the 'Accept Invitation' button on her computer.

Collapsing against the back of her chair, a heavy sigh of frustration escaped her lips. The puff of air moved a lock of purple hair that had fallen onto her face. She'd been staring at the screen for a good forty-five minutes and her decision was no sooner to being decided than it was when she stumbled across it.

For the past six months, Lochlyn had been involved in a role-playing, murder mystery club online. It was a fun way to escape the struggles of her life ever since leaving high school. It was safe to say her mother hadn't taken the news well when Lochlyn told her she wasn't going to college.

Her dad's reaction? Well, he'd have to be involved in her life to have one, and he hadn't been since the accident.

The online group consisted of nine players including her. There were only two rules really enforced. They only conversed as their characters, meaning no real names were used, and none of them were allowed to contact anyone else in the real world. It would break the glass and expose reality.

The way the game worked was they would play out scenarios similar to *Clue*. The game of cat and mouse would then ensue as they tried to uncover the murderer. Locklyn's character was Ivorie Jackson, the smart, beautiful, confident, witty, red-haired heiress. In other words, she was everything Lochlyn Jones wasn't.

Lochlyn tugged on a short lavender lock of hair with a sad smile. She definitely wasn't who she pretended to be within this group, but she knew that went for the other players as well. It was the point of the game, after all. It helped ease her nerves. Not much, but enough.

You are cordially invited to join Miss Featherton and company for a weekend of mayhem, themed dining, and a game of mystery.

Accept or decline.

Lochlyn's eyes studied the invitation once again. Though, she'd read it so many times now that she might have memorized it at this point. This was new territory. Their game had never bled over to reality before.

One of the other players, Kitty Featherton, wanted to bring their game to the next level. She suggested their group head to the mountains for a weekend of fun, games and, well, murder.

The usual rules would still apply according to Kitty's following messages. No real names, no real-world talk. Just them and the game. It sounded harmless enough.

Apparently, Kitty's uncle owned a small ski resort up in the White mountains. Since it was still considered the off season in late September, he was letting them use it for their trip for the weekend before maintenance showed up to start getting things ready for opening.

Crossing her arms, Lochlyn went over the pros and cons again. Pros were a weekend in the mountains at a fancy resort. Kitty had mentioned it could snow that far up, even in September. Which meant hot chocolate by the big fireplace, a blanket, and a good book.

A weekend away from her mother voicing her disappointment and making suggestions of colleges who were still accepting late applications was also a major pro.

Cons?

A weekend in the mountains at some resort with eight other *strangers*. They'd be completely isolated and reception was sure to be spotty with the upcoming rainstorm. If anything went wrong, they wouldn't be able to easily call for help. Roads wouldn't be easy to maneuver either since they flooded badly up there.

Twiggy had brought that up in the group chat.

While his game name was stupid, he was unequivocally the genius in their group. And she wasn't sure that it was just his character. He won most of their games because he was that good at catching certain patterns and clues.

They used character art as their profile pictures, but Lochlyn had always imagined Twiggy looked like Spencer Reid from Criminal Minds, social awkwardness and all.

Twiggy had a dry sense of humor and a knack for correcting the others in the game when they made a mistake. He was a know-it-all snob with piercing blue eyes and dark messy hair that she could imagine girls wanting to just run their fingers through.

Not that *she* wanted to be one of those girls.

Clearing her throat, Lochlyn rubbed her neck as she pulled the group chat up again. They were going over semantics since Kitty sent out the invitations. It was a big step meeting in person and people were rightfully skeptical. There were a lot of pieces to consider and details to straighten out before any decisions were made.

Twiggy brought up the flooding issue a few minutes ago. Kitty assured them there would be a small number of staff there to check in on them and help should anything go wrong. Procedures would be in place for any kind of incident. It would be safe, she promised. And with that, Twiggy dropped his concern and he accepted.

Oliver and Olive, the only two in the group who knew each other outside of the game, had already accepted the invitation to join. They were twins that shared a love for murder mysteries.

While Oliver enjoyed the act of playing the game, Olive was in it for the storytelling. When it was her turn, what she presented was always detailed and suspenseful, while her brother's were more heart twisty and thrilling.

Lochlyn had only chatted with either of them a handful of times, but from what little conversation they'd had it was safe to assume that Oliver was a big flirt and Olive was possibly the kindest person on the planet. Which made her the deadliest character in the game because no one would ever suspect her.

A sudden ping noise alerted Lochlyn that someone else had replied. Hovering her cursor over the '*coming*' side, she saw another name that sent a thrilling chill down her spine. Camden Craven was going. He was their group's wildcard. While Oliver was flirty, Camden's character just oozed charm and mystery.

They could never tell which way he would decide to go; whether he was a good guy or the villain. It was alluring, though she'd never admit that to any of them. Especially not Camden.

Lochlyn wanted to crack open his edges and find out the answers to her questions about him. He was probably the one she had interacted with the least. His games were usually more intense, and she never usually got very far in her sleuthing before someone else pieced the plot together.

If she accepted this invitation, it could be her chance to do so.

Lochlyn nearly hit *accept invitation* right there and then.

There was another con to this trip. She'd have to get her mother to agree to let her go. While she might be over 18, freshly graduated from high school, house rules meant her mother could refuse to let her go and she'd be forced to miss out. After the accident a few years ago, life in their house hadn't been the same.

Much to her surprise, there was already a *'can't come'* reply from Nik. With a quick scroll, Lochlyn saw she'd left a message in the chat saying she couldn't get out of work. Either work wasn't an issue for the others, or the weekend was far enough they could still request the time off.

Lochlyn had only had a summer job in town selling ice cream, but that had ended a week prior when the place closed for the winter. Maneuvering around a schedule wouldn't be an issue for her.

Nik was Kitty's right-hand partner. The two of them usually collaborated on their game's storyline. She'd seen a few of the others refer to her as 'Slick Nik' because she always managed to pull a good plot twist out of nowhere.

As much as Lochlyn understood why Nik couldn't join, it still felt like a disappointment. She was going to miss seeing one of her classic plot twists in person.

Soon after Nik's reply another one came in. It was from Pumpkin May. She was a sweet girl who loved everything spooky. October was her birthday month, or at least it was her character's birthday month, and she lived up to her name.

She included something pumpkin or fall related in every one of her games. It wouldn't surprise her if Pumpkin showed up all in a thick black and orange outfit even though it was only September. She was one of those '*I started decorating for Halloween July 5th*' kind of people.

The only other player's response that was unaccounted for, besides her own, was Boomer. Which wasn't unexpected. He would wait to reply until after everyone else had. He was always the last one to cast his vote. He just wanted to keep them all in suspense. It meant he wasn't going to answer until she did. Which meant Lochlyn needed to talk to her mom.

Taking a deep breath, Lochlyn pushed herself up onto her feet and headed for her door. Pausing at the door, Lochlyn reminded herself to just breathe.

What was the worst that could happen?

She could say no, Lochlyn thought bitterly.

Think positively, she reminded herself. There was a good chance her mom could also say yes.

As she headed out the door of her room, Lochlyn just hoped the odds were in her favor today. Moose Hollow Ski and Skate resort was in her future. This could be her chance to finally prove she deserved to be a part of the group and take a win.

Lochlyn suddenly had a good feeling about this trip.

Chapter 2

Three weeks later, Lochlyn was pulling up in front of the Moose Hollow Ski Resort with a trunk full of her belongings. Her talk with her mom had gone surprisingly easily. There had been some conditions for letting her go, but nothing that was unexpected.

The hardest one Lochlyn would have to come to terms with was finally making a solid plan for her future. Whether that was jumping into a career or going to college, her mom was letting her decide. A decision would be made either way.

Honestly, it felt like her mom was just happy to see Lochlyn making plans with friends. That, and she'd have the house to herself for a few days. She could enjoy the quiet with the occasional snoring of her Boston Terrier, Bubba.

In her trunk, Lochlyn packed a suitcase of her own personal clothes, but she also had a suitcase full of clothes she designated as *'Ivorie's wardrobe'* for the weekend.

Most, if not all, of said clothing was found at secondhand thrift stores. Ivorie had expensive taste, but unfortunately, Lochlyn didn't have the funds to support it.

As she put her car into park, Lochlyn shut off the podcast she'd been listening to, *The Twisted*, and reached over to adjust the red wig she had put on before she left home. She'd hastily tucked her hair into a wig cap before pulling on her red curls, but the wind had blown it around a little on the drive here.

Gazing forward, Lochlyn took in the sight of Moose Hollow and was blown away. This wasn't the little cottage size inn she'd been expecting.

Instead, this was a decently sized ski resort, and by 'decent', she really meant *huge*. The main building stood tall in the center. There were three large windows above the awning with an enormous chandelier glittering inside.

The building spread out on either side, five rows of windows extending in both directions. Those must be the rooms. It was easy enough to assume those went all the way around them, giving the resort guests a variety of options for views.

Lochlyn couldn't imagine someone willingly opting for a parking lot view, but it was a safe bet that those rooms were cheaper than the side overlooking the white, snowcapped mountains. It made her wonder briefly if it was snowy up there all year round or if it was fresh snow.

Giving her ensemble one last look over, Lochlyn deemed herself ready to leave the car and climbed out of the driver's seat. A sudden chill of September air hit her full on and Lochlyn immediately wished she'd worn a hat, or at the very least, something to cover her ears.

With any hope, they wouldn't be exploring the chilly outside much this weekend. Thankfully, the trek into the resort wasn't too far from where she'd parked, and Lochlyn knew she'd be toasty and out of the wind in only a few minutes. Perhaps she should have parked closer to the main entrance.

Dressing sensible over stylish wasn't something an heiress would consider. Lochlyn had chosen Ivorie's first impression outfit with fashion over warmth in mind.

As another cold breeze hit her, she was beginning to regret that choice. Pulling her jacket closer, a shiver ran down her spine and she let out a breath. Lochlyn was surprised to find that she could see it.

It was colder than she'd anticipated up here in the mountains. Even with it being the middle of September. Though, it shouldn't have been such a shock given Kitty had encouraged them to bring warmer clothes. She had warned them it snowed early this far up the mountain. The cold temperatures should have been expected.

"Ivorie, right?"

Turning, Lochlyn found she wasn't the only new arrival. Walking up the lot behind her was a boy who appeared to be around her age. His hair was mostly hidden under a beanie, but she could see a few peeks of dark strands poking out.

Immediately, Lochlyn knew this wasn't Camden, nor was it Boomer. At least, she didn't think so. Judging by their character art, she assumed they'd have a likeness to the images. Boomer had a darker skin tone, and his voice was deeper over the zoom calls.

Camden's hair was lighter, but that was easier to lie about in a drawing verse real life. He also came off more athletic, but she supposed that could be easily lied about as well. Now that she thought about it, there really was no telling if this was Camden or not.

This boy smirking at her was smug, but he didn't scream athletic or charming either with his chunky black frames and lanky build. He gave off more of a 'jerk-face' vibe to her.

Which left   Twiggy or Oliver.

"Hi, uh, yeah. That's me. What gave me away?" Lochlyn asked as she rubbed her hands together. "I'm sorry. Are you Twiggy or Oliver? An illustrated fanart profile picture can only help you so much, I guess."

Lochlyn hoped her nervousness was coming off more like a chill from the cold. If Lochlyn was being honest, she'd admit the shake in her hands were not from the gust of wind but from the anxiety charging through her veins instead. Her awkward laughter wasn't helping much either. Meeting new people always sent her nerves through the roof.

The smirk tilted further up on the right side of his face. "You look the part of heiress, although you don't have the '*I'm better than all of you*' arrogance of one. You're too   kind looking."

Lochlyn was taken back by the comment because she wasn't entirely sure that it *was* a compliment or not. "Do you know a lot of heiresses?"

The boy stuck his gloved hands into his pockets. "No, I can't honestly say that I do."

Lochlyn did something she normally never would. She raised her chin and straightened her stance. It was her attempt at her best unphased look, but she wasn't sure if she had quite managed to do it correctly.

"Then don't assume you know me."

The confidence in her voice surprised even her. She half expected him to laugh in her face. Anyone else back home would have, but this was Ivorie right now. So, Lochlyn spun on her heels and headed toward the main building.

Her brows scrunched together, her gaze falling to the ensemble she'd spent hours deciding on. The beige rain jacket fit her snugly. The middle was form-fitting, giving her more of an hourglass figure than just a shapeless stick of butter. The thin material did little to block the cold gust of wind, but the outfit looked chic so that was all that would matter to an heiress.

Anyways, she thought, who greeted a stranger like that? Insulting a person even before saying hello. Her earlier description of jerk-face was correct. This guy was exactly that.

Granted, the jerk was right. Appearance-wise, she looked the part, but as herself, Lochlyn would have never picked this outfit. Maybe she wasn't hiding her annoyance with the outfit as well as she should have been, but who was he to judge her? He was pretending to be something he wasn't just like she was.

He cleared his throat to regain her attention, causing her steps to slow to a stop. "You look fine. Beautiful, actually. I didn't mean to say you didn't."

Looking over her shoulder, Lochlyn watched as he pushed the chunky frames up his nose. It was a nervous tick, a tell. If she looked closer, Lochlyn might even say his cheeks had tinged a shade of pink.

"I'm Twiggy, to answer your earlier question," he added.

Maybe he was just as bad at making small talk as she was? It would explain his rude greeting. Maybe he'd meant it as a joke? She didn't know him well enough to know if he intended on being a jerk or if it was an honest accident.

A blush burned on her cheeks, but Lochlyn didn't dare turn her head again and let him see. No one had ever referred to her as beautiful before, least of all a boy her age. She immediately cringed at her inner thoughts. How pathetic was she?

Flattening her coat, Lochlyn avoided meeting his eyes as she kept her gaze straight ahead. "Pretending to be something I'm not isn't new for me." She didn't give him a chance to comment before she spoke up again. "Are we the first ones to arrive?"

A change of subject was needed.

Peering around the parking lot, Lochlyn noticed a handful of other vehicles spread about, but there was no way to know which belonged to the others in their group and which were employees.

Twiggy shrugged his shoulder. "I guess we won't know until we head inside."

Swallowing, Lochlyn nodded and turned back toward the resort. It loomed over them with dark windows and signs of a previous rainy day covering the roof. Whether it was welcoming them or warning them, she hadn't decided yet.

Lochlyn mentally smacked her head, realizing she'd been so concerned with her image, she'd forgotten to grab her bags from her car. She could come back for her things once she figured out where her room was. Sparing a peek over her shoulder, Twiggy motioned for her to lead the way and she rolled her eyes.

Her reaction only earned a snicker from him. "Ah, there's the heiress I was expecting."

Her fingers clenched the strap of the duffle bag she'd taken with her when she'd climbed out of her car. Her teeth clamped down on her bottom lip to keep from giving him the response he was looking for.

Squaring her shoulders, Lochlyn released a breath and pushed herself forward. He was in for a rude awakening if he thought she would be baited that easily.

Lochlyn didn't dare look back to check if he was following. If the squelch of mud behind her was any indicator, she'd say he was.

The double doors opened as she approached, and Lochlyn was surprised to see two employees standing there waiting.

One of them was a woman, possibly a few years older than Lochlyn. The sides of her head were shaved, and a tuft of blue hair fell into her eyes from the top.

The bellhop flashed her a mischievous grin and a wink as she took the duffle from her hands. "Good afternoon, Miss Jackson. Mr. Greenhorn. We've been instructed to bring your luggage to your rooms for you."

Her jaw flapped for a moment, too stunned to think of what to say. Lochlyn had never stayed in a place where the employees handled your things for you. Not to mention, knew who she was before she even stepped fully into the lobby.

She again heard a snicker behind her, reminding her that, as Ivorie, this shouldn't be new.

Closing her mouth, Lochlyn straightened and cleared her throat. "Right. The rest of my bags are in the blue Volvo. It's unlocked. Thank you."

The other bellhop with the brown hair and crooked nose nodded before slipping by them to retrieve the rest of her things. The woman who'd spoken reached to take Twiggy's suitcase but he pulled it closer to himself. "I'm fine. I'll keep mine with me."

If the woman was offended that Twiggy didn't trust her with his luggage, she didn't let it show. It wouldn't be a surprise to her if Twiggy wasn't the first or the last to refuse assistance. It was easy to believe people were uncomfortable about letting baggage out of their sight or leaving it with a stranger. The female bellhop merely shrugged and went into the back with Lochlyn's duffle bag.

"Oh, you're here!" a voice squealed.

Looking toward the main lobby, Lochlyn and Twiggy watched a small blonde bounced up to her feet, a smile exploding across her heart-shaped face. There was a man sitting beside her, a mirrored smile on his own face as he stood.

That wasn't all that was similar between them. They shared the same brown eyes so dark they were almost black. They had the same ears and chin too. That had to mean these were the twins, Olive and Oliver Le Blanc.

The biggest difference between them was their hair color, though she assumed Olive's perfectly straight Blonde bob was a wig much like her own. Oliver had a messy head of honey brown curls and Lochlyn found herself wondering if Olive's natural hair looked like that too.

Their height difference was staggering as well. The phrase *pixie size* came to mind now as Locklyn took in Olive's appearance. Though Olive seemed about an inch shorter than Lochlyn herself, Oliver loomed over her by a good foot and a half when he stood to follow his sister over. Lochlyn barely met his chest.

Seeing the twins standing side by side, Lochlyn couldn't imagine how she could have thought Twiggy was Oliver. Twiggy had been nothing but rude and he had a superior attitude. Oliver had a charming smile, and his eyes held a bit of mischief where

Twiggy's hadn't. Going off their character profiles, it should have been obvious who was who.

"We just got here like ten minutes ago. We were wondering if we were the first or last to arrive. Pumpkin got here just after us. That's her over there on the phone. She's on a work call. Good luck getting a good reception up here though. My phone's been in **SOS** since we got here," Olive barely paused to gasp in a breath before suddenly clapping her hands excitedly. "Oh, my god, Ivorie! I'm obsessed with your curls. They're like giant ringlets! Do you use curlers? Can you use curlers on a wig? Oh, or is that your real hair? Not that it matters. It's gorgeous either way."

Oliver shook his head, amused as he stopped a step behind his twin. "You'll have to excuse my sister. She was nervous and drank too much caffeine this morning. She doesn't react well to that mud, if you couldn't tell."

The look Olive gave her twin was nearly comical. "And you'll have to excuse my brother for his rudeness. He mistakes it for being charming and witty."

A snort escaped Lochlyn's throat before she could stop it, but she attempted to brush it off as clearing her throat. It was a very unheiress kind of noise, and judging by Twiggy's snickering she knew he hadn't missed it.

"It appears he and Twiggy took pointers from each other then," Lochlyn muttered, earning a soft giggle from Olive. "I take it you prefer tea over coffee, then?"

Oliver shrugged his shoulder, a playful smile on his lips. "You could say that."

Holding out her hand, Lochlyn intended on being formal with the twins, but Olive ignored her gesture as she hopped forward and pulled her into an embrace.

The abrupt motion stunned Lochlyn, and she wasn't sure exactly how to react. She wasn't a hugger. Especially not with people she was meeting for the first time.

In person at least.

They'd talked over zoom calls and the chat box for the game, but how much could you really get to know a person from that?

So, Lochlyn settled for awkwardly patting the girl on the back until she released her.

At least Olive had the sense to realize she'd overstepped. "Not a hugger then. Sorry."

Swallowing her nerves, Lochlyn waved off her apology as she attempted to force a smile. "Don't worry about it, darling. It's nice to meet you," she paused as her eyes flickered to Oliver. "Both of you. Officially, I mean."

Oliver's smile sent her stomach into flips, and she hated her body for betraying her. Though that might be more due to her anxiety about meeting new people. Granted he was handsome, but something else about him put her on edge.

Reaching out his hand, Oliver lifted her fingers and pressed a kiss to the back of her knuckles. "Pleasure's all mine, I can assure you."

Ah, there's the charm his twin was teasing him about.

"Oh, brother," Twiggy muttered behind her.

His scoff broke the spell Oliver's grin had cast upon her. Startled, she pulled her hand back and dipped her chin in greeting. "Right, sure. Um, you haven't seen Kitty yet? I would have thought she'd be here first."

Oliver stuck his hands into his pockets and shrugged. "If she's here, she hasn't made her presence known yet. Maybe she's waiting for everyone to arrive before her big entrance?"

Lochlyn took the chance to take in the entire lobby. It was a decent sized main room, not that she had many hotels to compare it too. She and her mom only ever stayed at *Evelyn's Seaside Inn* when they stayed up in Lakeside Cover for a week in the summer.

It was safe to say this ski and skate resort was nothing like that cozy inn. The resort strived for more of a cabin feel with rustic decor and neutral colors whereas the inn went for more of a nautical design.

Through the double doors, Lochlyn could see a massive fireplace in the lounge that was clearly the centerpiece of the room. She imagined a lot of guests gathering around after a day of skiing and warming up by the fire.

A girl she presumed to be Pumpkin was currently pacing in front of it, talking into her phone with barely a wave in their direction. Her chestnut hair was short and curly, but somehow, she'd managed to pull it into two tiny pigtails.

She'd chosen to pay homage to *Velma Dinkley* by dressing in a red quarter sleeve shirt with a pumpkin on it that complimented her curvy body nicely. *Hello Pumpkin* was written across the chest and she paired it with a mid-thigh length orange skirt.

Her legs were mostly covered by knee-high burnt orange knit socks and a pair of burgundy ankle boots completed the ensemble. For an outfit that shouldn't have worked, it somehow looked perfect on her.

All this girl was missing was the black framed glasses. Lochlyn wouldn't be surprised if she was one of those girls to own a fake pair of glasses though just because they went with her outfit though.

She didn't appear stressed over her outfit choice in the least. It felt so effortless for Pumpkin. Olive too appeared to be right at home, like this entire experience wasn't new for her. She was right at home.

They all were, Lochlyn noted sourly.

Lochlyn felt a wave of envy hit her remembering how long she'd painstakingly considered each piece of her planned outfits. The entire trip here had been nothing but a big panic attack.

The doors opened behind them, bringing in another gust of cold air. Lochlyn turned to see another man enter. The blue-haired bellhop was quick to head over to welcome him. Lochlyn watched as he lowered his sunglasses and took them all in before his eyes settled on her.

Well, not *her* specifically. On all of them.

"Well, ain't this cozy," he spoke up.

There was a hint of a southern accent in his voice, and Lochlyn wondered if it was for his character or if it was real. In this day and age, with the right amount of practice, anyone could have an accent. Whether it was believable or not was another question entirely.

Like the little ball of pure energy, she was quickly proving to be, Olive was the first to approach the newcomer. "Hi, welcome! I hope you had a good drive here. I'm Olive and over there is my brother, Oliver, and that's Twiggy and Ivorie. Pumpkin's over there."

Lochlyn must have missed Twiggy introducing himself to the twins, but that wasn't unusual. She tended to tune people out when her attention drifted onto something else. There were plenty of other things to focus on in this lobby, that was for sure. It was almost overwhelming.

She couldn't afford to allow herself to be distracted right off the bat. Even though the game hadn't officially started yet, these first impressions were what got the ball rolling.

Lochlyn was fully focused now though. She took in the sight of this new arrival. He had a mop of dark curls on his head, and a long face with eyes that reminded her of amber. He was dressed in an expensive looking leather coat with fake fur opposite the row of buttons that ran down the length of the jacket and his hood. Even his boots looked rich.

She now knew what Twiggy meant when he'd said she didn't come off like an heiress. Just by looking at this guy, Lochlyn could tell he really did come from money. This boy had that sense of confidence that just came from knowing you could afford anything you wanted. He didn't have a single worry wrinkle on his face.

A nervous chuckle rumbled in his chest as he overcame the startlement of Olive's sudden rapid-fire introductions. "Uh, hi. I'm Camden. Nice to meet y'all."

Yeah, he *definitely* had an accent.

Seeing him standing there while mentally comparing him to his character art, she was pleasantly surprised to see how accurate it was. Now that she thought about it, everyone's character art was oddly spot on. It was more unexpected, she realized as she was sure the opposite would occur considering catfishing was a real concern.

A sudden clap of hands interrupted their greetings. Spinning on her heels, Lochlyn turned her attention to the grand staircase that split in two directions. There was a person descending from either side.

On the left side was a tall slender woman, who Lochlyn quickly surmised was the one who'd clapped her hands to get their attention. Her hair was perfectly pulled back into a high ponytail, not a strand out of place. Her wiry frame was slender and tall, though Lochlyn could see that her shoes helped with the latter. She reminded Lochlyn of a younger Courtney Cox before all the Botox.

"Welcome, all, to a weekend of fun, mystery, and of course, murder. If you haven't guessed yet, I'm Kitty and that hunk of man over there is Boomer," she motioned to the man on the opposite side of the staircase.

Seeing Boomer in person now made her question how anyone could have mixed him up with the other guys in the group. He was the opposite in terms of size and build.

Lochlyn mentally swooned over Boomer's short dark hair, dark skin, and chiseled cheekbones. He was beautiful in a high school football player jock kind of way. Personally, it wasn't her type, but still, Lochlyn could appreciate his good-looking features. Would he be Ivorie's though? Rich athlete sounded right on paper anyway.

With a brief glance across the room toward Pumpkin, Lochlyn noted that she wasn't the only one appreciating the view of the cute boy. Her eyes were trained on Boomer with every step he took like a dog watching someone wave around their favorite bone.

Kitty continued, completely unaware of where Lochlyn's train of thought had gone. "I do hope you're ready to play because this game will not be one for the faint of heart. You'll remember this weekend for the rest of your lives."

Little did she know how much of an understatement that would come to be.

Kitty clapped her hands together again, her eyes running down the line of them. Oddly, when her attention caught sight of Lochlyn, it looked as if she'd momentarily forgotten how to breathe.

It was only a nano-second, but still. She'd seen it. Locklyn just didn't understand what it meant.

"Our game of murder and sleuthing starts tonight," Kitty began. "The first victim has already been chosen, as well as our murderer, and not even I know who either are going to be. The rules are simple. When the first murder occurs, the game is on. You have three days to piece clues together, follow leads, and decide who was the killer, how did they do it, and where it occurred."

"May the clues work in your favor," Boomer spoke up, grinning as he scanned the faces of the group before him.

Rolling her eyes at the bad pun, Kitty ignored the interruption. "My uncle is trusting us to leave this place as spotless as it is now. There are obviously going to be out of bounds areas, and we aren't allowed to use the ski lift. We're allowed to use the indoor pool and the hot tubs. There's a fire pit outside that we have access to as well. Everyone should have a key card in their room. Those are your keys to the world while we stay here. They will let you into any room and they also activate the elevators. Don't you dare lose them because they cannot be replaced."

As Kitty finished explaining the rules, she snapped her fingers and called for the bellhops to return. The lingering stare between the bellhop who'd welcomed them all and Kitty didn't go unnoticed by Lochlyn as the female bellhop passed an envelope to their host. It felt like the rest of the group were watching a silent conversation occur before their eyes.

Just as quickly as it happened, the moment was over, and the bellhop disappeared through another doorway. Lochlyn returned her attention to Kitty as soon as the door shut.

"We'll meet in one hour for lunch. These gentlemen will escort you to your rooms. Freshen up, unpack, enjoy the breathtaking views from your windows, and most importantly, enjoy yourselves   while you can, that is."

Chapter 3

Once the introductions were finished, everyone was directed to their rooms and each of them was given a key for their individual rooms. They were all reminded not to reveal their true identities and to keep in character. Although, given how little she knew about the other players, they could have been acting like themselves and Lochlyn wouldn't know the difference.

That was the downside of being the newest person to join the party. It was obvious the others had gotten to know each other outside of the group chat. It would be hard to remain total strangers after several years of talking to one another, she supposed. Either way, Lochlyn couldn't help but feel like the odd one out; like everyone else was in on a secret she didn't know.

Lochlyn had wanted to go into this weekend as confident as she felt online. It was easy to be Ivorie with the comfort of knowing they could never really get to know Lochlyn Jones. There was never a fear of being rejected before, but standing in front of them all? Boy, was there ever.

Without the computer to hide behind, Lochlyn had no doubt everything would change.

Lochlyn was at a disadvantage in terms of what to expect when it came to the other players. They would be able to pick up on each other's tells better than she would. She'd have to work extra hard to even have a shot at winning.

They would be immersed in the game for the next couple of days and as long as everyone followed the rules there would be no risk of that bubble popping until the end of the event. Typically, over zoom, each of them would have a board and dice. Kitty was usually their narrator, though occasionally others in the group took a shot at it.

Lochlyn had never been brave enough to give it a try, but this might be the encouragement she needed. Bringing their game to life left her with an exhilarating feeling. It would say a lot about her acting skills if she managed to pull off Ivorie's confidence and wit.

Ivorie was outspoken, charming, seductive, Lochlyn was none of those things. She didn't stand up for herself, or anyone else, when it mattered. Lochlyn was entirely fine being the wallflower, watching as everyone else lived their lives and had fun. She didn't like to rock the boat, at times even at her own expense.

Well, she was determined to capsize the boat entirely this weekend. She would solve the mystery first and out the murderer.

The nameless male bellhop had been the one to bring her to her room where her bags awaited. As the door shut, Lochlyn unzipped her rain jacket and let it slip off her arms. "Whoa," she gasped as she took in the room.

This was probably the fanciest hotel room Lochlyn had ever seen in real life or on tv. Kitty mentioned the girls would all be staying on the second floor in the West Wing and the boys would be in the East.

Their rooms were their safe places, Kitty had explained, where they could take their wigs off and put their characters away for a while. If they decided to let someone into their space, that was their business. She wouldn't stop them, but they couldn't let it affect the game.

Releasing a breath, Lochlyn shook out her nerves as she tossed her jacket onto the bed. Crossing the room, she stood at the wall-to-floor windows and took in the beautiful mountain range outside. It was breathtaking.

Her phone buzzed against her side, jolting her back to reality. Pulling it free from her pocket, Lochlyn saw her mom's picture lighting up the screen. Sliding the bar over, she raised her phone to her ear and smiled. "Hey, I just got to my room .... the drive was fine, Mom   yeah, I met everyone. They all seem nice."

A scraping noise caught her attention. Looking back, she saw a note on the floor in front of her door and realized someone must have slid it underneath. Lochlyn was so distracted, she missed what her mom had asked. "Uh, sorry. No, I'm fine. Just tired. I've got to unpack and get ready for lunch. Don't forget, the reception up here sucks. I'll call when I can .... okay, I will. Promise   I love you too. Bye."

Hanging up her phone, Lochlyn crouched down and picked up the note. Excitement shot through her, knowing this was it. The game was starting, and she couldn't wait to dive in.

Flipping it open, she let her eyes scan the lines of text.
Welcome to Moose Hollow,

Your host can't wait to dine with you tonight and officially start this thrilling whodunnit. This weekend will be full of games, twists, and secrets. It'll be a game to die for, or maybe to kill for.
Happy sleuthing,
Kitty

It was full of bad puns, which was on a par with its Clue homage, but Lochlyn had to admit it was cute. It was a nice touch. A sudden burst of excitement hit her as she held the card to her chest and squealed. A satisfied sigh slipped through her lips as she fell back into her soft mattress.

God, even the bed was like a dream.

Lochlyn would literally be sleeping on a cloud. This weekend was exactly what she'd hoped it would be, and it hadn't even officially started. It felt like all the stress and anxiety were leaving her body and it made her smile. For a weekend, Lochlyn could forget about the constant arguing about college with her mom and just relax.

None of them would be judging her looks or her quirks because they were now considered Ivorie's quirks and features. Everything was part of her character, and no one would think twice if something she said or did was weird. It honestly felt like a trial run at being on her own.

Maybe it wouldn't be college, but if she decided to save and move out on her own at some point, Lochlyn could start over and be someone new in a place where no one knew her or her history.

Before her body got too comfortable, Lochlyn rolled onto her stomach pulled her notebook and pen free from her duffle. Popping off the cap, she went about writing down the names of all the players.

Oliver, Olive, Boomer, Kitty, Twiggy, Pumpkin, and Camden.

It was a bummer Nik couldn't make it, but the show must go on, so to speak. This game was going to start with a murder, like all murder mystery parties do. Since it wasn't going to be *her*, that meant it would be one of *them*.

Earlier this week Kitty had everyone choose a number. She then put together an app to choose a number. They did this twice.

No one shared what number they had, but the first '*murder victim*' and '*murderer*' were chosen. It was the only way to make sure everyone, host included, could really enjoy the game.

Since her number was not chosen for either role, Lochlyn knew someone from the list she wrote was going to be 'killed off' tonight at dinner. And someone else would be the culprit. It was just a matter of who, how, and where. It was up to the rest of them to figure out the answers to those questions and for the murderer to drop clues and mislead.

Running her finger down the line of names, Lochlyn thought back to her first in person meeting with the others. Twiggy came off as arrogant and rude. He didn't appear to have a filter on his mouth. He was snarky too, Lochlyn noted bitterly, as she remembered all the little comments. He was also smart and detail oriented. It was how he won more games than he lost. She'd have to keep an eye on him.

Then there were the twins. Did she count them as individual players or as one unit? They had the ultimate advantage, seeing as they probably intended to be partners. Whether that entailed murdering or sleuthing was to be seen.

What did she know about the duo so far? Olive was a perfect Miss Muffet type and a little too caffeinated. The overly sweet and doe-eyed act could be a ruse to throw others off her trail, but it was too early to tell. Her brother, on the other hand, had soul searching eyes that a girl could just melt into.

Another dreamy sigh left her lips as Lochlyn remembered the way he'd kissed the back of her hand, flashing that smile that made her stomach flutter. He had unruly golden-brown curls she just wanted to run her fingers through and lips that made her wonder what it would feel like to kiss.

A blush burned her cheeks at the thought. None of that information would help her solve this game first. If anything, Oliver was going to be an obstacle for her; a distraction. She was not here for romance, though Lochlyn had to admit she felt a spark of chemistry between them.

Moving on to the next suspect.

Because Pumpkin had been struggling with the reception on her phone, Lochlyn hadn't been able to chat with her before they were dismissed. Even her own phone call with her mom had been pretty staticky, and with the storm coming in, Lochlyn wouldn't be surprised if it only got worse. It really added to the whole 'stuck in the middle of nowhere' vibes they were going for.

Then there was Kitty, their host, who was every bit the scream queen Lochlyn had imagined she would be. Her character carried the level of confidence that according to Twiggy, Ivorie was missing.

Given how long Kitty had been part of the group though, she was naturally comfortable in the role of leader.

Boomer appeared to be her right-hand man. He had clearly arrived early to help Kitty prepare for their arrival. She'd been expecting him to be the last to arrive, late even. There was always that one character who made a dramatic entrance during a tense moment or at the climax of an event.

In Lochlyn's mind, she'd expected it to be Boomer with his sly smile and seductive eyes. Instead, he'd been the first here with their host, descending the grand staircase like a power couple.

They were closer than Lochlyn had known about, or at least their characters were. It was a disadvantage for her. Like Olive and Oliver, they could be working as partners in the game. It didn't make Lochlyn's odds of winning look too promising.

Knowing she wouldn't be able to analyze anything else until the game officially started, Lochlyn twisted around and sat up. She would need to pick another outfit for lunch. Well, Ivorie did. This was going to be her official first impression. She had to make it count. Lochlyn just hoped Kitty didn't expect them to change three times a day or else she'd be an outfit repeater, which was a big heiress 'no-no'.

Grabbing the suitcase she'd designated as Ivorie's, she unzipped the bag and pulled out a few of the outfits she'd need to hang up. Lochlyn intended on making an impact during this first lunch that would help her to recover from the stiffness she'd held during the initial meeting. She needed to start over fresh, channel her inner Ivorie. *Become* the heiress.

Twiggy had thrown her off with his comment. Lochlyn wasn't about to let him ruin the rest of the game. Still, she didn't want to come off as trying too hard. So, after some debate, Lochlyn changed into a pair of plaid slacks that ranged in different shades of browns and a white button-down blouse. Once her buttons were fastened, she pulled a brown sweater vest over her head and looked at herself in the mirror.

There, she had her sleuthing vibe down. It was Nancy Drew chic and exactly what she was hoping to pull off.

Lochlyn still had to redo her hair. Brush out the wind-frayed curls and return them to their perfect ringlets, then somehow attach her beret to it with a few well-placed bobby-pins. Of course, she'd need to figure out accessories too, but other than that, she was ready to go.

Heading into the bathroom, she caught the reflection in the large mirror. The girl staring back at her wasn't Lochlyn. Her cheeks had a bit more color to them, though that might be because of the harsh wind outside. Her face also was caked in a layer of makeup, and she stood straighter.

This wasn't some eighteen-year-old introvert. This was a confident young woman in the making. Someone who knew what she wanted and wasn't afraid to demand it.

Lochlyn pulled the blood red wig off and set it down on the 'his and hers' sink counter. Meeting her stare in the mirror again, a heavy exhale released as she took in the purple hair and sad green eyes looking back at her.

In a second flat, that confidence was gone, and her insecurities had shot back in. That wasn't the first impression Lochlyn wanted to make with everyone. Twiggy's comments might have thrown her off, but if she intended to win this, Lochlyn would need to bounce back.

Kitty was scoring everyone's ability to become their character, their sleuthing skills, and their ability to improvise on a moment's notice. This weekend was a theater kid's dream.

Leaning against the counter, Lochlyn took a deep breath and let her nerves settle. She could do this. There was nothing to be worried or stressed about. Lochlyn wanted to be here, to take part in this game. She could handle this.

Ivorie could handle this.

Nodding, Lochlyn psyched herself up before freshening up. Grabbing the mannequin head from her other suitcase, she brushed out the ruined curls. Once the rollers were in, she tucked the escaped purple strands back into her wig cap.

Placing a beret on top of her wig, she fastened it in place with a few bobby-pins. Hopefully this looked alright when she put it on.

Next, she touched up her makeup. Lochlyn smiled at herself in the mirror as her desired look came together. Ivorie went heavy on the red lick stick, but the rest of her makeup was supposed to appear natural.

Pulling on a pair of closed toed wedges, Lochlyn fumbled for a moment before she righted her footing. To say Lochlyn wasn't a heel kind of girl was an understatement.

But Ivorie would be, Lochlyn reminded herself. She probably would have been wearing heels before she could properly walk.

So, Lochlyn committed to her part and had practiced walking in these silly death shoes all week.

Hopefully it paid off.

After securing her wig back on her head and making sure the beret was on correctly, Lochlyn knew it was time to rejoin the others down in the dining room.

"You can do this, Loch. It's just a game," she whispered to herself. "You're playing a part in a game and you're going to win. You *will* win this."

Shaking her nerves out one last time, she took a deep breath before turning and heading for the door.

Ready or not, here she comes.

Chapter 4

Since she had time before lunch, Lochlyn took a detour to check out the rest of the lodge. She wanted to get a better idea of the layout. Maybe she'd sketch the layout of the place and keep note of where particular rooms like the pool, gym, ballroom, lobby, etc were. It wouldn't be a bad idea for when she started investigating for clues.

So far, all she'd found were a few conference rooms probably used to host events throughout the season. Lochlyn imagined business conventions were popular up here.

Wandering to the lower levels, she followed the arrows pointing toward the pool area. Slipping through the doorway, Lochlyn smiled at the sight of the huge pool sparkling inside.

Reaching down, she unbuckled her shoe straps and pulled them off. Rolling the bottom of her slacks up her calves, Lochlyn crept closer toward the edge. She couldn't wait to take advantage of spending time in this room.

Near water was her favorite place to be. Whether it was a pool, a bath, or the ocean, Lochlyn would soak up every second she was submerged in some kind of body of liquid.

Not wanting to get her outfit wet, she grabbed a white fluffy towel from the rack and headed for the poolside. Laying it out on the edge, she set her shoes aside and sat down.

Lochlyn smiled happily as she dipped her feet into the pool and let herself relax. Leaning back on her hands, she closed her eyes and inhaled the smell of the chlorine. She'd have to wander back down here after dinner tonight and go for a real swim.

"There you are."

Startled, Lochlyn went ridged before twisting her body and found Oliver standing in the doorway. He hadn't changed out of his off-white shirt and brown sweater combo. His dark slacks were rolled at the ankle much like her own were.

His head tilted, his gaze consuming her into the dark chocolate abysses of his eyes. It felt like he could strip her naked and read every secret she kept buried inside. It was intense.

"Is everyone waiting on me for something?"

Oliver shook his head, chuckling as he stuffed his hands in his pockets and closed the distance between them. "No. I think

Kitty's checking in with the staff. The storm's coming in quicker than anticipated and she wants anyone who isn't staying overnight to leave early."

"Oh," she said, worrying her bottom lip.

A spark of worry filtered through her at the mention of the incoming storm. They'd been checking the weather the entire week and knew it was supposed to downpour the rest of the day and into tomorrow. The roads flooded badly up here in the mountains and given that there was only one road up and down, the lodge was isolated from the nearby town.

Although it made the weekend more exciting, there was still a part of her that recognized the danger.

Oliver crouched down beside her, though given the height difference between them he still loomed over her. "Can I join you?"

Not wanting to appear too eager, Lochlyn pretended to consider the question as if she might possibly say no. "I suppose I don't see the harm in it. Just don't go prying any information out of me. The game hasn't officially started yet."

A chuckle rumbled in his chest as he took the spot beside her. "Fair enough. I think I can keep it strictly causal. No sleuthing talk before dinner."

Slipping off his own shoes and socks, he set them down beside her wedges and rolled his pants up further before dipping his feet in the water.

To her amusement, Oliver jolted in surprise as he immediately pulled his feet back out. "Holy crap that's freezing."

Her laugh echoed through the room. "Sorry, I should have warned you."

His dark eyes studied her, taking her in from toe to head. It didn't miss her attention how his eyes lingered in spots that made her blush. Yeah, it was clear her earlier thoughts about this boy were going to be proven correct.

Oliver was going to be a big distraction for her this weekend.

Lochlyn tried to think of how Ivorie would react to the attention. Given that she was an heiress, she was probably used to it. She couldn't take his lingering stare too seriously. His character of Oliver could just be a major flirt, and this could mean nothing to him.

It was going to be hard to keep that line between fantasy and reality from blurring this weekend. This was the perfect example of how feelings could be hurt if they weren't careful. They were playing out how their characters would react in certain situations.

Right?

Still, it would be easy to mistake his flirting for real attraction. It would be best to keep that in mind. Especially with Oliver.

This flirtation could be good for the plot line of Ivorie's game, but it could spell trouble for Lochlyn. For all she knew, this was his strategy to win the game. If Oliver distracted her, it would keep her from playing to the best of her ability and therefore might cost her the win.

Lochlyn wasn't about to let that happen. But it didn't mean she couldn't enjoy herself while she was here either. "Are you just going to sit there and stare at me until lunch or actually say something interesting?"

His brow raised with amusement. "Talking's definitely one option."

Lochlyn hoped her blush wasn't giving away her nervousness. She wanted to come off as casual as he was. "Do you have another option?"

Oliver opened his mouth, ready to answer her question, when the door opened behind them and killed the moment. Both turned their heads to look for the culprit to their interruption.

There stood the blue-haired bellhop from earlier.

The girl was still in her work uniform, but her shocking blue hair had made her unforgettable. Most of the time, hotel employees blended into the background, but this girl stood out. Now having more time to study her, Lochlyn noticed she had two earrings on her left earlobe and one dangling from the right side.

"Sorry to interrupt, but Miss Featherton would like everyone to gather for lunch now," the girl announced, a tenseness in her voice Lochlyn couldn't understand.

Lochlyn noted how the bellhop's eyes seemed to be locked in on Oliver alone rather than both of them. Turning her attention toward him, she saw the way his jaw had clenched. A sour expression had replaced the grin that had been there a moment before.

Following his glare, Lochlyn returned her gaze to the bellhop and took note of the smug grin on her face. She got the impression this girl was far from sorry to interrupt them.

"We'll be up in a few minutes. Thank you," he spoke up in a clipped tone.

It was clearly a dismissal but if this woman was annoyed, she didn't show it. If anything, she appeared to be amused by his aggravation.

The bellhop nodded and took a step to leave but paused in the doorway and turned back to them. This time, her gaze landed solely on Lochlyn. "Be careful with who you put your trust in.

Sometimes a pretty face is just as bad as a scary one. If not worse since you don't see the betrayal coming."

With that, the woman disappeared from the doorway. A chill went down Lochlyn's spine, but she wrote it off as excitement about the game beginning. That was all the warning was about, right? It had to be.

Lochlyn pulled her feet from the pool, stood, and grabbed her shoes from where they sat beside Oliver's. "I suppose you'll have to get back to me about that option B after lunch," she said, giving him a wink as she headed for the door.

His laughter sent her stomach in a flutter, but Lochlyn did her best to ignore it. "Another time then."

Little did they know that next time wouldn't be coming.

Chapter 5

Heading for the dining room, Lochlyn felt anxious. It felt like a vice of fear was clenched around her heart. This would be the first time she really interacted with the people she'd been talking to nonstop the last several months.

"It's okay to be nervous," a voice said from behind.

Turning, Lochlyn saw Pumpkin walking to catch up to her. Her short hair was still pulled up in two small pigtails, but upon a closer inspection, she could see there were strips of reds and oranges in the girl's hair. It made her hair look like a living flame.

Lochlyn noticed that Pumpkin had freckles drawn across her face. It was makeup trend she never saw the point of, but to each their own. If she had squinted, Lochlyn might have even noticed how they seemed to create little pumpkin shapes on her cheeks.

"Oh, um, I'm fine," Lochlyn stumbled over her words. A silent cringe shot through her. Stuttering was not very heiress like. "I'm good."

Pumpkin waved her off, immediately seeing through her. "You don't need to be embarrassed about being nervous. This can all be a lot. I'm sorry I was on the phone earlier. I didn't get to properly introduce myself. I'm Pumpkin."

Brushing her palms against her sides, Lochlyn accepted Pumpkin's outstretched hand with a firm shake. "Ivorie."

Pumpkin nodded toward the doors behind them. "Shall we?"

Swallowing the lump of nerves in her throat, Lochlyn nodded and motioned for her to lead the way. "After you."

Pumpkin stood straighter, a new air of confidence overcoming her. With a small dip of her chin, she pushed open the dining room doors and headed inside.

It wasn't more than a second before Pumpkin's voice broke the silence of the room. "Olive, darling. I was hoping you'd be the first here. It's simply been too long since we've caught up properly."

Lochlyn watched from the doorway as Pumpkin crossed the room and headed straight for the chatty girl from earlier. Pumpkin leaned forward, pushing air kisses towards both sides of Olive's face.

"Behind you," Oliver warned as slipped by her in the doorway.

He seated himself to the left of his twin, kissing her cheek with a quick hello. Olive shot him an accusing glance before returning to her conversation with Pumpkin.

With a quick scan around the room, Lochlyn could see Olive wasn't the only one here. On either end of the table sat Kitty and Boomer, respectively. They were playing the parts of hosts perfectly, Lochlyn thought to herself.

"Having second thoughts already, Heiress?"

A scowl slipped over her face as she turned to see Twiggy now standing beside her. "Not at all. I don't get spooked that easily."

His grin widened, and his canine tooth winked at her as a dimple appeared on the left side of his face. "Noted."

With that, Twiggy tucked his hands into his pockets and entered the dining room with a head nod in Kitty's direction. Her gaze lingered on him for a lingering moment, Lochlyn noticed, before Kitty joined in the conversation. Twiggy took the free seat to Boomer's right and settled in as he unrolled his silverware and set the sage napkin down across his lap.

"Jerk," Lochlyn muttered under her breath as she followed.

Taking the open seat to Olive's right, she flattened out the creases in her pants and tried to relax. The more she acted on edge, the more she proved Twiggy right. Her nerves over meeting so many new people were getting the best of her. It didn't mean she was spooked.

On the contrary, Lochlyn was pretty excited about this weekend.

Lochlyn wished her mouth would function right. Even though the game wasn't officially beginning until dinner, they were supposed to be in character until then. Heiresses didn't stutter or stumble. Her own nerves were hurting her ability to play. Did pretending to be someone else get easier? Everyone seemed to be settling into their parts like their roles were a second skin.

Camden was the last to arrive, taking a seat to Twiggy's left. It didn't miss Lochlyn's attention that there was an open chair between him and Pumpkin.

It was meant for Nik, Lochlyn realized.

Nik hadn't been able to get the time off work though, and she wouldn't be able to join them. It was disappointing, but as Kitty had said in the chat, the game must go on. If this went well, they could always plan another game where everyone could partake.

The sound of silverware clinking against glass turned her attention away from the chair and over to Kitty, who stood. Like most of the girls, Kitty had also changed. The sleek black dress looked magnificent on her tall slender frame. Her straight chestnut hair fell past her shoulders and down her back as she pushed a lock of it behind her ear.

"I know the game doesn't technically start until later, but use this time to get to know the suspects ... I mean *guests*. Use your sleuthing skills to find tells or to make alliances. There may only be one winner by the end of this weekend, but that doesn't mean you have to work alone," Kitty explained.

There was a devious grin on her face, but it was all a part of the game. At least Lochlyn thought it was. As their host, Kitty was supposed to be ominous and suspicious. She'd lured them here just as Mr. Body from Clue had once lured others to his mansion.

Now that Lochlyn thought about it, in every horror movie she'd ever seen, it was usually the host looking to enact revenge on their guests for some reason or another. Going off that logic, Kitty already had a motive in place. It would be easy to point an accusing finger in her direction as more information was revealed this weekend.

Something odd that only added fuel to her running theory happened then. Kitty's body tensed as her eyes landed on Pumpkin. To add to the weirdness of that reaction, Pumpkin appeared smug as she raised her glass slightly.

As if nothing had just occurred between the two women, Kitty's forced smile was back in place as her gaze continued down the line of people around the table. With a call over her shoulder, she summoned the wait staff with their meals.

It was the quickest of reactions, but Lochlyn was sure she hadn't imagined it. Was it on purpose? A misdirection planted to throw the players off? Or could it have been a genuine slip of her calm, cool, collected mask? Was Pumpkin's response a clue they were supposed to catch, a secret passed between the two women?

Lochlyn knew there was no way to tell for sure given they had all officially met in person for the first time today. It was easy to hide unspoken drama over a zoom call or in a group chat.

It was something to keep an eye on though, Lochlyn pondered to herself as her lunch plate was set down in front of her.

*

Lunch went over without a hitch and Lochlyn enjoyed getting to know the other players a little better. Well, as much as she could given the situation. It was hard to really connect with any of them since the question of '*is this just their character's personality or their own*' loomed over her.

Like Kitty said earlier, the time before dinner was meant to get to know the other suspects. She'd have to assume anything anyone did from the moment they stepped foot in the resort was as their character and not as themselves.

Being this immersed in the game was going to take some getting used to. Lochlyn was hoping it would become more comfortable as the weekend went on. It was hard to get to know someone who wasn't acting like themselves to begin with.

It was one thing to gain a sense of someone's personality over a computer, or even an audio only zoom call, but it was another to see the person face to face.

It was an entirely new ballgame now.

What if she came to really like these people yet none of them turned out to be anything like their characters? Then again, they never broke character with each other. Kitty would always be Kitty to her.

Maybe this was why the rule was in place? To keep feelings from getting confused or hurt? They did audio-only zoom calls for their game nights to keep the illusion alive. It was easier to imagine a character without how they really looked getting in the way. So far no one had disappointed her mental image of them.

"You look like you're in deep thought," a voice spoke out from behind.

Lochlyn turned to see Kitty now standing there, watching her as a predator would its prey. "Oh, uh, I suppose I was. Sorry, were you trying to say something?"

Shit, she really had to catch her stutter.

Kitty's smile was forced, and she tried to hide that well. If Lochlyn had been anyone else, they might not have noticed that detail. Her love for mysteries made it easier for her to read people. Though, that wasn't always a good skill to have.

Most of the time it was her habit of overthinking everything that got the best of her.

"I just wanted to welcome you personally to the lodge. We didn't get a chance to really talk when everyone arrived," Kitty said, flashing another forced smile as she pushed her hair behind her ear. "Being the newbie, I know this all can be overwhelming. I wanted to make sure you settled in okay."

Hair touching was a nervous habit, a tell, as Kitty had mentioned earlier, Lochlyn had noticed her doing earlier. But why would she be nervous about talking to her? Lochlyn wasn't anyone important or intimidating.

"This place is beautiful. I can only imagine it looks even better once it snows. It's so nice of your uncle to let us spend the weekend here for this," Lochlyn said as she let her attention move around the room. She hated making eye contact, but Ivorie wouldn't have that issue. It was another thing she'd need to work on over the weekend.

"Yes, it was. He's pretty great."

Lochlyn couldn't explain why she felt the sudden urge to bolt, but it would be rude to run off like that. Instead, she went a different route. "So, have you done anything like this before?"

A thankful smile crossed the other girl's face, grateful for the subject change. "Once or twice. It gets less awkward as you get more comfortable. You're with a good group too."

Her mind immediately went to Oliver flirting at the poolside. A small smile slipped over her lips before she could stop herself. "Can I ask you a question? About the game, I mean. I know we're supposed to be in character, but it's been bugging me since I got here."

Kitty's smile strained. Perhaps she didn't want to answer any more of Lochlyn's questions? It would understandable if she didn't. Just asking her previous question was breaking the fourth wall.

"I suppose not."

Lochlyn chewed on her bottom lip, another nervous habit she'd need to work on erasing this weekend. "How do you keep from getting too caught up in the game? I mean, is it weird to get to know someone knowing they're not actually the way they're acting."

Kitty gave her a knowing smile, but again, Lochlyn couldn't help but notice that something felt off about it. "That line can get blurred easier than you'd think, but just relax and have fun. If you're worried about someone taking the game too seriously, don't. I've had Twiggy running background checks on all the members before accepting them into the party. It helps having a computer nerd in the group."

How deep did Twiggy dig into a person's background and why did that unnerve her more than ease her concerns? The thought of him knowing personal details about her past didn't sit right with Lochlyn. It felt like she was at another disadvantage. He and Kitty knew more than she was aware of.

Kitty must have caught the look of terror on her face because she was suddenly grabbing hold of Lochlyn's hands. "Don't worry your pretty little head, darling. He just makes sure there's no criminal record or severe mental illness issue. It's just a precaution to keep everyone safe, you know? No surprise skeletons hanging in the closet and all that."

She said it as if it was entirely normal for someone to go digging into someone's private life over a game, but then again, Lochlyn also understood the reasoning behind it. Throwing a murder mystery game could turn deadly if the wrong person was invited.

Still, Lochlyn didn't appreciate the sudden change of tone in Kitty's voice, like she was placating a child. It was like her mood had switched in a moment. Something about this girl just didn't sit well with her, even though there was no specific reason Lochlyn could pinpoint. Kitty just rubbed her the wrong way.

"Well, this pretty little head is gonna go check out the lodge. If you'll excuse me," Lochlyn attempted to leave, but Kitty's hand wrapped around her wrist, yanking her back.

"I would stick to the indoors. It looks like the rain's about to start any minute. I would send out any good night texts to any boyfriend or girlfriend cause the connection gets nearly impossible to use up here in the mountains. You wouldn't want to keep anyone at home waiting and worried about why you've suddenly gone silent, would you?" she warned with that too big smile of hers.

Her statement almost felt too pointed and out of nowhere to be meaningless. There was a splash of anger behind her words, a burning hatred in her amber eyes. That fury was pointed toward her, and Lochlyn couldn't figure out why that was.

They were supposed to be in character now, weren't they? Maybe this was a part of Kitty's narrative? It left an unsettled nagging feeling in her stomach. The moment of playing a good host was over and clearly Kitty was falling into her role as an ominous leader.

After a lingering moment, Kitty eased her death grip around her wrist. Lochlyn wanted to believe this was just Kitty playing her part, but a little voice in her head was warning her to be cautious of this girl. Her ability to switch from helpful to frightening was too good.

Maybe Twiggy wasn't as good at his screening job as he claimed to be? That is, if he even bothered to screen their own host.

Either way, she was going to make a point of staying clear of Kitty and her rudeness.

A silence bordering on awkwardness fell over them. Lochlyn was itching to get back to her room to get some rest before she changed for dinner, but it felt as if Kitty wanted to say something more. But after what had just occurred between them, Lochlyn wasn't sure she wanted to hear anything else.

Rubbing her sore wrist, Lochlyn tried unsuccessfully to control the shakiness in her voice. "Well, I should get going."

Kitty opened her mouth, ready to speak, but the words appeared to die in her throat. Whatever she'd wanted to say was left behind as she said, "Go rest up before dinner. I have a feeling you're gonna need it.

Hesitating, Lochlyn accepted that Kitty wasn't going to say whatever was bothering her and nodded. "I'll see you at dinner then. Bye."

Chapter 6

After her run-in with Kitty, Lochlyn escaped to the third floor of the lodge where she discovered a little tucked away library. Since she couldn't keep herself hidden away for longer than five minutes despite the lodge being massive, Lochlyn found herself wondering who might stumble upon her next.

She seriously hoped it wouldn't be Twiggy and his aggravatingly smug grin.

Was this part of the game, or was it just a coincidence that she couldn't seem to get more than two minutes to herself? Maybe it would have been a better idea to just head back to her room like Olive and Boomer had after lunch? They'd wanted to decompress before dinner when the first murder would take place.

At least if she'd done that, Lochlyn would have had some peace and quiet to unwind.

Trailing her fingers along the spines of different books, Lochlyn perused the different shelves in search of something interesting. She'd brought some books with her, though only one or two. If this had been a normal vacation, she might have brought a third just to read by the poolside, but it wasn't an ordinary trip.

To be fair, they were supposed to interact with each other to help lay clues or suspicion as the game went on.

So, Lochlyn had packed away a few different notebooks to jot down different clues and theories instead. She added an entire pouch of different pens, markers, sticky notes, and red string too. It was entirely possible Lochlyn had even overpacked, at least in the office supply department, but it was better to be over-prepared than under-prepared.

Lochlyn was pleasantly surprised to find a shelf entirely of Agatha Christie books. Kitty probably made sure the books had a home here in this library. She'd mentioned over their group chat last week how her uncle was a big mystery lover as well.

It was probably why he'd agreed to let them have the run of the lodge to themselves.

Finding a Halloween themed title, Lochlyn pulled it from the shelf and made herself comfortable in a big, dark blue armchair facing the huge floor to ceiling windows. Outside she could see the sun was starting to disappear behind dark rain clouds.

The incoming storm felt like a further warning to run while she still could. It should have scared her, but instead it only brought her excitement about the game.

The ominous view out the windows just added to the setting and it was the exact reason they'd decided on this weekend to have their game. Lochlyn couldn't imagine a more beautiful sight as the backdrop to the story. It was an added bonus that the ski lodge would empty of other guests too.

Curling up in the armchair, she pulled her phone out and pressed the camera button. Holding it up, Lochlyn angled it so that she captured the mountains behind her and the book in her free hand as she smiled as she hit the bar on the side of her phone.

Taking two shots to be sure she got the right one, Lochlyn lowered her phone and pulled open her photos app. Sliding between the two shots, she deemed the second one better and was just about to delete the first when something caught her eye.

There was a reflection in the glass of the window that didn't belong to the back of her head. Lochlyn squinted her eyes as she held her phone closer to her face.

Zooming in on the background, Lochlyn did her best to make out the bizarre form. Because it was a faint reflection, she couldn't make out details. It didn't help that the photo was pixelated from being so zoomed in either.

But it was *definitely* a face, she realized.

And not just any kind of face either. It appeared to be a stark white mask with hollow eyes and a pink pig snout and ears. It was a thing of nightmares.

As soon as she made out that much of the reflection, a gasp escaped through her lips as her eyes darted up to the shelf it had appeared behind only to see nothing there now.

"Hello?" No answer.

Lochlyn slowly uncurled her legs and dropped them to the floor as she quietly stood from her chair. "Twiggy, if you're trying to spook me before the game starts, I wouldn't recommend it. I have a book and I'm not afraid to use it."

Still no reply as she crept closer to the shelf in question. Thunder boomed, vibrating through the large room. A frightened squeak escaped from her mouth and her startled body jolted. As the thunder rumbled again, she swore she heard the doors open and shut, but Lochlyn couldn't be sure.

Raising the book up in her hands, Lochlyn held onto it as if she was holding a bat. It wouldn't do the same amount of damage that a heavy hardcover would, but with the right amount of force, it would still stun an assailant long enough to make a run for the enormous mahogany double doors.

Just then, a shadow moved behind the shelf, confirming someone was still in here with her. Lochlyn launched herself around the side, ready to strike before stopping instantly.

A startled Olive was standing there with wide brown eyes as she took in the sight of Lochlyn and her weapon of choice.

Pulling out an ear pod, her dark eyes traveled up from the book in her hands to Lochlyn's own green eyes with a raised eyebrow. "Were you about to hit me with .... Agatha Christie? Fitting choice for a murder weapon considering we're here to play a murder mystery game."

Shock came over her as a blush burned her cheeks. Lowering the book to her side, Lochlyn couldn't hide the look of guilt on her face. Did she explain what she saw in the picture? How crazy would she sound? Olive barely knew her.

Would she think Lochlyn was crazy and paranoid? The game hadn't even started yet, but she was already panicking. Lochlyn hadn't had a chance to prove her ability to handle this kind of stress. Olive would have every right to judge her in this situation.

What if the pre-game jitters were just getting to her? She was so worried about messing this up, she was working herself into a frenzy trying to fix it.

That photo was so blurry and grainy, she could have made a mistake. Olive's Blonde wig was light, it would be easy to mistake it for white in a grainy picture. Yeah, Lochlyn was sure that was all it was.

It probably didn't help that she'd been doing a scary movie binge to prepare for this long weekend.

"Sorry, I don't do well with thunderstorms," Locklyn said, choosing to brush off her panic as no big deal. That wasn't unheard of for an heiress, was it? "I thought I saw someone watching me and then no one answered when I called out. Now that I see your ear pods, I'm realizing you just didn't hear me."

Lochlyn couldn't convince her mouth to stop talking even though she was fully aware she was now rambling. The amusement over Olive's expression only made her more nervous. She was absolutely sucking at playing her part as an heiress. Lochlyn could only hope her nerves settled and she got more comfortable in the role.

"Well, you're not wrong about seeing someone. Sorry, I'm trying to get into the zone listening to this murder mystery podcast, but I'm just not clicking with it. They've got a monotone voice and I'm practically falling asleep here," Olive said, motioning to her phone in her hand.

"Have you given *The Twisted* a try? The narrator covers *tons* of cases that have these epic twists in them. Her last one covered that gruesome murder investigation about the cornfield a couple of states over. It was pretty interesting, but I won't spoil it for you," Lochlyn said as she pulled up the podcast on her own phone and showed it to Olive.

The blonde, though Lochlyn was sure it was wig, scanned the screen of her phone before another burst of excitement filled her. "Oh, I've heard of this one. She covered that one about the summer camp murders, didn't she? I love her."

"Yeah, I think she's got a great storytelling voice. She knows how to hold your attention. Here, you should give this season a try. I'll send you the link to it," Lochlyn said, motioning for her to enter in her number so she could text the link to her.

Olive seemed hesitant to take the phone, but before Lochlyn could take back the offer, Olive accepted it and typed in her phone number. The hesitation was expected, given the rules, but did this count as breaking them with the no personal stuff? Was it considered a grey area? Lochlyn didn't know and before she could ask, Olive had already handed the phone back.

"Thanks for the recommendation," Olive spoke up. "I hope you're not hiding in here. We're really not that scary of a group."

How do you tell someone it wasn't them, per say? That it was more of a 'her' issue without sounding corny? It's not you, it's me felt too much like a breakup.

Sometimes Lochlyn just needed a minute to relax and recover from socializing. Not to mention all the stress she'd felt on her way up here. All the excitement and nervousness about today was starting to wear on her mentally.

Having a few minutes to recharge and to find her peace of mind did her wonders, but how did she explain that? Not everyone could understand. While it only had been a few hours since arriving, the entire process of this trip and getting ready for it was exhausting for her too.

"No, no, everyone's wonderful," Lochlyn started. "Well, mostly everyone. It's just been a long morning with the drive, introductions, and lunch. I'll be fine by the time dinner starts."

A small smile tugged on Olive's lips. "I'm assuming that 'mostly' refers to Twiggy. He's not everyone's cup of tea. He's more like black coffee, bitter and harsh. He can be kind of blunt too with his thoughts, but he's not as mean as he pretends to be."

"I would say kind of blunt is a pretty accurate way to describe him," she muttered.

Olive chuckled, alerting Lochlyn that her voice hadn't been as quiet as she'd thought. "Don't sweat it. Just remember to have fun this weekend. That's what all of this is about, right? To relax and do what we love to do. Solve a murder. Well, a pretend murder, but still."

"Right, yeah. Sure."

A twinkle of something shined in Olive's eyes. Her smile appeared almost forced and fake. Totally opposite to the happy energetic girl she'd been up until this point. Just like Kitty earlier.

"I should get ready for dinner. I bet it's gonna be a *killer* meal. Enjoy your book." Olive laughed at her own bad joke, which seemed to go well with the ball of energy Lochlyn had encountered earlier today. She seemed like a nice person.

Or that was what Olive wanted them all to think.

Always keep an eye on the nice bubbly ones, Lochlyn reminded herself.

They got away with more because no one would think to suspect them of such a horrible crime as murder. They were either the first ones killed off or behind all of it. If Lochlyn had learned anything. It was to never trust a smiling face.

Watching as Olive left the library, Lochlyn felt a chill run down her spine. Even with Olive gone, she couldn't ignore the gut feeling she was still being watched. Another rumble of thunder echoed through the room, putting her nerves further on edge. She hadn't been lying when she told Olive thunderstorms upset her.

Maybe the game was already getting to her? It was possible, but also disappointing considering it hadn't even officially started yet. She was psyching herself out by over analyzing every detail and every word spoken.

Swallowing her fear, Lochlyn put the book back where she'd found it and collected her things. She no longer had any desire to sit and read in here. Not with the storm brewing and the game starting so soon.

Pausing in the doorway, Lochlyn looked back, scanning the empty room one last time. If she had strained her ears, she might have heard the floorboards creaking as someone shifted their weight. She might have seen another shadow twitch with anticipation as they waited for her to leave.

If she lingered any longer in that doorway, Lochlyn might have seen the hollowed-out eyes of a pig man mask staring back at her from the shadows.

But Lochlyn didn't do that, didn't hear or see any of it. Instead, she turned and left the room. The doors clicked shut behind her, trapping the hidden monster inside.

Chapter 7

When Lochlyn got back to her room, her body was abuzz with a new-found energy. The desire to get in a nap before dinner was forgotten and instead, she pulled out one of her notebooks and got to work.

Kitty had bulletin boards left in all the rooms with a sticky note with the words '*Time to create your murder board. Hope you brought your red string*' on it.

Lochlyn wasted no time in setting the board up on the table and retrieving her supplies. Her suspect list was really all she could put on it right now. Anything else would have to wait until after the first murder occurred. Still, she put a notecard beside each name with her first impressions of the other.

Twiggy – Arrogant, smart, tech-savvy, annoying.

Pumpkin - Snobby, secretive, diva.

Oliver – Charming, kind, handsome (just an observation), flirty.

Olive - Sweet, bubbly, fake.

Kitty - Queen B attitude, stunning, hiding something.

Boomer - Jock, intimidating, Kitty's second hand.

Camden – Gentleman, charming, is the accent real?

It wasn't much to go off, but it was a start. Until the game started, this was really all she could do. Still, first impressions in this sort of environment said a lot. These were the personalities the players wanted to come off as.

Over the weekend she'd have to figure out motive, place, and weapon. The more she got to know these characters, the better equipped she'd be in doing so. They'd be studying her in the same way. Her character of Ivorie was going to be judged and critiqued just as harshly as she was being with theirs.

Twiggy's earlier comment about her lack of confidence came back to mind. Had she already blown her first impression? She certainly wasn't off to a great start. There would be no way of knowing for sure though until the end of the weekend when Kitty tallied the scores.

Running a hand through her fake red curls, Lochlyn itched to pull it off and let her purple locks breathe. It was too much of a hassle to take on and off though. She would just have to wait until after dinner when she's in for the night.

Speaking of dinner, it wouldn't be long now. Lochlyn glanced at the time on her phone and realized she'd been going over her board for the past hour. It would probably take her another hour to change and freshen up her face.

Heading for the closet, Lochlyn pushed a few hangers aside before deciding on which outfit she wanted to wear to dinner. If her first impression was off, she would need to up her game. That meant attitude, look, and confidence. She couldn't be snarky, shy, nervous Lochlyn.

It meant she couldn't be herself.

She'd have to be better at catching her stuttering or exposing any nervous ticks like fidgeting with her hands. Things like that were going to affect her game strategy.

Taking the new outfit into the bathroom, Lochlyn went about cleaning her face, and wiped away her old make-up so she could apply a fresh look. It didn't make any sense to her why women caked their faces with all this gunk.

Even Lochlyn had to admit, though, she did look more like the beautiful heiress she was pretending to be. Lochlyn had been afraid she was going to look like a clown, but she'd been watching tutorials all week. Lochlyn could happily say she was pleased with the result.

Once her makeup was finished, Lochlyn carefully stripped out of her afternoon ensemble and into the outfit she'd chosen for dinner. As she slipped the straps of her romper into place, she studied herself in the mirror. Between her freshly applied make-up and the clothes, Lochlyn found she didn't recognize the girl looking back at her.

She was beautiful, posed, an heiress ready to strike.

Lochlyn wasn't used to showing so much leg and she knew the shorts were going to ride up even more while she walked. Things were going to chafe! Never mind having to use the bathroom.

Not to mention how it fit against her frame. She suddenly had curves and a shape Lochlyn didn't know existed. It felt too revealing, too noticeable. It was completely opposite to how she usually dressed.

But that was the point, wasn't it? That was why she bought it.

Lochlyn might want to blend in, but Ivorie was literally born to stand out. She would want all eyes on her. "Well, this outfit will definitely achieve that goal," Lochlyn muttered as she turned and twisted to examine the outfit in the mirror.

Still, like with the makeup, Lochlyn had to admit she looked pretty. The romper had a similar beige tone like her raincoat. The straps fell off her shoulders, creating a sweetheart neckline. There was a red belt clinched around her waist, giving her an hourglass shape. At the waist, a darker sand colored skirt descended to the floor with an opening in the front to reveal the shorts.

Lochlyn knew she'd have to wear some kind of heel to keep the skirt from dragging behind her, but it'd be worth it. She looked, and *felt*, badass in this outfit. If she could stand tall and keep her nerves at bay through dinner, they might even believe Lochlyn had the confidence she was pretending to have.

Glancing at the time, Lochlyn met her reflection in the mirror once more and inhaled a deep breath.

Showtime.

*

Dinner was silent and awkward, to say the least.

Much to her unfortunate luck, dinner was being thrown in a different room than lunch. She eventually found the dining room after two tries of searching for it. As a result, it was no surprise that she was one of the last ones to arrive.

The twins, Pumpkin, and Camden were already there, and Olive had taken it upon herself to fill the silence with chatter. Twiggy arrived just after Lochlyn got there. He still hadn't changed since this morning. He remained in the black turtleneck she'd seen him wearing earlier at lunch.

It grated her how much effort she put in with wearing three different outfits today when guys like Twiggy didn't need to worry about that detail. It wouldn't be blasphemy like it would be if she'd chosen to stay in her traveling clothes.

Kitty arrived soon after with Boomer in tow. She called for the staff and for everyone to take their assigned seats. Lochlyn found a little card with Ivorie's name scribbled in a fancy font beside Oliver and across from Twiggy.

Olive sat to her brother's left while Camden was on Twiggy's. Pumpkin sat on the other side of him, diagonal from Lochlyn. There was an empty seat open on her other side, no doubt meant for Nik if she'd been able to come.

Lochlyn found it odd there would be a place set for her seeing as Kitty had known for three weeks that Nik would not be attending. She may have just assumed it was an extra seat if not for the fact the spot open on the other side was missing a chair.

Boomer and Kitty, being the power couple they were, took the two end seats, completely their group of seven players.

As the food was brought out, Lochlyn took the chance to study the other players better. Pumpkin and Olive were still chatting away, seeking Kitty and Boomer's attention, respectively.

Camden tried to interject a word into both conversations every so often, but he wasn't having much luck. Oliver merely rolled his eyes at his twin and turned his attention to Boomer.

Boomer.

He was the only one she hadn't had the chance to really talk to before they were escorted to their rooms. During lunch, he hadn't said much to anyone and had gone directly to his room as soon as it ended.

His tousled dark hair appeared to have been positioned to appear dishelved, but somehow it was still perfect. His dark skin nicely complimented his forest green t-shirt. The short sleeves showcased his muscular arms, something she couldn't help but appreciate. Sitting there, he was like a Greek god. It was exactly how Lochlyn had pictured him.

Boomer had a lazy grin on his lips as he listened to Pumpkin drone on about something Lochlyn could only assume he couldn't care less about, but he kept a smoldering gaze on Pumpkin and gave her his full attention anyway.

Well, maybe not his *full* attention, Lochlyn noted as she watched his eyes flicker to Kitty and give her a playful wink. Kitty, in turn, rolled her eyes before returning her attention to Olive, who wasn't the wiser to the fact her words were landing on deaf ears.

That little exchange made him appear every bit the playboy his character was notorious for being. He and Ivorie would be a dangerous pair if they were to team up. At least, on paper they would be.

In reality, Boomer and his hypnotic blue eyes intimidated her. He was the oldest in their group. He and Kitty were the only ones legally allowed to drink while everyone else was still 18 to 20 years of age. They were technically considered the 'adults' in their party, which was how Lochlyn talked her mother off the ledge when she started to stress about the lack of supervision.

Still, Boomer wasn't the knight in shining armor that Lochlyn would look to for a rescue. He came off more like the devil in disguise. The one who was more likely to take you by the hand but then stab you in the back when your guard is down.

She'd have to keep an eye on him for sure.

As if sensing her stare, he lifted his gaze from Pumpkin and shot a wink in her direction. Lochlyn quickly averted her eyes, which unfortunately turned her attention to Twiggy.

He was watching her with a curious twinkle in his eye. He'd caught her spying on the others, and he was smugly making sure she knew it.

"Why are you looking at me like that?" she quipped.

Her tone took her by surprise, but Lochlyn quickly realized Twiggy seemed to just have that effect on her. Even though she'd only known him outside of their group chat for a mere few hours he truly brought out the worst in her. He took pleasure in getting on her nerves and all he had to do was merely sit there and smirk.

"I can't admire the heiress in our presence? I mean, it's not every day I'm in the company of someone who's basically royalty. Wait, should we be calling Princess Ivie?"

Her jaw clenched. "Ivorie. Not Ivie."

The way he shrugged a shoulder only annoyed her more. "Potato, patato, and all that."

Lochlyn was about to snap at him and tell him where he could shove his potato when Oliver wrapped an arm around the back of her chair and squeezed her shoulder. "So, Ivorie, tell me, how was the drive here? I meant to ask earlier, but the time got away from me."

Grateful for the interception, Lochlyn flashed him a small smile. "It was fine. Quiet. How was yours?"

His grin stretched across his face then. "We passed through this darling seaside town and got some saltwater taffy for the drive. Olive *had* to find a keychain. She gets one in every state we visit. She has about 24 of them at this point."

Oliver was diffusing the tension successfully. In the process of doing so, he was also pissing Twiggy off, which was absolutely a bonus in her eyes.

Upon hearing her name, Olive turned her attention to the rest of the table. "Oh! Yeah, how cute is this keychain?"

Pulling something free from her pocket, she dangled a small ring over her finger. The charm was of a red and white striped lighthouse with the words *Pinewood Point Lighthouse* written across the bottom of it.

Lochlyn recognized it. "You stopped in Lakeside Cove. It's a cute small beach town but it certainly has some bloody history."

That appeared to get everyone's attention. She wondered how many of them were from the area other than her. From the curiosity in the twins' and Camden's eyes, she figured it was safe to assume they weren't.

Kitty cleared her throat, gaining everyone's attention. "As riveting as Lakeside's history is, we're here to solve our own crime. As it turns out, Moose Hollow has its own frightening history. It's why I knew our game had to be set here."

That peeked Lochlyn's intrigue. Everyone on the East Coast knew of Lakeside Cove's tragic history with the Camp Pinewood murders, but it was news to her that Moose Hollow had its own tainted past. Was Kitty legit, or was this purely for the game's benefit?

"I feel a ghost story coming!" Camden was nearly giddy in his seat as a waiter set a new plate of food in front of him. He immediately started to dig into the salad without a glance.

Kitty sat back in her chair like a queen on her throne, a smug grin on her face as she scanned those around her. "Moose Hollow used to be home to one of the richest families on the East Coast back in the late 40's. They hosted grand parties here every winter. Their events were always legendary because of the beautiful backdrop of the mountains and, well, the parties were never dull. One year, they decided to host a masquerade ball. It was supposed to be the event of the year, but it ended in tragedy when the guest of honor was found murdered by her scorned lover."

Twiggy spoke up, breaking the trance Kitty's story had enchanted upon them. "You're full of it. I did my research on this place. There was a tragedy here, but it wasn't some fairytale horror story like the one you're describing."

Lochlyn swore she saw Kitty's eye twitch, but her tense smile never faltered. "If you know so much, then why don't you share?"

It was a challenge, a dare Twiggy stupidly appeared ready to accept. "Kitty's right, as far as there being a rich family who threw a lot of shindigs, but it wasn't as grand as all that. During one of their dinner parties, a snowstorm hit. It wasn't anything new or something they weren't prepared for. They offered rooms to all the guests who weren't comfortable driving. At some point during the night, they all awoke to a scream. Upon investigating, they found a young girl lying in blood in the dining room. On the wall, written in blood, was one word. Liar. And that was only the beginning."

Before he could continue, Kitty took back control of the story. "The remaining guests were terrified, but by then the storm was so bad that the only road up and down the mountain wasn't drivable. At some point the power had gone out. So there was no way for them to call for help either. They all locked themselves in their rooms until morning when the storm passed. All was quiet until the next body was found. The word 'Thief' was written on the wall this time. Three more bodies turned up as the night went on, their crimes announced much like the first two. No one was safe. One of the family members took a chance and found a working snow mobile so they went into town for help. When they returned hours later, everyone was dead, whether because of the murderer or because they risked the elements trying to leave."

Everyone sat totally engrossed as they hung on Kitty's every word.

"Did they ever figure out who killed them?"

It was Olive who asked what they had all been thinking. Lochlyn sat forward in her chair, waiting for whatever answer Kitty gave them.

"For years, it was theorized that it was the family member who'd gone for help, but he swore he was innocent up until the day he died. But since he was the only survivor no one could argue with his story. I've read some articles claiming it was someone else in the house that night. Someone who wasn't accounted for because they were never supposed to be there. Possibly it was one of the staff members who claimed to have left before the storm got too bad. There's always been a third theory though. My personal favorite, if you ask me," Kitty confessed.

Lochlyn nearly fell out of her seat with anticipation. "What's the other theory?"

Before Kitty could continue, a sudden choking sound alerted everyone. Lochlyn's attention shot to Camden to see him holding his neck. He was coughing, struggling to breathe. That bellhop from earlier was suddenly behind him, having popped out from the shadows, and was thumping his back with her hand.

Kitty and Twiggy both moved to help him when it didn't appear to be working.

"Oh, my god, talk about timing!" Olive gasped.

Kitty wasn't remotely as excited. "This isn't the game! He's really choking! Hey, Cam? Cam, is something stuck? Does anyone know the hymnlike maneuver? Gab?"

Lochlyn couldn't even process the fact Kitty had just called the bellhop Gab, as if they were two friends and not strangers. All she could do was watch as Camden's face turned red as he shook his head.

Twiggy stood and pulled Camden up with him with the help from Gab. He got behind him and wrapped his arms around his frame. Gab muttered something about keeping the staff out of the way before rushing out of the room. Lochlyn sat frozen in her chair, hand to her mouth, as she watched Twiggy move.

"Why isn't it working?" Kitty panicked. "He still can't breathe!"

Boomer ran around the table, his hands searching the table. "Does anyone know if he was allergic to anything? Kitty, did he tell you?"

Kitty was shaking, her eyes wide as saucers as a purple tone colored Camden's face. He couldn't get air in, and Twiggy's help wasn't working. "Uh, uh, yeah, he-he said he was allergic to nuts. I-I had everyone email me a list of allergies so I could inform the cooks."

Oliver stood then, shaking off a distraught Olive's arm. "He should have an EpiPen with him then. Where's his room?"

Kitty's body shook with tremors. "Uh, um, I-I don't-"

"Kit, focus! Where's his room?" Boomer snapped.

Trembling, she nodded as she made herself focus. "Uh, second floor on the left. Room 201, next to the elevator."

Oliver didn't wait a second before he sprinted off. Olive had scooted over and latched onto Lochlyn, but she barely noticed. Pumpkin sobbed across from them. Even if Oliver had super speed, he wouldn't make it back in time. Camden had already been struggling for air too long.

Twiggy held onto Camden as they both collapsed to the floor. "Come on, man. Hold on a little longer. Keep fighting! It's going to be okay. Kitty, call 9-1-1!"

"I left my cell in my room. Th-there's a landline at the front desk," she stuttered, fumbling into a run as she raced out of the room.

Camden could only wretch as he strained for breath, but his throat was swollen, blocking his air passage. His cheeks were red and splotchy, his eyes filled with fear and bloodshot as he fought to keep them open.

Boomer paced, his eyes shooting to the doorway every other second. Pumpkin had turned to pacing, muttering to herself as fat tears ran down her cheeks. Olive still clenched onto Lochlyn, sobbing into her shoulder. And her? Lochlyn felt numb as the rise and fall of Camden's chest slowed before stopping all together.

"He-he stopped breathing," she whispered, too stunned to speak any louder.

Lochlyn wasn't sure anyone heard her over Olive's crying, but the way Twiggy's head snapped up and his eyes turned to her immediately told her that he had.

"Shit," he cursed under his breath.

He shifted Camden's body to lay him down. "Ivie, come here! Quickly. Come on, come on!"

Shaking, Lochlyn jolted into action as she slipped out of her chair and maneuvered around the table. "Wh-what can I do?"

Twiggy pushed his hair out of his eyes as he moved to kneel beside Camden and pushed up his glasses. "We need to start CPR. Here, kneel behind him. Keep his neck elevated. Just like that."

Lochlyn did as he instructed as she got to the floor. He lowered Camden's head and tilted it back. "I'm going to start chest compressions and when I tell you, I want you to pinch his nose and blow air into his mouth. Okay?"

Her eyes were focused on Camden's red mouth. It was the allergic reaction from whatever he'd ingested. He was going to die. He wasn't breathing and-

"Ivie, focus! Can you do this? Cause if you can't, Boomer can take your place, but Camden doesn't have time for you to freeze up," Twiggy shouted through her thoughts.

Shaking, she nodded firmly and wiped her eyes. Not wasting another moment, Twiggy went forward performing CPR on Camden. Lochlyn focused on his voice as he counted out the compressions. When he told her to go, she did as he instructed her and blew air into Camden's mouth.

Nothing.

Twiggy didn't give up. They went again and again. As he readied for another round, Boomer set a heavy hand on his shoulder. "He's gone, man."

Twiggy shook it off with tears running down his face as he shot a glare at the older boy. "We have to keep trying! We can't just let him die!"

"He's already gone, man," Boomer reiterated. "You did everything you could."

Lochlyn covered her mouth, a sob racking through her body. The door opened and she was hoping to see Oliver come charging in with the solution to save Camden, but it was the wrong entrance and was just Kitty running in. "I can't get through on the landline. Is he   " She trailed off as she took in the sight before her.

Horror filled her eyes, a hand flying up to her mouth.

"No!" she cried.

Another door opened and Oliver came running in holding Camden's EpiPen. Sweat poured down his face, his chest heaving as he caught his breath. "I've got it! I've got it!" he shouted as he skidded to a stop just feet from them.

Boomer shook his head, silently telling him it was too late.

Camden was dead.

Chapter 8

The group of seven moved to the lounge. Gab, or Gabrielle as Kitty later mentioned, told the staff to stay out of the dining room until they could call for help. Most of the staff had left before dinner and the kitchen staff had left as soon as the dishes were put out, but apparently there were still some overnight staff that were hanging around.

Keeping the staff out of the dining room wasn't their most pressing issue though. There seemed to be a connection problem. The landlines weren't working, and their cells weren't getting any service.

There was an incoming storm that the group had initially been excited for, but now they wished for nothing more than for it to miss.

Sitting in the bay window, Lochlyn hugged her knees to her chest and stared out into the darkness on the other side. The rain started to fall a few minutes ago and had already turned the road leading out of the resort into small ponds of muddy water.

No one else would be able to leave, let alone get here, until the thunderstorm passed, and considering they were in the mountains, there was no telling when that would be.

With the shotty cell service this far up, there was no chance of calling 911, and anyone who wasn't initially intending on spending the night had already left by the time the incident occurred. That meant there was no sending anyone back to town with a call for help either.

Someone started a fire in the lounge in an attempt to warm them up, but Lochlyn knew that the chill that had overtaken her wasn't from the cold. She couldn't get Camden's haunting expression out of her mind. Every time she closed her eyes, she could still see the fear on his face. He knew he was dying and he couldn't do anything to stop it.

"Did he have the wrong plate? Maybe they accidentally gave him someone else's dish." Oliver was trying to figure out what happened, but there was no way to make this make sense.

Kitty was sitting on one of the couches, her blank stare focused on the fireplace. "No. I didn't want to risk it so I made sure none of the meals served this weekend would have nuts in it."

That new piece of information sat like lead in her stomach. Camden's very real death hadn't been a part of the game, and it wasn't an accident either. Suddenly their fun had turned into a nightmare.

With the storm quickly becoming worse, Lochlyn had a feeling their current situation would follow its lead.

Boomer was pacing in front of the fire. "Well, that doesn't mean it was murder, right?"

Lochlyn's attention snapped up, horror etching itself across her face as soon as the words left his mouth. How did he jump to that conclusion so quickly?

Boomer quickly backtracked as he caught sight of the horrified looks that he'd received from her and a few others in the room. "I mean, mistakes happen. Maybe one of the kitchen staff misunderstood or it was genuinely an accident. Human error."

Lochlyn heard Twiggy snort and looked over in time to see him rolling his eyes. He was twisting some sort of coin charm necklace between his fingers. "That's one big error and pretty unlikely. I mean, what are the chances the *only* salad that had nuts in it went to the *only* person who couldn't eat it? I think we've all watched and read enough mysteries to know it was on purpose. I mean, that's the entire point of this weekend, right? Because we love murder mysteries. Maybe someone wasn't happy with it only being pretend. How did you even know he wasn't faking it?"

He'd said what they were all thinking. Someone had taken the game a step too far and crossed the line between fantasy and reality. There were the questions of how Kitty immediately knew something was wrong or where Gab had suddenly come from too. Olive's reaction of assuming Camden was just playing his part was reasonable to understand. Lochlyn had thought so too.

Kitty's red, puffy eyes lifted, gliding over the other faces.

"Because *my* number was picked for the murdered player. Not his. As for her, Gab isn't a player. She's been helping me put everything together all this past week. She was supposed to keep the story moving forward."

Lochlyn felt a chill go down her spine. Of course that was why Kitty knew something was wrong. She would have been the only person who knew it wasn't part of the game. If Kitty's story was to be believed, she and Gab were the only ones who knew she was supposed to be the one to 'die' and not Camden.

Lochlyn's eyes scanned the rest of the group. Olive and Oliver were sitting on the other couch. He had his arm wrapped around his twin to comfort her. Olive hadn't stopped crying since this all began. She was hysterical and Oliver was doing his best to calm her as he rubbed soothing circles on her back.

Pumpkin was curled up on the loveseat to their right, staring numbly into the fire. Every so often a piece of firewood would crack, and her body would flinch. Lochlyn wasn't even sure Pumpkin was aware she was doing it.

Boomer ran a hand through his hair. The same perfectly mused hair she'd noticed before was now a real mess. "And you're sure we can't leave? I mean, the storm hasn't been going that long. I've got my truck."

Kitty shook her head. "The roads up here are dangerous during severe storms like this. They completely flood."

Pumpkin's eyes lifted from the dancing flames. "We should at least try. The worst that could happen is that his truck is stuck overnight."

The others mumbled in agreement, and it was decided. They had to at least try to get out of here or at the very least get help. Kitty's eyes narrowed on Boomer, as if annoyed he'd suggested a new plan.

It must have been her imagination though because, why wouldn't she want to get out of here? Why wouldn't she want to get help? It wouldn't bring Camden back to life, but it could save anyone else from dying tonight.

Gab and Kitty retrieved rain ponchos for everyone from the storage closet. It could be risky to head off to the rooms and collect their coats since they don't know what was happening. All they knew for sure was that Camden was dead and it was starting to look like it wasn't an accident.

Lochlyn didn't move from her spot at the bay window. The longer the two women were gone, the antsier everyone else was becoming. Boomer had returned to his pacing, anxious blue eyes darting to the doorway every few minutes.

Lochlyn might have assumed he was worried about them, if not for the look Kitty had just given him.

And, if she had glanced up, Lochlyn might have noted the bitter look of jealousy on Pumpkin's face. Not that she would blame her. Pumpkin came off as the type of person who was looking for a hook up on a vacation like this one was supposed to be. The girl had clearly been intending on setting her sights on the broody athlete. It appeared Kitty beat her to him though.

A throat cleared and Lochlyn shifted her attention to the person now standing beside her. Olive had finally pulled herself together enough to move from the couch.

"You've noticed the death glare too, huh?" Olive immediately winced, as if she instantly regretted her word choice.

It probably was in bad taste to talk about murdering, death glares before Camden's body even had a chance to cool.

"I was under the impression none of us had met, but "
Lochlyn trailed off, realizing now wasn't the time or place to gossip.

But still.

Kitty had been clear on the rules of the group since day one. No one was supposed to break the fourth wall and get personal. Getting to know each other intimately was explicitly over the line.

Olive chewed her lip, deciding her words carefully as she lowered herself to the spot beside Lochlyn.

"The rule is kind of more like a guideline," Oliver started. "It's safer for everyone's privacy, which is why it's there and stressed, but it's not a a deal breaker. It just can't interfere with the storyline for the game. No jealousy if you're into other people while in character and don't bring internal fighting into it either."

It sounded great on paper, but how did it work in action? If Pumpkin and Boomer's characters were supposed to get close in this game, did that create conflict between them and Kitty? Or was she able to separate game from reality and let it go?

Lochlyn couldn't imagine watching her own boyfriend cozying up to someone else for the sake of a game.

"Have there been any issues before?"

She'd only been in the group several months, but the others had been in the game for much longer. She wasn't sure how long the group had been going or who started it originally. Maybe the rule had been created *because* an incident had already occurred.

"There's always been tension between those three, but they've kept it out of the group. Hopefully tonight doesn't end that truce," Olive whispered as her attention flickered to the two in question.

"Does anyone else know?"

In a blink-and-you-miss-it moment, Olive grinned, but it was gone before Lochlyn could analyze what it could mean. Was Olive pleased that she'd asked? Lochlyn must have misread the twitch in her mouth.

"Camden overheard them earlier. After lunch, Pumpkin had gone to find Boomer and walked in on him and Kitty in a heated moment. She allegedly confronted them about keeping it in their pants this weekend. It could interfere with the game. Kitty accused her of being a jealous troll, her words not mine," Olive whispered, her eyes darting across the room to make sure no one was listening to their conversation. "He didn't hear anything else because Boomer had dragged them both into the room and shut the door."

Camden had overheard a conversation he wasn't supposed to hear and now he was lying dead in the dining room. Lochlyn's attention shifted toward Pumpkin and Boomer and she couldn't help but note how on edge they were.

Not like Twiggy, who was watching the fire, still with the coin-like charm at the end of his necklace twisted between his fingers. Or Oliver, who was trying to get Boomer to just chill and sit down while they waited for Kitty and Gab to get back.

How long did it take to retrieve two handfuls of ponchos?

"If you two are done gossiping over there, maybe you'd like to share with the rest of the group whatever you're plotting away?" Pumpkin spoke up, her narrowed gaze now zeroed in on them.

A blush of embarrassment burned across her face, but Olive didn't appear to share the same guilt and just rolled her eyes. "Oh, get over yourself. We were just chatting about the storm."

It was a lie, but only she and Olive knew it. Lochlyn wasn't about to point it out.

Pumpkin went ridged, a bitter smile stretching across her face. "So, sweet sobbing Olive does have claws. I knew that innocent act was just that   an act."

Olive went tense, her fingers clenching the cream-colored billowy pants she'd changed into. "You're one to talk."

Before Pumpkin could reply, the double doors to the lobby flew open and Kitty and Gab returned with two stacks of folded ponchos in their arms.

The two of them paused, taking in the tension filled room. Kitty's gaze immediately turned to Boomer with a raised brow. He subtly shook his head, warning her not to ask.

Clearing her throat, Kitty subtly dipped her chin and turned her attention back to the rest of the group. "If we're going to do this, it needs to be now before the road floods entirely."

Twiggy was the first to stand, tucking his necklace back under his shirt before clapping his hands together. "Well, I, for one, am more than ready to end this experimental disaster of a trip early. Anyone else?"

Pumpkin merely huffed and rolled her eyes as she accepted a rain poncho from Gab. Though, Lochlyn couldn't help but notice how she tossed another glare Kitty's way as she did it.

Oliver, Olive, and Lochlyn all followed suit and accepted the ponchos as well. Unfolding the weird material, Lochlyn noted its plainness except for the lodge's logo in its center. The red and white planks appeared to pop amid the foggy white poncho. In the center of the board was a moose shape with the name of the ski lodge on it. It was a simple logo design, but it was unique enough to be memorable.

Slipping it over her head, Lochlyn noticed Boomer accepting the last poncho from Kitty. Their gazes locked and their fingers brushed, as he took it from her. The stare held for longer than necessary, but with a brief glance toward Pumpkin, Lochlyn knew she wasn't the only one to notice.

Tensions were running high ever since Camden started choking on his dinner. It wouldn't surprise Lochlyn if tempers reached their limits and the anger and fear of the situation got the best of them.

Hopefully, they made it to town before that happened.

Chapter 9

The group of eight filed out once everyone had their ponchos on over their clothes. They decided to stay together as they ventured out into the drizzling rain.

If Boomer's truck was going to make it through the flooded road, it would be better to not push their luck and try to make it in one trip. It was going to be a tight squeeze, even with Twiggy and Oliver volunteering to huddle in the bed of the truck.

Lochlyn shouldn't have been surprised to see the kind of truck Boomer drove. It screamed privileged athlete with its cobalt blue paint job and the outline of white flames along the sides.

Kitty snagged the passenger's seat as she effortlessly pulled herself up into the vehicle. She settled in and turned the heat on full blast. It didn't appear to be the first time she'd been Boomer's co-pilot.

With a sour expression, Pumpkin grabbed onto the handle and lifted herself up into the backseat. Locklyn noted it was going to be a tight fit with Pumpkin, Olive, Gab, and herself as she saw Olive wiggle into the back next. Even as small as she was, there wasn't much room left for Locklyn. Olive would basically be on their laps when Gab joined them.

"Come on, there's no time to waste. The longer we sit here, the more the road is flooding," Kitty urged, motioning for Lochlyn to hop inside next.

Nodding, she grabbed hold of the handle, lifted one of her legs onto the truck, and bounced on the tip of her toes before basically launching herself inside the back. Lochlyn landed in the small wedge of space left with an '*oomph*'.

Olive gave her a small smile as she settled in beside her. "The leap into Ollie's truck is so bad. At least Boomer has a step to help us minion sized people."

A snort escaped Lochlyn's lips before she could think better of it. This was not the time or place to be laughing. Especially not with Camden's body lying in the dining room. Judging by the glare Pumpkin had leveled on them, Lochlyn could assume she agreed.

Lochlyn was startled by the door shutting beside her, and she spun her head around. "Where's Gab going to sit? Wait, where is she anyway? Didn't she come out with us?"

Kitty twisted around in the passenger seat. "Gab's gonna stay behind with the other overnight crew. We can send help back once we get to town."

"*If* we get to town," Pumpkin muttered.

It didn't sit right with Lochlyn that they were leaving someone behind. Even though they just met and Gab was part of the staff, it felt wrong to leave her behind. Though, it wasn't like they were inviting the other staff members to jump in either.

There was still a chance Camden's death was an accident, Lochlyn tried to remind herself. There was no reason, no motive. It was simply a human error with the food. That's all.

But if she was being honest, a part of her wasn't sure if she really believed that or if she was trying to convince herself that was all it was.

The truck shifted under new weight. Turning around, Lochlyn saw Twiggy hopping into the back. Oliver had his hand stretched out, giving him a hand. As if sensing her stare, Oliver turned his head and gave her a subtle nod of his chin.

Lochlyn returned the acknowledgement and shifted back around in her seat. Her heart felt like it was thumping against her rib cage. Clasping her hands on her lap, she tried to control her breathing. Closing her eyes, Lochlyn attempted to relax her mind but found the tactic to be useless.

A hand dropped over hers and startled Lochlyn as her attention jumped upward and landed on Olive. "It's all gonna work out. I promise."

How could she know that for sure, let alone realistically be able to make that kind of promise? There was no way Olive could be this confident that everything would work out in their favor. The chance they'd make it through the flooded road was already slim.

Still, Lochlyn appreciated the sentiment. "I hope you're right."

Olive opened her mouth to say something but stopped herself and settled back into her seat. Lochlyn's attention drifted out the window, taking in the sight of the mountains in the distance.

She could barely make out the silhouette of the ski lift, stationed in place for another few weeks until the winter season officially arrived. Not that she'd been hoping to use it. The thought of dangling from that high up in the air with nothing to cushion her fall terrified her.

Something else in the distance caught her attention. Out there by the lift something moved. Lochlyn couldn't clearly make it out, but she swore it looked like a person straddling what looked like possibly a four-wheeler. Whoever it was appeared to be watching the truck.

"There's someone out there," Lochlyn muttered mainly to herself.

She must have said it loud enough for the others to hear, which wasn't too surprising. A moment later Olive and Pumpkin were pressed against her back trying to get a look. Even Kitty was straining to look out her own window.

"Where? How can you make out anything out there? It's already getting dark," Kitty said, skeptical as she kept her eyes trained on the darkness around them.

Lochlyn started to point to the person, but when she looked again, no one was out there. Confusion befell her, feeling strongly that she'd seen someone out there. At least, she was pretty sure. Perhaps she was seeing things like earlier in the library?

"They were on a four-wheeler. I could see the headlights shining at us," she tried to explain, but as the two behind her settled back into their spots she knew they didn't believe her.

"It was probably a security guy checking the grounds," Kitty offered, though she didn't sound too sure about that.

Lochlyn knew she didn't believe her either. A nameless staff member was more of a comforting explanation though than a possible murderer stalking them.

Lochlyn sat back into the seat, crossing her arms. She swore someone was out there, but there was no way they could have disappeared that quietly. Not on a four-wheeler. Those things were not stealthy in the least. It wouldn't go unnoticed, that was for sure.

Could the combination of the rain, wind, and distance have confused her though?

The last door to the truck slammed shut as Boomer slid into the driver's seat. "If we're done playing *I Spy*, I suggest we get going."

Irritation passed over her and her teeth clenched. They were acting like this was one big joke. Lochlyn felt pretty sure she'd seen something out there, but she wasn't going to fight them on the matter. For all she knew, it was possible it was some employee.

In the end, if they managed to get off this mountain in one piece, that was all that was important. The sooner they were out of here, the sooner she would be home.

Boomer shifted the truck into REVERSE and checked his mirrors before pulling out of the parking space. Shifting into DRIVE, the truck jolted forward as he started driving. Lochlyn found herself latching onto the door with a white-knuckled grip.

Boomer wasn't the worst driver, but he certainly didn't mind going a few, or many, miles over the speed limit. The truck jerked sharply as he made a turn. Lochlyn held on for dear life.

Looking out the window again, Lochlyn attempted to focus on the tree line as it passed by. They were moving too fast to see anything other than green blurs.

When she squinted her eyes, Lochlyn thought she saw headlights hurdling through the woods, but she didn't bother speaking up this time.

Chapter 10

The truck jostled as they traveled down the muddy road. Holding her stomach, Lochlyn prayed that her dinner stayed inside of her. Peering over her shoulder, she could see Oliver and Twiggy holding onto the sides of the truck as if their lives depended on it. Which, to be fair, it honestly might have.

Lochlyn would have laughed if not for the fact she wasn't certain opening her mouth wouldn't have allowed her stomach contents to travel upward.

"I understand we're all a little freaked," Pumpkin started, gritting her teeth as they hit another bump. "But could you drive a little more smoothly?"

To her horror, Boomer just laughed. "If we're going to make it through the flooded sections, we're gonna need speed on our side."

He wasn't exactly wrong, but Lochlyn and her flipping stomach wanted to protest.

A thud from the truck bed caused the three in the backseat to turn their heads in unison. Twiggy was laid out on his stomach, grinding his teeth as he adjusted his glasses.

"I'm pretty sure Twiggy just went airborne," Olive noted.

Pumpkin held back a laugh, as did Kitty, who kept her gaze forward. Lochlyn might have joined them, but her stomach again reminded her that was a bad idea as they hit another bump in the road.

"Things are about to get hairy. Hold onto your seats, ladies!" Boomer almost sounded excited for this part.

Looking past him, Lochlyn could see that the road was taking a turn. On the way up to the resort, she'd noted how beautiful the winding road was, but now she hated it.

"Oh, my lanta," Pumpkin gasped as she grabbed simultaneously onto the door and the back of Boomer's seat. "We're going to die."

Lochlyn wasn't sure Pumpkin's exclamation was that exaggerated. If Boomer hit the turns at the wrong time, they could spin out or lose traction and slide off the side of the mountain. Never mind if they made it through the flooded sections of the road.

As they made it around the first bend, Lochlyn didn't dare breathe a sigh of relief. She probably wouldn't until they were safely at the bottom of the mountain and out of Boomer's terror truck.

His tires skidded out around the second bend, but he was able to keep the truck moving forward and regain control. It wasn't until they got to the third turn in the road that trouble hit.

Boomer cursed under his breath, struggling to turn the wheel. Lochlyn could feel the tires sputter beneath her as they tried to find traction, but there was too much water and mud around them.

"Everyone, hold on!" Boomer shouted as he sharply turned the wheel.

Suddenly they were spinning around and screams filled the cramped space of the interior. Lochlyn had one hand on the emergency handle and one hand latched into Olive's, whose hand was holding onto her seatbelt. Pumpkin was pressed to Olive's other side screaming.

Peeking an eye open, Lochlyn could see Kitty gripping onto Boomer's arm, as if that would keep him safe if they crashed. She didn't dare check how Oliver and Twiggy were hanging on.

With a hard thump, her side of the truck slammed into the side of the mountain, bouncing as it settled back on its tires. Her arm screamed in pain from connecting with the door so hard, but she flexed her fingers and knew it wasn't broken.

Her vision doubled for a moment as she watched two Boomers shift the truck into PARK. Closing her eyes, Lochlyn pressed her hand to her throbbing head. Something warm coated them. Opening her eyes, she realized there was blood on her hand. She must have hit her head.

Kitty was rubbing her own arm, but other than a new bruise she seemed fine. Still, Boomer was immediately on top of making sure as he checked her over with more concern than a stranger should. It added to the theory that they were already well acquainted before today, and not in the sense of talking online for years.

What was odd was the moment Kitty recoiled away, as if his concern disgusted her. The emotion was quickly erased as her body forcibly relaxed, and she gave Boomer a reassuring smile instead. "I'm fine. Seriously," she reassured.

Olive twisted around. There was panic etched across her face as she opened the small window. "Are you guys alive back there?"

Following her lead, Lochlyn turned to peer into the back and saw both boys laid out flat. Oliver groaned but gave them a thumbs up before rubbing the back of his head.

"You know that scene in *Toy Story* when Woody gets tossed around the back of the pizza truck?" Twiggy spoke up as he shifted to push himself into a sitting position.

Olive shot Lochlyn a look before nodding. "Yeah?"

Twiggy rubbed his arm, wincing as he rolled his shoulder. "I can now say I know how the guy felt, and I can strongly say I never want to again. One of you guys can sit back here next time."

Pumpkin rolled her eyes before shifting to look out her window. Her eyes widened and before they could question what was happening, she pushed open her door revealing the water almost level with the tires. "I don't think we'll be driving back from here," she noted.

Leaning over, Lochlyn's face scrunched up at the sight. There was no way they'd be getting the truck out of this water even if they tried pushing. The thought of jumping into the mud wasn't appealing to her either.

"We're gonna have to walk from here. It'll be dark by the time we get down to the bottom, but I have emergency flashlights in the bed of the truck," Boomer instructed as he opened his door and hopped out with a splash.

Kitty slid over the middle console and into the driver's seat since she and Lochlyn were trapped against the mountain. Boomer, seemingly unphased that he was knee deep in muddy rainwater, held out his hand to help Kitty down.

Glancing back, she noticed Twiggy and Oliver both hopping over the side of the truck. A moment later, Oliver extended a hand to help Pumpkin out. Except Pumpkin's attention was narrowed on Boomer lifting Kitty down into the water beside him.

Lochlyn noticed him lean forward and whisper into Kitty's ear, to which she rolled her eyes with a small smile and shook her head. Olive cleared her throat pointedly, reminding them there was an audience for their otherwise cutesy moment.

Pumpkin ignored Oliver's offered hand and hopped down, splashing the disgusting water as her feet hit the ground. Olive scooted over and accepted her brother's hand and hopped down next.

Sliding over the length of the seat, Lochlyn swung her feet out the doorway and grimaced at the brown slop awaiting her.

"Ah, now there's the heiress rearing her stuck up nose," Twiggy taunted as he took Oliver's place as he extended a hand to help her down.

His eyes were daring her to jump into the water. Pushing back her disgust, Lochlyn pressed her lips firmly together before pushing herself off the seat before she could regret her decision.

The water was warm around her legs, and she suddenly wished she'd taken off her shoes before hopping out of the truck as her heels slid over the sole of her shoes. Seeing the irritation on Twiggy's face as he wiped off his glasses made it all worth it though.

"Oops, sorry," she apologized with a quick flash of a smile.

Yeah, that was a lie, she thought to herself. And she had an inkling Twiggy was *well* aware of that fact.

Reaching down, Lochlyn undid the strap around her ankles and took her wedges off one at a time. As she lost a good two inches in height, she didn't let it show as she held her chin up high and bumped shoulders with him as she passed by. Lochlyn silently pleaded with her legs to not buckle under her weight and ruin the satisfaction she got from showing Twiggy up. Her head was still throbbing from the impact.

Olive did a poor job of hiding her chuckle behind her hand as she nudged her brother who was doing an even worse job of hiding his laughter. A part of her should feel guilty for embarrassing Twiggy, but he'd thrown the first shot. If he couldn't handle a jab back, then he shouldn't have opened his mouth.

Where was this boldness coming from? Lochlyn wasn't outspoken or quick on her feet with a retort. Normally she wouldn't have bothered responding to his taunting, but something about Twiggy drenched in mud brought out the confidence to stand her ground.

Twiggy grumbled, rolling his eyes as he went around to the back of the truck to help Boomer find the flashlights. Lochlyn kept walking to the edge of the road to get free from the water. As much as she enjoyed being knee-deep in it.

Her knees threaten to crumble beneath her. Lochlyn felt herself sway, but she quickly caught herself and used the closest tree for support before anyone could see.

"He's intimidated by you," Oliver offered as he approached. Lochlyn's body went ridged as she leaned against the tree. "I don't think anyone else gets under his skin like you seem to be able to. It doesn't hurt that you're pretty either."

Her cheeks felt like they were suddenly on fire. Oliver thought she was pretty? Or did he just know Twiggy did? Not that it should matter. Given the events so far tonight, that should be the last thing on her mind right now.

Lochlyn opened her mouth to say something when he suddenly raised his hand to her face, pushing a red curl behind her ear. His touch sparked a shot of pain against her head.

"Ouch."

She flinched, wincing as she touched the tips of her fingers to the sore spot. When she pulled her fingers away, there was a rusty red color covering them. She was still bleeding. *Shit.*

"It doesn't look too bad, but you'll have one hell of a headache. Do you feel woozy or unsteady?" Oliver asked, holding up his pointer finger. "Follow my finger."

Lochlyn did as he requested, even though she knew this was a waste of time. They needed to keep going before   her thoughts trailed off as something beyond him caught her attention.

Squinting, Lochlyn moved around him and stepped forward. "Please tell me someone else sees that," she spoke out though didn't dare shift her attention.

Down the stretch of road stood the figure straddling a four-wheeler. The headlights weren't blinding, but they were bright enough to obscure the person's face.

"Who is that?" Oliver spoke up as he stood behind her.

Lochlyn took another step forward, trying to get a better look. She could barely make out the points of pig ears and a glow reflecting off the white materiel of the mask she'd seen in the library window's reflection earlier.

Her eyes widened as the memory rushed back. Panic seized her as the rumble of the four-wheeler's engine broke the silence.

"We need to go back. Guys, we need to move. *Now.*"

Reaching behind her, she gripped Oliver's hand as she turned and made a run through the water.

Given the intense splashing, Lochlyn knew the others were following close behind. The water was heavy and dense, but soon enough they managed to free themselves from its grip and made a run back up the pathway toward the ski lodge.

Peering over her shoulder, Lochlyn noticed the person hadn't moved from their spot. Whoever was under that mask wanted them to go back to the lodge.

Thunder rumbled in the sky, laughing at their attempt to get back safely. Or was it a warning to stop and find a different way down the mountain?

Lochlyn didn't pause to figure it out.

But maybe she should have.

Chapter 11

The large doors burst open as the group all but fell inside. Boomer was quick to shut the doors behind them, panting as he leaned against the oak giants. Lochlyn felt like her heart was going to explode out of her chest as she tried to catch her breath. With a brief glance, it appeared the others weren't in any better shape.

"What the hell happened to you guys?"

Lochlyn's head snapped up, her eyes settled on Gab as she came out from one of the other doorways. Her jacket was soaked and her hair was damp against her face. Mud dripped off her hiking boots. Boots she hadn't been wearing a half hour ago.

Had Gab been outside since they departed? What was she doing out there? Could she have been the one following them on the four-wheeler? Even with a running head start, it wouldn't surprise her if the maniac on the four-wheeler beat them back to the lodge.

There was genuine concern and confusion on Gab's face though and Lochlyn might have taken back her suspicion if not for the fact her whereabouts were unaccounted for.

"Some lunatic just chased us back up the mountain on a four-wheeler. Know anything about that?" Twiggy snapped, apparently having come to the same conclusion as Lochlyn had.

Gab's jaw twitched, her eyes narrowing on Twiggy's scornful expression. "Can't say that I do. I was grabbing firewood in case you lot ended up back here, which, by the way, you did."

Kitty pushed through the group, her chest panting as she tugged off her poncho. "Well, someone doesn't want us off of this mountain. I'm really starting to believe that Camden eating those nuts wasn't an accident."

None of this made any sense. Why would someone be targeting them here and why now? What about their group brought out a murderous side in someone? Were they all being targeted, or did they just have the misfortune of accepting the wrong person to their group? Maybe someone had a vendetta against one of the other players in the group?

Maybe Twiggy wasn't as great at weeding out the weirdos as Kitty thought. He was only a freshman in college, not some fancy FBI agent trained for this kind of situation after all.

"Guy," Olive interjected and snapped everyone to attention. "Does that mean we're stuck here until the storm ends?"

Boomer scoffed. "This is a snow resort in the mountains. If that psycho managed to find a quad, there must be a bunch more. Kit, would your uncle have them locked up in some storage unit around here? We can take those."

Lochlyn watched as Kitty accepted a towel from Gab and wiped her face. "Yeah, there's a storage unit down by the ski lift with a few quads the staff use to get around the grounds. It should be locked, but maybe it's not. I'll get the keys on the off chance it still is."

Boomer was nearly bouncing with energy now. He wasn't the only one. Twiggy looked ready to bolt on a second's notice. So did Pumpkin and Olive.

"Great. Gab and I can go out with you. Everyone else should stay here," Boomer instructed. "Don't go off alone."

Pumpkin's scoff wasn't subtle, but Kitty ignored it as she rounded the front desk and searched for the keys.

"Just point out the obvious here, but we all know splitting up never ends well. Why don't we all go out there?" Twiggy had a point.

If Lochlyn knew one thing about murder mysteries, it was that you never split up. It was one thing she always shook her head at while watching the old *Scooby Doo* cartoons.

Still, Boomer disagreed. "We don't even know if we can get to them or how many there are. Just stay here, keep warm by the fire. We won't be long. Ready, Kit? Gab?"

Lochlyn watched as he extended his hand toward Kitty. The slender girl hesitated before placing her hand in his and nodded as she came back around the desk and motioned for Gab to follow them. It didn't miss Lochlyn's attention that their hands stayed intertwined as they left the room. Pumpkin's glare trailed after them.

This moment cemented the fact those three were far from strangers in Lochlyn's mind.

Boomer was already here when everyone else arrived. They didn't act like strangers. Olive had mentioned sometimes they paired characters in the games. Maybe it had something to do with that? They could have gone over possible plot points before the trip.

Earlier, Kitty had mentioned that she was the one who was supposed to die during the game. Perhaps that played a part in this too? Pumpkin's obvious distain of Kitty and Boomer's characters' connection gave her own character motive as the killer. She didn't know enough facts to know that for sure, but it held up as a theory for now.

If it was just a plot line for the game, why did it feel like it was leaking over to reality? Any plot for the game should have ended the second Camden released his last breath. Hell, shouldn't it have been over the minute he took the poisonous bite of his dinner? There was more going on here, Lochlyn just couldn't see the full picture yet.

But there were those raw nano-second moments where Kitty let her disgust slip through the cracks of her mask. Like she couldn't stand being close to Boomer. Was that how she really felt about him? If that was the case, then why would they still be continuing the narrative that they were intimate? It didn't make sense.

There was no way of knowing without flat out asking Kitty about it, and after the last time when her entire personality shifted on a moment's notice? Lochlyn wasn't racing for another one-on-one with her any time soon.

Silence fell over them while they traveled into the lounge where the fireplace was crackling with flames. Lochlyn returned to her earlier spot at the bay window, staring out into the darkness on the other side of the glass.

A shadow loomed over her, pulling her attention away from the outside as she noticed Twiggy standing beside her with a cloth in his hand. "For your head," he said, motioning to the drying blood crusting against the side of her face.

It had finally stopped throbbing. To be honest, she had nearly forgotten about the wound in the panic of getting back to the lodge. "Oh, um, thank you," Lochlyn said, her voice barely above a whisper as she accepted the cloth.

Twiggy pulled at the back of his neck. "No problem. I doubt Kitty wants you bleeding all over the furniture."

Lochlyn's mouth tightened, flattening to a thin line. Even when he was attempting to be kind, Twiggy couldn't manage to keep his snide comments to himself.

She was ready to tell him off when she noticed the shake in his hands. So, the know-it-all jerk was affected by all of this after all. Twiggy was human and maybe his snark was his way of keeping people from seeing the cracks? He didn't deserve her pity, but he still had it.

"No, I doubt she would," Lochlyn chose to say instead. "I think I can manage from here."

His piercing blue eyes widened for a second before any emotion he might have accidentally let slip disappeared altogether. Twiggy tugged at his wet clothes and nodded before returning to his spot on the couch without another word.

Locklyn did her best to clean herself up using her reflection in the window, but there was only so much she could do. Thankfully the cut on her head didn't appear to be too deep, meaning it wouldn't require any stitching. The thought of trusting anyone in this room to stick a needle and thread into her head didn't settle right in her stomach.

Tapping her finger against her knee, the deafening quiet started to get to Lochlyn after a few minutes. It felt like a month had gone by since Kitty, Gab, and Boomer left the room.

Not able to sit still any longer, Lochlyn tossed her feet off the window seat and stood. The sudden movement made the others jump, but she couldn't find it in herself to care. She needed to move. Her head protested the quick movement, but it did little to slow her down.

Crossing her arms, she paced the length of the floorboards and landed in Boomer's spot. This weekend had so much potential yet had quickly taken a U-turn and went south. Now it felt like a bad dream they couldn't get out of. Camden's corpse was lying on the floor of the dining room. He was alone and getting colder by the second.

"Did anyone know his name?" Olive spoke up, cutting through the silence. "I mean, Camden was his character name, right? It feels, I don't know, wrong to keep calling him that."

Guilt hit her hard then, causing her to stop her pacing. Her eyes shifted between Oliver and Twiggy. She was the last to join the group when a spot opened. Twiggy and Kitty had the advantage of already knowing everyone given she received the initial applications, and he did the background checks.

Lochlyn had no idea how long the others had known each other or how close they were. There was no way of knowing how much the others knew of each other. She knew the rules about keeping private, real-life information out of their games, but how long could you get to know someone without knowing their real name?

"Peter. His real name was Peter."

Her gaze shot toward Twiggy. But his eyes weren't meeting anyone elses's as he stared into the fire. A blank expression had fallen over his face since settling back in, dancing flames created shadows that gave him a sinister appearance.

Oliver grunted as he pushed himself off the couch and stood. "I don't know about you lot, but I could use a drink. Anyone else?"

Lochlyn watched with wide eyes as Oliver crossed the room to the bar. Tugging on the delicate doors to see if they were locked, he found they were not. He pulled out a few glasses and a crystal vessel with some kind of dark liquid and set them down on top of the marble counter.

"Do you really think that's a good idea, Cas-Oliver?"

Olive almost said his real name. She wondered how weird it was, for them especially, to call each other fake names.

A scoff erupted from Twiggy's throat as he joined Oliver. "It seems silly to keep pretending we're our characters, doesn't it? Given there's a body lying in the other room and some psycho just chased us back up here. I'll have one."

Oliver nodded and poured Twiggy a glass. He peered over his shoulder at her, but Lochlyn just shook her head. Shrugging, he turned back and finished preparing drinks for him and Twiggy. Who happened to have a point.

"I suppose that depends on whether we trust each other. I mean, the no-real-names rule is safer, that's why we came up with it in the first place," Oliver countered. "Given the circumstances, playing it safe feels like the right direction to go. Don't you think?"

Lochlyn couldn't tell whether he was just playing devil's advocate or if he truly believed that. She turned her attention to Pumpkin, and wondered where she landed on the matter. She'd been awfully quiet since Boomer, Kitty, and Gab left.

"I think Oliver's right," Olive commented, wiping her eyes as she stood. "It's safer if we just keep to our character names. There's less of a chance our home lives will be affected after all of this is said and done."

Nodding, Lochlyn rubbed her arm as she looked between them all. "So, we stick to game names for now?"

Twiggy didn't seem to agree, but he didn't argue either. "I guess so. Pumpkin, that good with you?"

The girl in question merely rolled her eyes, pulling her knees up to her chest and wrapping her arms around them. "What does it matter? If someone's trying to kill us, who cares what we call ourselves?"

A deafening silence fell over them as the rain grew louder outside. No one argued with her point, but no one changed their mind either. It appeared they'd stick with their characters names for the time being.

Lochlyn returned to the window, her eyes searching as best she could for any sign of Boomer, Gab, and Kitty. "When do you think they'll be back?"

Just then they heard a door slam.

Chapter 12

The sound of the double doors of the main entrance slamming shut echoed throughout the lounge. All five of the heads turned toward the noise. There stood Kitty, Gab, and Boomer, all shaking off the excess of rain covering them as they removed their hats and gloves.

"Well?" Twiggy asked with a faint twinge of hope.

From the crestfallen expression on Kitty's face, Lochlyn knew they weren't going to like whatever answer they were about to give. Boomer tossing his gloves on the check-in desk in a huff confirmed that fact.

"The lock to the storage space was busted open. All the four wheelers inside were damaged and   " Kitty trailed off, sharing a look with both Gab and Boomer.

Lochlyn turned fully, taking a step forward. It felt like she was waiting on edge for whatever piece of bad news was yet to come. "And *what*? What else did you find?"

The trio shared another look before Boomer spoke up. "One of them was missing."

So her earlier theory had been right. There was someone out there who didn't want them to make it off this mountain. None of this had happened by mistake. Someone planned every accident. Maybe even Camden's death.

It wasn't *just* anyone targeting them though. It was the same masked pig man Lochlyn caught watching her in the library earlier. At the time, she'd convinced herself she'd imagined it, but it wasn't the case now. He was real and not just her paranoia getting the best of her.

This masked monster had taken one of the four-wheelers for himself and destroyed the other so they couldn't use them.

The pig man had sabotaged them.

It felt like the air had been sucked right out of Lochlyn's lungs. Holding her stomach, a wave of nausea came over her. "I need some air," she spoke up, though she wasn't sure if it was loud enough for anyone to hear.

Not waiting for anyone's acknowledgement, Lochlyn raced out of the room. She wasn't sure where she was going, but Lochlyn couldn't stand being in that room another second. The fire made it too sweltering. The walls seemed to be closing in on them.

Lochlyn could vaguely hear her name being called. No, not *her* name. They were calling for Ivorie because to them *that's* who she was. She was the heiress, the rich spoiled girl with a taste for mystery solving and who didn't want to get her shoes muddy.

Tears rimmed her eyes. That girl didn't exist. *Ivorie wasn't real.* Had it really only been a few hours ago that she'd been excited to shelf Lochlyn for a few days and embrace Ivorie? It might have well been a lifetime ago.

While Lochlyn loved reading about murder mysteries and watching scary movies, this was too much. *Too* real.

Lochlyn wanted nothing more than to take her silly wish back. Ivorie was no longer wanted. If only shredding the persona would fix any of this. Even if she tore off her wig now, there would still be a dead body in the next room and a maniac stalking them.

Lochlyn just wanted to be alone so she picked up her pace. Looking briefly over her shoulder, she realized Oliver was coming after her. She wanted to tell him to go back, to let her be alone for a minute, but Lochlyn wasn't even sure if that was what she really wanted.

As she pushed the swinging door into the dining room, her choice of destination registered a second too late.

She was back at the scene of the crime.

As Lochlyn halted to a stop, her eyes immediately dropped to where they'd left Camden, more specifically, Camden's body. Her blood ran cold and her eyes widened. Her entire body froze except for her heart, which was beating so hard it pounded in her ears.

The door behind her swished open. "Ivorie, you can't just …. oh, shit."

Oh, shit indeed.

The spot where Camden's body had been lying, was now nothing but a few specks of dried blood. His body was gone, which clearly didn't make any sense. He couldn't just be gone. Bodies can't simply get up and leave the room.

Kitty had instructed the remaining staff to keep out of this room until they got help. Speaking of the left over staff, she'd yet to see one other employee since arriving other than Gab. Kitty had said it'd be a skeleton crew staying overnight, but still it was odd.

Stumbling back, Lochlyn jolted when she bumped into Oliver. "T-that's not possible. How   where did he go?"

The door swung open again and the rest of the party rushed inside. She knew without turning that they too were shocked by what they saw. Better yet, what they *didn't* see.

Kitty was the first to question out loud what they were all wondering. "Where is Camden?"

"Well, this certainly took an interesting turn," Twiggy added.

An interesting turn indeed.

Lochlyn turned to face the others. "I thought you told the staff to stay out of here?"

Horror struck Kitty's face at the accusation Lochlyn had thrown her way, her attention flickering between Lochlyn and Gab as if her friend would have the answers.

"I did!"

Shifting from one foot to the other, Lochlyn crossed her arms. She needed to do something to hide the way they were shaking. "Then where is-" she paused, catching herself from saying '*the body*'. "Where is Camden?"

He hadn't been dead long enough to be '*the body*'. He was still Camden, *Peter*, the guy she'd been crushing on just a week ago. She'd been excited and nervous to meet him, and barely got in more than one conversation with him before he died.

Oliver rested a hand on her arm. "I'm sure there's an explanation for all of this. The staff probably just moved him somewhere cold to keep the smell at bay. It's not like a corpse can just get up and walk off, right? Besides, Kitty was with us. She couldn't have moved the body."

Except she could have. Boomer, Gab, and she were all gone long enough to go check the storage unit and move the body. Hell, they could have put Camden's body in storage and been lying about the four-wheelers being sabotaged. Kitty could've had Gab do it while everyone else was out in the truck.

Maybe that was why she'd opted to stay behind? That would explain her muddy boots and wet clothing.

"Maybe not alone, but Kitty, Gab, and Boomer had plenty of time to move the body when they left to check out the shed," Pumpkin spoke up, her glare shifting toward Gab next. "Or she had her crony do it for her. How do we know Gab didn't have Camden moved and then followed us back in the quad to scare us?"

The sudden expression of insult across Kitty's face made her think Pumpkin might have crossed a line, but it didn't mean she was wrong. She'd just implied Kitty, Gab, and Boomer could have moved a dead body and lied about it. Worse, that would also imply they had something to hide.

Lochlyn might have thought it, but it was totally different to say it out loud. It didn't matter now. The line was officially crossed, and there was no taking her words back.

"Considering what game we were here to play, I'd like to think that if I was to hide a body, I wouldn't be so obvious about it." Kitty mocked her with a tense and bitter tone.

Swallowing her nerves, Lochlyn scanned the room in an attempt to gauge the others' expressions. She was the newbie so she didn't really know any of them well enough to make an educated guess.

Pumpkin had some solid theories, but no actual proof to back up them up.

Either way, Kitty had a point. They were here because they all loved murder mysteries. They knew all the tropes, all the tricks, and it wouldn't make sense for Kitty to make such an obvious mistake.

Boomer took a cautious step between the girls, his hands raised in peace. "Look, I get you're not happy about this weekend, but your jealousy isn't a valid reason to start accusing people of murder."

Lochlyn saw Pumpkin's face go red with embarrassment and anger. She felt bad for the girl. It wasn't like she had the full history on Pumpkin, Boomer, and Kitty. Though, Lochlyn wasn't entirely sure she wanted to know.

To be honest, Lochlyn assumed their little act had been a part of their game plot, but clearly that wasn't the case. There were legitimate feelings getting tangled up and hurt. Realizing that made Boomer's comment even more uncalled for.

Was Pumpkin out of line first with her accusation? Maybe, but she didn't deserve this humiliation. Lochlyn took a step back, joining the twins and Twiggy as onlookers.

SMACK.

Boomer's head turned from the impact of Pumpkin's hand. The sound of it vibrated through the room, causing the group of onlookers to wince.

"I am *not* a lover scorned. You are far from worth it, Boomer. You better believe *that*," Pumpkin snarled before turning on her heels and leaving the room.

Boomer took a step to follow, but Oliver cleared his throat and moved between them. "Tensions are high, yeah? Why don't we all just go to our rooms and wait out the storm? As soon as it's safe, we can all pack in one of the other cars and go to the cops in town together."

Ever the helpful, Twiggy scoffed and interjected. "I thought we already established splitting up was a bad idea? Besides, it didn't work out so well for the last group of party guests who were stuck here after a murder. It's bad enough Pumpkin just went off on her own."

It was then Lochlyn realized Kitty and Gab were bickering quietly in the corner. If she had to guess what about? Lochlyn would say it was safe to assume it was about Pumpkin.

Gab raised her hand, waving off Kitty's concern. "I'll go talk to her and convince her to come back."

Without waiting for anyone to argue, Gab was out the door and disappeared into the hall on the other side.

Lochlyn shot Twiggy an irritated look. "What do you suggest then, oh wise one?"

He didn't answer right away. The silence lingered long enough that she assumed he wasn't going to. Just when she was about to turn back to Oliver, Twiggy spoke up. "We stay in pairs. No one sleeps alone. Best case, no one's alone and we all make it through the night."

"And the worst-case?" Olive spoke up.

Even Twiggy didn't voice what they were all thinking. Awkward glances passed among them all before Boomer cleared his throat. "Worse case? One of us is the killer and we'll know who it is when their bunk-mate doesn't make it through the night," he added, putting their fears into words.

A chill ran through the group and Lochlyn doubted it was from the cold. Anxious glances continued to shift among them, with a few lingering on her longer than she liked.

Did they think she was behind this? Did being the newest member of their group automatically make her the number one suspect? What about the points Pumpkin made? At this rate, the culprit was anyone's guess.

"Should we *Scooby Doo* it then? Girls in one room, boys in the other?" Twiggy suggested after a long pause.

A strange expression flashed in Olive's eyes as she immediately turned to her brother. "Ollie ..."

Oliver merely shook his head. "It'll be fine, Ol. You'll be fine."

It didn't miss her attention that Olive didn't appear to agree with her twin. If nothing else, she looked annoyed that she'd be separated from him. Which, fair, but Olive appeared more agitated than fearful in that moment.

That was a curious reaction, Lochlyn noted.

Panic, fear, that was natural given the circumstances. It made sense Lochlyn wouldn't want to be apart from the only person in this room she knew and trusted either, but that wasn't the feeling she got from Olive.

The five foot nothing blonde was definitely annoyed, as if being separated from Oliver was an inconvenience for her.

Kitty crossed the room and wrapped her arm around the younger girl. "Your brother is right, honey. Us girls have to stick together. Isn't that right, Ivorie?"

That pointed glance was loud and clear. It would do them no good if they turned on each other and started throwing accusations around. Although, Pumpkin had already thrown the first punch when she accused Kitty of being behind this. The two of them sharing a room was definitely going to make for an awkward night.

Swallowing, Lochlyn didn't trust her voice and merely nodded in agreement. Satisfied with her approval, Kitty plastered on a forced smile and dipped her chin with satisfaction.

"One hitch in the plan. Just one," Twiggy piped up yet again. "Should we hang out down here until Gab comes back with Pumpkin? Last thing we need is for them to come back and wonder where everyone went."

Twiggy had a point. Staying In groups until the storm passed was the right move, but with Pumpkin and Gab unaccounted for, they couldn't head up to the rooms yet.

"Given that there's a murdering, body snatcher on the loose, I'm gonna have to agree with Twiggy, even though I hate to say it," Olive sighed and tugged at her sleeves nervously.

Oliver rubbed his neck. "Yeah, I also agree. Although, knowing Pumpkin, it could be a while before Gab can drag her back.

She's not thinking rationally, and it'll take her a few minutes to calm down and see reason."

A laugh-laced scoff erupted from Kitty's throat. "Believe me, I'm well aware of how long her temper tantrums can last."

Lochlyn's gaze shifted to the duo. Her interest piqued as she processed their teasing. They were talking like they'd been friends for years and not just meeting for the first time tonight. Maybe they'd just gotten to know each other throughout the years playing the game, but something felt off about it.

Their laughter quieted as a silent conversation passed between Kitty and Boomer. They'd said something they weren't supposed to. If it hadn't already been obvious since her arrival that they knew each other, the truth was now there wrapped with a pretty bow on top. At first Lochlyn had assumed it was a plot point for the game, but now she wasn't so convinced.

Studying the room, Lochlyn wanted to take in everything and remember as much detail as she could in case they were questioned about it later. Their plates from dinner were still scattered down the length of the dining table. Scraps of forgotten salads and chicken had long gone cold.

Someone had tipped their glass over in the chaos and a dark stain ran down the tablecloth. It was truly an eerie sight given the circumstances of why it was left behind in such a state.

While the others continued murmuring how to go about the rest of the night as Lochlyn turned and moved toward the table. She was careful as she moved around the spot where Camden had coughed up blood. Dark stains were speckled across the floor.

His salad plate was mostly untouched. He must have only had a bite or two before his reaction hit.

Had Camden been so engrossed in Kitty's story that he wasn't paying attention as he took a forkful of food? It was possible. Looking further around the table, Lochlyn noticed something odd. There was a peculiar item on the floor between Kitty and Camden's seats.

"Huh?"

Crouching down, she grabbed a butter knife from the table and used it to flip over the wrapper. The logo on the bag was for Seaside Caramel Sea Salt-flavored walnuts. What if the nuts in his food hadn't been there when it'd been placed in front of him? What if someone had taken advantage of the distracting conversation and emptied this bag into his food?

"Did you find something?"

Startled, Lochlyn turned to see Oliver standing a few steps behind her, a look of curiousness on his face.

Hesitating, Lochlyn nodded as she moved to stand. "Uh, yeah. I think so."

One of his brows rose to a perfect arch and his head tilted just slightly. "What is it?"

Before she could answer, Twiggy walked over as well. "You wanna share with the entire class or are we keeping secrets over here?"

Her mouth set into a firm line as her anger started to boil. She would need to keep her cool in front of these people though. "There's an empty bag of walnuts on the floor. I don't think the kitchen staff made a mistake. I think-"

"You think someone added it after they set down the plate in front of him," Twiggy finished.

A blush burned her cheeks when she realized they were all watching her. It suddenly felt like she was presenting an essay in front of a room full of teachers ready to judge her.

Lochlyn suddenly wished the shine from the wrapper hadn't caught her eye and she hadn't gone to investigate what it was. She hated being the center of attention.

Still, Lochlyn nodded. "I do. We were all engrossed in Kitty's story, and we were still high on arriving. Everyone was taking everything in and excited to start the game. It isn't hard to imagine Camden was so distracted that he didn't see someone drop a few nuts into his food."

To her surprise, Oliver appeared impressed. *Not* to her surprise, Twiggy didn't. Not wanting to give him a chance to counter her theory, she continued. "I think when we were all scrambling, the bag fell out of someone's pocket, and they had no idea."

Lochlyn took another chance to study their faces. Olive's eyes were wide with glassy tears rimming them. Her hands trembled in front of her, though that could be because her clothes were still soaking wet.

Looking past her, she saw Kitty fidgeting. Boomer stood beside her with a calm, cool expression on his face. He appeared stone-cold but it was clearly a mask because how could anyone be calm during a moment like this? Unless they were the murderer themselves.

No, she couldn't jump to conclusions.

"Ivorie?"

Lifting her head, Lochlyn hadn't realized they were trying to get her attention. How long had she been absently staring at them? Did they notice? Was it obvious she was taking a mental list of the suspects? Though, she supposed they were all doing that same thing.

Clearing her throat, Lochlyn straightened as her gaze passed over them again. "Sorry, I spaced out. What did you ask?"

The doubt in Twiggy's expression told her he didn't believe she'd simply zoned out, but he didn't call her out on it.

"We're supposed to stay together in the lounge until Gab and Pumpkin come back. Makes no sense to go out looking for them when we don't know where to start. Are you okay?" Oliver asked, his eyes studying her with apparent concern.

He seemed to genuinely want to make sure she was okay, and it made something inside of her flutter. It was an ill-timed feeling, and she could feel fire-like warmth creep up her neck.

"I'm fine. You don't have to worry about me."

Oliver took a step toward her and instinctively she took a big one back. Flutter aside, he was still a stranger and there was a missing dead body.

Lochlyn could see her realization hitting him as he paused and held up his hands. Oliver was treating her like a spooked animal. Truth be told, she wasn't sure how far off his assessment was.

He tentatively reached forward and took hold of her hand and held it against his chest. If Lochlyn wasn't blushing before, she absolutely was now. "Nothing is going to happen to you. Or any of us. We know every trope and trick in the book, right? This guy is going to regret messing with us."

Lochlyn wanted to swoon over his words of comfort, over the way he tilted his head, and how his deep brown eyes enchanted her. He did have a point. Whoever was messing with them, whoever killed Camden, had chosen the wrong group to mess with.

It meant Lochlyn was right to question everything and everyone. Which, unfortunately, included Oliver and his sweet words.

Twiggy's scoff broke their stare. She peered over Oliver's shoulder in time to see his predictable eye roll. "Oh, kill me next if Oliver's going to swoop in and play Prince Charming for the new girl."

"Don't joke about that," Olive scolded. "That's not even remotely funny."

Pulling her hand back, Lochlyn flashed Oliver a sheepish smile before crossing her arms. "I appreciate the attempt, but I don't think any of us will feel safe until Moose Hollow is in the rearview mirror."

The left side of his mouth twitched as he nodded. "I suppose you're right."

The sight of his half-grin made her stomach flip and Lochlyn put some distance between them in order to think clearly. She had to remember he was just as much a suspect as she was to them.

Oliver had even mentioned how he and Olive stopped in Lakeside Cove and had picked up some saltwater taffy from Deb's

Sweet Shop. It wouldn't be too hard to also pick up a bag of walnuts there too.

They hadn't been sitting beside Camden, but that didn't mean either of them were innocent of the crime.

"Back to the lounge, right?"

The others all nodded, and the group headed back through the doorway. Boomer led them inside. Lochlyn peered over her shoulder, watching Twiggy for a moment as he begrudgingly followed behind them.

Twiggy was quick to ruffle her feathers, get her on the defense, like he was trying to put a target on her back. It felt like he wanted them to see her as paranoid and skittish. Unstable. Nothing like this had happened before she joined their group. It would be easy for him to pin this on her if she didn't prove it to be otherwise.

As if feeling her stare, Twiggy's eyes lifted from the floor and a smirk twisted his face. He raised an arched brow, as if challenging her stare.

Flustered, Lochlyn turned her attention back to the space in front of her. Just in time too, because Kitty and Boomer had come to a sudden stop. Looking ahead of them, she tried to see what had caused the pause.

Then, multiple gasps were released at once. Lochlyn's blood ran cold, now twice in a matter of minutes. Dark red lettering dripped across the wall. A chill went down her spine and her knees quivered.

All eyes were on her.

There, just feet away, one word was written in either paint or worse, blood. Either way, it was a sight that would haunt her forever.

Ivorie.

Chapter 13

The crude sight of her character's name painted on the wall made her stomach roll. If Lochlyn had just eaten, she might have thrown it right back up. Something about this was wrong. She'd seen this plot play out before in the movies.

Looking around the room, she couldn't find guilt written on anyone's face, but that meant nothing. Plus, one of their players was still missing. Where had Pumpkin gone and why was it taking so long to come back?

There was also Gab, who could have done this while they were outside. She was currently unaccounted for. Again. It could be a coincidence, but Lochlyn wasn't going to brush it off as nothing.

Like Oliver said before, the people in the group knew every trope and trick in the book when it came to murder mysteries. That included Pumpkin and possibly Gab too. She was Kitty's friend after all.

Lochlyn jolted when a hand touched her arm. "Don't touch me!"

Oliver again raised his hands to show he wasn't intending to hurt her, but what did she really know? He still could just be lulling Lochlyn into a sense of comfort before pulling the rug out from under her.

The murderer was usually the one least expected; the person they would all swear up and down it couldn't be. Charming, sweet, flirtatious Oliver fit the description perfectly. But then again, so did distraught, frightened, and sobbing Olive. Maybe they were in on this together? That was a possibility too.

There was also the drama between Kitty and Boomer, and Pumpkin too. Olive had mentioned that Camden overheard a private conversation and then he turned up dead.

In theory, all the evidence was pointing at one or two parts of that trio. Given that Pumpkin was unaccounted for when Lochlyn's character name was written on the wall, she was tempted to put her money on her.

Still, she couldn't cross anyone else off her list yet. But Oliver was currently the one in front of her.

"Come on, Ivie," he pleaded. "I was with you when you took off to the dining room. I couldn't have double backed and done this and still beat the others into the other room. This wasn't me."

"That doesn't mean you weren't distracting me while Olive did it for you," she accused. "And didn't you say you stopped in Lakeside for taffy? That bag of walnuts was from the same shop."

He took another step forward, his hands still raised where she could see them. "Don't panic and jump to conclusions. Come on, think this through. You know it wasn't me, and it wasn't Olive either. I can explain the nuts."

Her attention dropped to his hands. The cleanliness confirmed it couldn't have been him. At least when the question of painting her name on the wall was concerned.

Her eyes darted over to his twin and noticed hers were clean as well. Even if she had washed them off, that would have taken some time to do so. Too much to fail to notice she had been gone.

Raising a brow, she motioned for him to go on and explain the bag she'd found. Oliver released a breath, though she couldn't tell if it was full of annoyance or relief. "The bag was mine, but I gave it to Twiggy during dinner. He had them when Cam went down," he confessed.

His voice was too low to be overheard, which was probably for the best considering he'd basically just pointed the blame at Twiggy. Twiggy, who'd been sitting next to Cam during dinner. Twiggy who did all the background checks and would have known Cam was allergic to nuts.

Twiggy who was treating this like a game and acting like a jerk to everyone. Bad manners didn't make him a murderer though. Did it?

"I-I believe you," Lochlyn finally spoke up. "I don't trust you, but I do believe you."

His lips twitched again and a small chuckle escaped his mouth. "I wouldn't believe you if you said you did. You have no reason to. None of us have any reason to trust the other. We're all practically strangers who happen to share a love for mystery."

Her stare flickered to Boomer and Kitty as she reminded herself that not everyone was strangers. Olive and Oliver's connection was expected, but no one else was supposed to mix their fantasy with real life.

Obviously, like Olive had mentioned earlier, that rule was more of a guideline than anything else, but something seemed to run pretty deep.

"It's fake blood. Not human," Twiggy's voice cut through the silence. Lochlyn's attention turned toward him as his finger popped free from his mouth. "It's also not too new. Maybe done earlier today, but it's not wet enough to be freshly done."

They all watched as Twiggy raised his hand where spots of redness now stain his skin. If he had any of it on him before now there was no longer a way to know for sure. He'd just contaminated the site, making it useless to help uncover the culprit.

If Twiggy was to be believed, it meant that someone must have done this either while they were outside like she'd thought earlier or possibly even before that. There were several hours since arriving that were unaccounted for. They could have covered it up somehow and unveiled it before heading back to the dining room with the others.

Whoever had done it would have had time to paint this and then clean up before anyone was the wiser. Someone who was here and blended into the background   like an employee.

"I don't know whether it's a relief that it's fake blood or not," Kitty spoke up. "But, also *ew*, Twiggy. I can't believe you tasted it."

Regardless of whether it was fake or real, the effect was still the same. Someone was clearly doing this to mess with her. It was her name that was written out. Not Oliver's or Boomer's. *Hers*.

The question still remained: why? Why not Olive or Twiggy? Why not Kitty, or everyone? It made no sense. She wasn't anyone special. There was nothing she could think of that made her stand out from the others.

Except …. *no*.

There was no way anyone could know about that. Especially not the people in this room. They didn't even know each other's names.

Only, they did.

Clearly, Kitty and Boomer were close. It wouldn't surprise her anymore if Pumpkin was close with them either. Olive and Oliver were actual siblings. They were all friends to some extent and had been for years. Only Lochlyn was new and unknown.

There was also the fact that Twiggy ran all the backgrounds checks before they were accepted into the group. How detailed did his searches go? He might be a computer genius, but could he get into court sealed cases?

Her throat closed with anxiety at the realization. Could Twiggy know about her brother's accident? Could he know her part in it?

Lochlyn suddenly jumped when a hand touched her shoulder. She turned to see Oliver standing there but she pulled away without thinking.

With a quick scan, she realized the others were discussing details of what to do next. His eyes widened with hurt but soon enough she saw understanding sink in as he lowered his hand. Even after his pleas and reasoning, Lochlyn still didn't trust him.

"Sorry," he muttered, suddenly embarrassed as he dropped his arms back to his sides.

"It's fine. I just   I'm not big on touching," Lochlyn quietly confessed.

He waved her words off. "You don't have to explain yourself. I just wanted to make sure you were okay. You have that '*I'm going to bolt since there's a crazy masked freak out there*' look in your eyes."

A blush crept up her neck and her head tilted as a small smile snuck up on her lips. "Oh, is that what my eyes say?"

Her breath caught in her throat when he took a step forward. Oliver raised his hand, as if he was reaching to touch her, but paused as his fingers hovered over the cut on her head. Thinking better of it, he lowered his hand and settled for leaning closer instead.

"They might be saying other things," he whispered into her ear.

The feeling of his breath against her cheek sent the butterflies in her stomach aflutter again. Swallowing, Lochlyn leaned back and studied the dark chocolate orbs watching her curiously.

There was a glint of something in there that sent a chill further down her spine. Guilt? Excitement? Amusement? Maybe a mix of the three? Whatever it was, it made her want to run far away from him yet also move in even closer. Her body was at a crossroad with her head.

"Yours are keeping secrets," Lochlyn whispered. "It was a pig mask too, by the way."

And like that, the trance between them was broken and Lochlyn took a step back as confusion settled on his face.

"A what?"

The question had come from Kitty, who was now watching her with a strange expression. They were all watching her now, Lochlyn realized. Her private moment with Oliver was no longer just that   private.

"I think the guy outside was wearing a pig mask. A weird, white, latex one with hollow eyes. But it had the snout and ears of a pig," Lochlyn described.

Twiggy scoffed. "How could you have possibly seen that from where we were standing? It was raining and too dark to make out any details."

Did Lochlyn tell them about how she might have seen the same masked figure in the library earlier? Olive was there too, and she hadn't seen him. Would it be better to keep it to herself then? Perhaps she was wrong about what she'd seen? Twiggy was right. It was too dark and rainy to make out anything when they were out there. Lochlyn could have made a mistake.

"Never mind, I'm probably wrong. Forget I said anything."

Lochlyn chose to lie instead.

The others returned to their earlier discussion over what to do while they waited for Pumpkin and Gab to return. Oliver didn't leave her side though.

Neither did Twiggy's stare. It felt like he was trying to break open her chest and discover all the secrets she was hiding. It was unnerving, to say the least.

Intrigue filled Twiggy's expression as he tilted his head, a knowing smirk on his face. "I guess I'm not the only one keeping secrets. Although isn't that the point of hosting a murder mystery game?" he challenged.

Lochlyn assumed the game had ended when Camden fell to the floor, choking for air until his body no longer needed it. Now she wondered if that was when the game truly began, and someone was playing with a set of rules she wasn't privy to.

Chapter 14

The next hour went by in an anxious silence. There was still no sign of Gab and Pumpkin returning, and people were starting to get antsy. Lochlyn reclaimed her spot at the bay window, watching the rain steadily pouring outside.

It was so majestic looking; peaceful even. She could understand why people enjoyed coming up here. Lochlyn wasn't a fan of thunderstorms, and for good reason, but when it just rained like this, she could understand why people felt a kind of peace when watching them.

Would rainstorms be tainted forever now? Would rain always remind her of Camden's death and how violent and scary it was? Not to mention Boomer crashing his truck while a pig man chased them back to the lodge.

Would she ever be able to listen to the rain again without seeing the fear in Camden's eyes as he took his last breath? Or the panic on Olive's face when they caught sight of the pig man.

"You've been awfully quiet over here."

Lightning flashed, illuminating Oliver's form behind her in the reflection. "Am I supposed to be acting a certain way after someone's been murdered? Not to mention Pumpkin is still missing and so is Gab. I know she'd not part of the group, but I just have a bad feeling."

The bitterness was a reflex: a defensive reaction. Oliver didn't deserve it. Twiggy, maybe, but not Oliver. He'd been nothing but nice to her since meeting only a few hours ago.

A moment of awkwardness fell over them before her guilt got the best of her. "Um, I-I'm sorry. My go-to defensive side is sarcasm and snark."

Judging by the way he brushed her off, he wasn't offended by her tone. "You don't need to apologize for reacting like a human being. I guess it is pretty stupid to ask how you're holding up."

Pushing her hair behind her ear, she gave him a small shrug. "It might be, but I appreciate you being worried about me. How's Olive?"

Olive had finally stopped shaking, but the energized ball of happiness from earlier was now a vacant shell of a girl who sat in front the crackling fire.

Kitty sat beside her with her arm wrapped around the younger girl. Twiggy and Boomer had taken spots at one of the tables and were passing the time playing chess, of all things. It actually bothered her how unconcerned they were that Pumpkin hadn't come back.

Oliver crossed his arms, watching his sister for another moment. "I think she's in shock. I don't think any of us were prepared for how real this weekend would be."

Lochlyn's eyes narrowed in on the duo across the room. "Everyone reacts differently, I suppose."

Oliver followed her gaze and raised his brow. "You think one of us killed him."

It wasn't a question, she noted. He was stating a fact.

Lochlyn dipped her chin just enough for him to know she was nodding. "You said it yourself, Oliver. We know every trick and trope in the book. While that makes us bad targets to go after, it could also make us great killers."

Oliver swallowed, his skin visibly paling as her words sunk in. "I wish I could say you were wrong about that. It doesn't help that we're all basically strangers going by fake names. Pumpkin wasn't exaggerating earlier either. Her points weren't out of nowhere."

Lochlyn shifted, her eyes scanning the group again before returning her attention to Oliver. "Don't you think it's weird no one else seems to be concerned that Gab and Pumpkin haven't come back yet? Can you *honestly* tell me there's nothing to be worried about?"

He couldn't. There was something to be troubled over and Oliver knew it.

Oliver took a deep breath and placed his hand on her knee as if he was consoling a child. "Pumpkin's known to be dramatic. I mean, this isn't the first game you've played with her. I know you haven't been with the group that long, but we've played enough games at this point, right? You know how she is. Everything's going to be-"

She was quick to cut him off. "Don't you dare finish that sentence with the word 'fine'. Nothing is ever *fine* after someone says that."

Oliver held up his hands in defeat again, pretending to zip his lips and toss away the key. The seriousness of her comment disappeared as a small smile cracked open across her face.

How could she be smiling, let alone almost laughing at something so silly after the night she'd had? Lochlyn wasn't entirely sure. Maybe it was a sign her mental state was cracking under all the duress?

All Lochlyn wanted was to be back home, curled up on the couch with her mom and Bubba, watching some silly reality TV show. She'd choose that kind of night over the nightmare she was currently living through.

Olive was the one who broke the latest silence. "So how do we know who to trust if everyone isn't who they say they are? I mean, what's to say the killer isn't just telling everyone else what they want to hear? There's no way to know."

That was the million-dollar question.

"There's one way to break the ice," Twiggy spoke out from across the room.

Lochlyn's body became tense, realizing he'd been listening to his surroundings much more than she'd realized. She'd assumed everyone was in their own world, passing the time until Pumpkin returned and they could all go to bed.

Could he hear what she and Oliver had been discussing? If so, how much did he overhear and did he have his own theory about what was happening?

"And that would be?" Lochlyn asked, sharing a curious glance with Oliver.

Twiggy shrugged his shoulder. "We play a game. Truth or truth. No dares. Just brutal honest truth."

His suggestion sent a chilling spark down her spine. A game like that could go wrong in so many ways, but he was right. It might help eliminate people from her suspect list. Everyone had their tells. Even if they were lying through their teeth, they might slip and make a mistake.

"You can't seriously be suggesting we play a game right now," Kitty snarled, her attention snapping back to the boys. "Are you mental? Someone just *died*. Their body is *missing*, two other people are unaccounted for, but you want to play truth or dare? No way!"

"Let's play," Lochlyn suddenly spoke up. "Twiggy's right. How can we trust each other if we don't know anything about each other? We can leave real names out of it, but I think we should play."

If nothing else, perhaps they could figure out who was lying. It was a solid plan in her mind.

The shocked expressions from Kitty and Olive were valid given that she had to be insane to agree with Twiggy. Oliver didn't move a muscle, waiting to see what happened next.

Boomer remained impassive, but Twiggy looked intrigued and suspicious. "You agree with me?"

Lochlyn couldn't hold back her eye roll. "Don't get too excited. It won't happen again."

His chuckle should have irritated her more, but Lochlyn found herself fighting back a smile instead. Clearing her throat, she spared Oliver a glance before standing and heading over to the couch.

Kitty and Olive followed, turning from their spots on the floor, as Twiggy hopped over the back of the couch and Boomer took the open armchair.

Oliver sat on the arm of the furniture beside her, his hand resting on the back of the couch behind her head. "Who wants to do the honor of starting us off?"

Silence. No one happily volunteered. Boomer coughed and crossed his arms as he shifted in his seat. Kitty avoided making eye contact with anyone.

Lochlyn cleared her throat, fidgeting with her shorts. The idea of offering herself up to be first felt like a bad idea. It was one thing to agree to play, but she didn't want to be the one to go first. It meant she'd be the first one to show her cards, and Lochlyn wasn't going to do that.

Two minutes passed before the tension of the silence got to be too much for them. Twiggy was the first to break.

"Oh, this is silly. I'll go first since the game was my idea," he said. "Come on, heiress. You've accused one person of murder already. Ask me something."

He twisted his body to face hers, his brow raised with challenge, as she was startled at the sudden spotlight upon her. Lochlyn hadn't meant to accuse anyone of anything. Okay, maybe she did, but still. Why did she have to answer the first question?

Lochlyn could feel her cheeks flush with embarrassment. Her eyes begged the others to save her from making more of a fool of herself than she already had.

"Are you really a know-it-all genius or are you just a sarcastic ass who thinks she'll be impressed by your *I don't care* attitude?" Oliver's voice spoke up in her place.

Lochlyn twisted to look at him with surprise and a smidge bit of gratefulness for the save. Oliver didn't meet her gaze. His focus was solely on Twiggy, waiting for his answer.

Turning her attention back to Twiggy and she saw his smirk was no longer present. His lips had straightened out into a tense line. But they didn't open to answer. It appeared then even though it was his idea to play, he wasn't any happier to go first than she was. Going first went giving everyone else the power.

Time ticked by and the silence was nearly deafening. This ice breaker appeared to be doing the opposite of its purpose.

Lochlyn twisted around again, shifting her attention to Olive and Kitty. "Kitty, are you a cat or dog person?"

Surprise engulfed Kitty's expression before a small smile replaced it. "Ironically, I'm allergic to cats. I have a bearded dragon though. His name is Steve Scalington."

A few chuckles rumbled around the group and Lochlyn knew the ice had finally been chipped at. Barely, but it was a start.

"Oh, I love Stranger Things. Steve is just perfection," Olive gushed, her usually perky self starting to return.

"I have a red and white Boston Terrier named Bubba. Well, he was my brother's before he   before Hunter left. Now he's glued to my mom's hip," Lochlyn admitted, though she'd almost revealed too much of her real life than she was comfortable telling a group of strangers.

The weirdest part was the way Kitty's eye twitched and how her jaw clenched, like she was holding something back. If she did have something to add, though, she kept it to herself as the game continued.

Still, just like that, the tension was somewhat defused. Even Boomer let a chuckle slip when Oliver revealed his school volcano disaster two years prior.

Half an hour went by, and it felt like they might actually succeed in passing the time until Pumpkin returned. For a moment, it felt like they could pretend that two people had yet to return, but the thought that they could simply forget that someone had died and that a corpse was missing was just ridiculous. A fool's dream.

The laughter from Boomer's tale of his ski trip last winter quieted immediately when the bay windows suddenly blew open. The wind hissed as it broke through and rain invaded the safety of the fireplace's warmth.

Oliver and Boomer immediately jumped to their feet. Lochlyn sat frozen as she watched them hurry to the windows. "Quick, get that side! Kit, help me with this one," Boomer ordered, while motioning for her to help as well.

Kitty scrambled to her feet and sped around the couch to help. Lochlyn leapt, shook herself from her daze and jumped to assist Oliver with the other side. Together the four of them pushed the windows shut. As soon as they closed, Kitty and she moved to flip the locks back into place.

Breathing hard, Lochlyn narrowed her eyes on the two who hadn't attempted to help before she peered outside. She couldn't see anything besides the blinding rain, but just then there was something solidified against the blurred background. It wasn't just something though.

Squinting in her eyes to get a better look, Lochlyn gasped as she realized what it was. It was an outline of a person.

"What the hell?"

"What? What's wrong?" Oliver asked.

Lochlyn blinked, shifting to nearly press her face against the glass. "I-I think there's someone out there! Over there! By the rental place."

Suddenly there were three other faces against the glass. It was like the truck ride all over again. By the time Olive and Twiggy made it to the window though, the flash of a person was gone. She hadn't even seen the figure move. The rain was too dense. The figure merely vanished.

"Nothing's out there," Kitty scoffed, squinting as she still searched the outside.

Something had been there though. Lochlyn hadn't imagined that silhouette, just like she hadn't earlier. "There was someone there! Maybe it's the pig face guy, or maybe it was Gab and Pumpkin, but there was someone out there. I swear! Oliver, did you see it?"

Oliver had been right beside her. There was no way he didn't see it. Right?

Except, judging by his guilty expression Lochlyn knew what he was going to say before he said it. "Sorry, Ive. I don't see anything but rain out there. I'm surprised you could see anything through it."

Darting her eyes around, she noticed they were all giving her a look of pity. Maybe it had just been nothing, but she could have sworn it was   no, she couldn't be *that* character. The paranoid one that jumps at every shadow. That's the one that ends up quickly meeting their doom in every horror movie.

"Maybe it was just a tree or something. I didn't mean to freak everyone out," Lochlyn apologized. "I think knowing there's still a guy somewhere in a mask is making me jumpy. It doesn't help that Pumpkin and Gab haven't come back yet. Seriously   where are they? I know Pumpkin was upset, but it's been almost an hour."

Twiggy huffed, rolling his eyes as he climbed back to his feet and moved back to the couch. "I guess we know who's the paranoid one out of our group now."

Lochlyn hung her head sheepishly. Ivorie was supposed to be smart, brave, cunning. So far, she was letting Lochlyn's fears leak through.

Except she stopped being Ivorie the second someone slipped nuts into Camden's food. It stopped being a game when someone was still out there stopping them from going down the mountain for help. It stopped when someone decided to write out Ivorie in red paint on the wall and move Camden's body.

Lochlyn's fear was genuine and she shouldn't be ashamed of it. So, why was Twiggy's comment getting under her skin?

Because she still didn't want him to be right.

"That's not even remotely fair, Twiggy," Olive spoke up. "Someone *was* out there earlier on the road, and we all saw him. It's possible he's still out there now. This isn't just a case of the girl who cried wolf. Camden died tonight. If you're not freaked out over that, something's wrong with *you*. Maybe you're the one we need to be concerned about, seeing as you're still treating this like a game."

Lochlyn didn't know what to say. Twiggy could be right. She was acting paranoid so maybe Olive was too. But it was hard not to since their game became reality. Olive hadn't only come to her defense, though. She'd also put the spotlight squarely on Twiggy.

Oliver was quick to chime in next. "She's right. You're surprisingly calm about all of this."

"Maybe we should go up to our rooms and if anyone sees Pumpkin, we'll just tell her what we're doing," Kitty suggested, trying to ease the tension. "Throwing accusations around isn't helping anyone's nerves."

Tensions were running high, and it was only going to get worse until they were able to get out of here and go for help. Being stuck in a room together wasn't doing them any favors. Neither was the fact Pumpkin and Gab were *still* missing.

Shaking her head, Lochlyn didn't want this. She didn't want the accusations to start and their group to squabble. None of this was supposed to be happening.

"I mean, it could be worse. At least we don't have to deal with psycho phone calls," Boomer broke through.

As if taunting fate, a phone rang.

Chapter 15

All eyes turned to Kitty, seeking an explanation since the phones weren't supposed to be working. By the way her face had paled several shades, Lochlyn got the impression she didn't have an answer. Either that, or it wasn't going to be an answer they were going to like.

The phone went silent for a moment, but within a minute it started again. The noise seemed to jolt Kitty out of her silence. "That's one of the landlines. It's mostly for employees because they don't work well out of range. There's usually too much interference because of the mountains. Calls out drop too often for them to be reliable," she explained, her voice barely above a whisper. "I honestly forgot about them. Only the staff know about them. Guests just think they're part of the old fashion charm."

They all stared at the rotary phone hanging on the wall beside the doorway, waiting with bated breath as it continued to ring.

"It could be Gab. Maybe she and Pumpkin were able to get through to the cops and they're calling to tell us," Boomer offered, though Lochlyn noticed he chose to whisper as well.

Kitty swallowed, nodding as she stood up. The others shared a look before hesitantly following as she crossed the room.

"Or, she's calling because something's happened to her and Pumpkin," Twiggy muttered, followed by a soft curse when Olive swatted his arm.

"Think positively," she scolded.

Taking a deep breath, Kitty picked the phone up and held it among all of them. Lochlyn was the closest, giving her the best chance to overhear the conversation.

"Hello?" Kitty answered with a slight tremble. "Gab, is that you? Did you find Pumpkin?"

Lochlyn strained to hear anything, but there was nothing but silence. At first. Wait, was that breathing? It was too faint to tell.

Suddenly a voice spoke up. "Tick tock, pumpkin season is almost over. You better find yours before someone else decides to carve into it,"

CLICK.

A dial tone took place of the silence. Lochlyn and Kitty exchanged a panicked glare. Whoever had called, was not Gab or

Pumpkin. And their message was clear: Pumpkin was next if they didn't find her first.

"Forget '*Scream*' vibes, we've officially dived into the '*I Know What You Did Last Summer*' waters," Twiggy piped in, huffing as he flopped onto the lounge chair and dropped his head into his hands.

Looking around, Lochlyn noticed Olive sharing a glance with her brother, and a hint of knowing passing between them. Continuing, she watched as Boomer moved behind Kitty and rubbed her back. He was trying to comfort her, but Lochlyn wasn't sure if that was possible.

"Except this isn't a game or some movie anymore," Lochlyn countered. "Kitty, how much of the staff is left in the off season?"

Kitty pondered the question for a moment. "Only a few. A skeleton crew was how my uncle described it. Most went home before the storm hit. They cooked dinner and breakfast ahead of time for us and the ski lifts are off limits. Gab was supposed to get out before the storm hit too, but now she's stuck here."

If Kitty was telling the truth about the phones, then whoever called just now was in the lodge with them. At least having only a small list of staff would make their suspect list short. If they could eliminate anyone, it would help even more.

"Can you write down exactly who they are?" Lochlyn asked as she turned and searched for a pen and something to write on. "Whoever that was knew about the phones and they're in close enough range to get through clearly."

Kitty's hands shook as she accepted the bar napkin and pen. "I don't know all of their names, but I'll do my best. Maid, lifeguard, that kind of list. The only one I know personally is Gab because we both interned here one summer."

While Kitty thoughtfully took her time writing people down, Lochlyn stood in front of the fireplace, rubbing her bare arms. Just a minute ago, it felt too warm in here, but now she felt a permanent chill in her bones that refused to let up.

A jacket dropped onto her shoulders, and she realized it was the white jacket Oliver had been wearing when they arrived. Peering behind her, Lochlyn attempted to give him a smile, but even a small one was exhausting. "Thanks," she muttered, dipping her chin as she tugged it closer around her.

Oliver's pools of dark brown eyes were illuminated by the fire. The shadows darkening across his face made him appear more sinister. "This was not how I was hoping this weekend was gonna go," he confessed.

Raising a brow, she glanced over. "You didn't expect there to be murder and mystery at a murder mystery event?"

A snort escaped his lips. "Touché. I just didn't think it would be the real deal."

Her gaze found the crackling flames again. "Kitty did promise it'd be a weekend we'd never forget."

Silence fell over them. Oliver was right. This weekend that promised so much fun and an escape from the real world had turned into a nightmare worse than anything she could have ever dreamt.

"Do you think Pumpkin's okay? They didn't even mention Gab. What if she's already .... I mean, she has to be okay, right? Maybe this person just has them tied up somewhere looking for a payday? If they think they can black mail a couple of rich kids for a quick payout, that's not so farfetched, right?" Lochlyn was falling down another rabbit hole of speculation, but she couldn't help herself.

Oliver ran a hand through his dark hair, loosening his curls. He bit his lip as he pondered her idea. "It's not a bad theory, but there's nothing to back it up. We can pass blame around all we want, but at the end of the night? We don't have even have any solid clues."

Her shoulders dropped with disappointment as a huff of frustration passed through her lips. "Well, we're not going to find either of them while we're holed up in here the entire night playing games like someone wasn't murdered."

He turned to her with intrigue and a raised brow. "What do you suggest then?"

Peering back at the others, she made sure no one was paying attention. Boomer was leaning against the desk Kitty was writing her list on, while Twiggy poured himself a glass of what she hoped was water and Olive went back to Locklyn's previous spot at the bay window.

Returning to Oliver, Lochlyn lowered her voice to a whisper. "You were right when you said we're not the group someone should be doing this to earlier. The phone call, the missing body, the vague threat, it's all textbook horror movie stuff. If this guy wants to play, we'll beat him at his own game."

"So, what's the move?"

That question made Lochlyn pause. If they were playing an actual mystery game, what was the next step to take? The initial crime was set, the suspects were known, the first phone call was made, what was next? Find clues. They needed to find clues in order to narrow down their list of possible murderers and find their missing player.

Players, Lochlyn corrected herself. Gab might not have been on the initial roster of players, but she was not going to be collateral damage in this mess. She was officially on the game board.

So far, they had the weapon and place. They just needed one last missing piece left to figure out. The murderer.

"We split up and search for them," she said quietly. "And look for any clues while we're out there."

Oliver paled beside her, swallowing whatever refusal he was thinking. She knew it was a crazy idea, but they didn't have a better one.

The psycho clearly knew where they were. Safety in numbers was ideal, but what if it wasn't in this case? If they were all together, this creep could take them out all at once.

Lochlyn could see the doubt clearly written across his face. "I know that's like the worse idea in horror movies, but just sitting here like a group of ducks waiting to be slaughtered isn't a good move either, right? Especially not for Pumpkin and Gab. We need to find them."

Oliver couldn't argue with her there.

Reaching over, Lochlyn touched his arm. "Please, just hear me out."

Silence lingered over them like a knife waiting to fall. When he didn't say anything, Lochlyn was sure he was going to shrug her off and tell her she was nuts. Which, maybe she was, but that didn't mean she was wrong. Not about this anyway.

Dropping her hand, Lochlyn was ready to apologize and tell him to forget what she said, but before she could, Oliver grabbed hold of her hand and squeezed. "I'm listening," he said with a a small but encouraging grin.

Relieved, Lochlyn dipped her chin in thanks. "I think we should turn this trope on its head. Splitting up is a bad idea because he could pick us off one at a time, but what if we're ready for him? He won't have the element of surprise if we know he's coming. Especially if we go in pairs and have him out numbered."

"Hey, Nancy Drew, you wanna share with the group?" Twiggy called over. "Or do you plan to just conspire over there all night?"

Startled, Lochlyn put space between her and Oliver and turned to find they were watching her now. "Oh, uh, we weren't, um, conspiring."

None of them looked convinced. If she was being honest, she wouldn't be either.

Oliver angled himself in front of her. "Ivorie's right. We should be out there trying to figure out who's doing this or finding a way to help Pumpkin and Gab."

"You realize that's, like, breaking the biggest how-to-not-get-murdered rule, right?"

Twiggy wasn't the only one skeptical of their plans. She could see conflict written on the others' faces too. He was just the only one willing to voice his doubts.

Lochlyn moved around Oliver, giving him a thankful nod. "Waiting for this guy to find us won't keep us any safer than trying to figure out what's happening. It won't help Pumpkin and Gab either. He already knows exactly where we are. It's just a matter of time before he makes his move. Wouldn't you rather have the upper hand?"

Much to her surprise, Olive voiced the next question. "How are you so sure it's a guy? I mean, downloading a voice changer app isn't hard. For all we know, that was Pumpkin on the phone trying to lure us out or maybe it was Gab and Pumpkin's already dead."

She had a point.

"You're right," Lochlyn agreed. "Even though they clearly know about us, we don't know anything about this person. If we look around for Pumpkin and Gab, maybe we can change that? It's worth a shot at this point."

Only Oliver looked ready to agree. Even Boomer showed apprehension. If she could convince Kitty to join though, Lochlyn knew he would too. Olive would help because her brother was planning to. That just left Twiggy.

He was going to be the hardest to convince. He was the most cautious of the group. It was a miracle Kitty had even talked him into joining this weekend to begin with. Lochlyn was sure he regretted that decision right about now.

The lights flickered as thunder rumbled outside. Lochlyn tried to hide the way her body flinched at the sound, but she wasn't sure how well she succeeded.

"There's, um, there's walkie-talkies behind the front desk," Kitty piped up. "They keep them there in case of power outrages. We could use those to keep in contact with each other."

Kitty was in. This meant Boomer and Olive would be too.

The look of disbelief on Twiggy's face made it clear he couldn't believe the turn this conversation had turned. "You guys can't be seriously on board with this plan. You realize it's basically sealing our fates, right?" Twiggy's voice raised.

"*Enough*! Enough, okay?" Lochlyn snapped. "We're not in a movie. We'll keep in contact and be careful."

Twiggy let out a growl of frustration and rolled his eyes as he flopped back onto the couch. "You idiots can have fun dying out there. I'm not going anywhere."

As if further proving his stance, Twiggy crossed his arms and huffed. Lochlyn was ready to let him stay behind and pout like a child, but she knew it wouldn't be right. Looking around the group, she tried to come up with another plan.

"I'll stay with him," Olive offered.

Oliver looked about to tell her no way, but he stopped himself when Olive preemptively settled a pointed look back at him. The glare was enough to cut him off. Lochlyn had to admit, it was kind of impressive.

"So it's settled," Kitty said. "Boomer and I will take the rooms in the East wing. Oliver and Ivorie can take the West. You two can stay here, or if Twiggy decides he wants to help, you can check out the ground floor. I'll grab the walkies and be right back."

"Gahhh, don't say those words!" Twiggy groaned, putting his hands over his ears.

Rolling her eyes, Kitty motioned for Boomer to follow her and the two of them went to retrieve the walkies as they shut the doors behind them, silence fell over those left.

Lochlyn noticed Olive and Oliver moving to the side to talk in private, no doubt to make sure the other is careful and stays safe. It was sweet to see how protective Oliver was of his twin. Not only that, but he respected her decision.

"This is a stupid idea, heiress," Twiggy reiterated. "You know that, right?"

Even if it was, they couldn't just stay here waiting to be hacked up by Pig Man.

Nodding, Lochlyn crossed her arms as she dragged her attention from the twins over to the boy still seated in the chair. "Maybe, but it's the only one we've got. Someone's targeting us and Pumpkin and Gab need our help. Besides, don't you want to figure out what's going on?"

Twiggy shrugged his shoulder. "Curiosity killed the cat, didn't it?"

A chill ran down her spine. Was that supposed to be a threat or a warning? Coming from Twiggy, it could have been either. Either way, Lochlyn didn't have an answer for him, and she wasn't sure he really wanted one anyway. He was just determined to get under her skin as much as possible.

Maybe that was just how Twiggy delt with situations he couldn't control? It would explain why he was so detached to the seriousness of crimes committed. Even if so, Lochlyn didn't think it gave him a right to treat her the way he was.

They might have just met this morning, but he had already figured out which buttons to push to get under her skin. Lochlyn didn't like how easy it was for Twiggy to coax a reaction out of her. The sooner Lochlyn was away from him, the better.

After a minute, the missing duo returned with three walkies in hand. Lochlyn took one from Kitty. Muttering a quiet 'thank you', Lochlyn turned her gaze to Oliver.

"Ready?"

Oliver dipped his chin as he squeezed his sister's shoulder one last time before joining Lochlyn's side. "Should we have a meet back time?"

Lifting her eyes from the walkie, Lochlyn glanced around the room. The others shrugged their indifference. No one appeared to be against the idea, but no one was jumping to assume leadership either.

Sighing, Lochlyn figured, since this was her idea, she should do it. "Realistically, it'll probably take more than an hour to have a thorough look around. How about we say two hours? If we haven't heard anything from the other, we call a regroup over the walkies. Sound fair?"

"Yeah, sure." Boomer didn't even look up as he spoke.

His entire focus was on fussing with the device in his hand. When he was satisfied with whatever he was doing, he handed it to Twiggy before reaching for the one in Kitty's hands.

"I'm setting them all to the same channel. That way if this creep has their hands on one, they won't hear us," he explained as he adjusted the walkie he and Kitty would be using.

When he finished, he returned it to her and reached for the one Lochlyn was holding. Hesitating, she debated. For all she knew, he was setting it to the channel this creep was already on, although that could be her paranoia again. She had to trust that he wasn't. They weren't going to get anything done if they didn't trust each other.

Nodding, Lochlyn extended her hand and let him take it. "Good idea," she murmured, tucking her hands into the folds of her arms to keep herself from drumming them against herself.

It would come off as impatient, but it was more a nervous tick. She didn't always do it. The twitchy fingers started when her panic attacks did last year, but Lochlyn wasn't going to let those thoughts in right now. Not in front of all these strangers.

After a moment, Boomer handed it back and Lochlyn tried not to snatch it too quickly. With a forced smile, she nodded before clipping it onto the belt loop of her romper. It weighed down her clothes, but she'd take mild discomfort over no communication.

Oliver lifted his arm up and whispered into his watch. Her brow raised, watching him apparently set an alarm and then lowered his wrist. He noticed her staring a moment later and chuckled. "I'm just setting an alarm for two hours," he explained.

Satisfied with his answer, she inhaled deeply before turning on her heels. "Let's get moving, yeah?"

Lochlyn turned on her heels and didn't look back as she headed out into the main hall. If she stopped, she might talk herself out of doing this and hide away in that room with Olive and Twiggy. But hiding wouldn't get them through the night alive or find Pumpkin and Gab. Only action would.

It was time to solve a mystery.

Chapter 16

The wind howled against the lodge and lightning crackled as it erupted from the sky and bolted to the ground. Its flash lit up the empty hall as Lochlyn and Oliver wandered down it. Thunder rumbled immediately after.

One Mississippi. Two Mississippi. Three Mississippi. Four Mississippi. Five Mississippi. Six Mississippi. Seven Mississippi.

BOOM.

"The storm is just over a mile away," Lochlyn noted, though it felt like she was reassuring herself more than it was to inform Oliver.

Thunderstorms always put her on edge. Rain was fine, but the thunder sent her scurrying away under her covers every time.

Lochlyn hadn't always been afraid of thunder. When she was little it excited her, but at some point over the years it became something she feared. If she really thought about it, Lochlyn knew the source of her terror, but she was more than happy to leave it locked behind the dark, wooden door in her head.

It was the place in her head where she locked away all her bad memories. Her dad leaving, the arguments she overheard, the glass breaking, *that* night, all of it was locked behind that door never to be thought about again.

Her body flinched and instinctively moved away from the windows as another rumble of thunder exploded above them. Her feet fumbled and fell out from underneath her as she tumbled into Oliver. She closed her eyes, waiting for the embarrassing moment of impact as she hit the floor, but after a moment Lochlyn realized it never came.

Opening her eyes, Lochlyn raised her eyes from the floor to Oliver's grinning face as he loomed over her. He had slipped his arm around her before she could make an utter fool of herself.

"Careful there, darling," Oliver spoke as if he was calming a spooked rabbit, and Lochlyn supposed that was exactly what she was.

Attempting to recover from her fall, Lochlyn fought down the blush threatening to burn its way up her neck as she refused to meet his gaze. If she looked into his dark eyes too long, Lochlyn was afraid she'd be trapped her in their shadowy abyss.

"I'd blame it on the shoes, but I don't think you'd believe me."

It was clearly a deflection and they both knew it, but thankfully he didn't call her on it. Instead, he merely righted her onto her feet and pushed a fallen red curl behind her ear. She tried to ignore the way her skin tickled from his touch.

"We should keep moving. There are still a few doors we haven't checked in this hall. Pumpkin and Gab could be anywhere."

Not wasting a moment putting some distance between them, Lochlyn stepped around him and kept moving. When Oliver didn't comment, she hoped that meant he was going take the hint and drop whatever had just occurred.

Unfortunately, Lochlyn wasn't going so lucky.

"So, not a fan of thunderstorms?"

Her lips pressed together firmly, trapping her frustration inside. Still, a few words managed to slip out. "Not a fan of long silences?"

The moment that followed gave her false hope that he would finally get the message, but it was not meant to be. "Not entirely, no. I can't say that I am. Upside to having a twin, I suppose. There's always someone to talk to."

"It must be nice always having someone around. You two seem close," Lochlyn said back as she opened one of the doors on the right and entered cautiously.

The room was dark. Not to mention *empty*. Spotless, in fact. There was no sign of Pumpkin or Gab. There wasn't even a pillowcase crease to be seen. It was just like the other rooms they'd searched.

Still, they checked all the nooks and crannies before continuing onto the next. It only took missing one spot, one closet, and they could be leaving Pumpkin and Gab to their deadly fates.

"There were a few off years that we were each other's worst enemy. My sister has a jealousy streak that can be ...." Oliver paused, as if considering his words. "Well, frightening. She's a wicked little thing, my sister. For example, Oll has driven off just about all of my ex's. The thought of not being the most important person in each other's lives, it scares her."

"But not you?"

Oliver shrugged before opening the next room. "We'll always be twins. It's a connection like no other, as I'm sure you've heard. Nothing and no one can change that. If she was truly happy with someone, I'd like to think I'd welcome them with open arms."

Scanning the room, Lochlyn wasn't surprised to find it exactly like the rest. It was clear this wasn't the room Pig Man had tossed Pumpkin and Gab into.

She was about to leave when something caught her eye. "There's something peeking out of that top drawer," she noted curiously.

Oliver's eyebrows scrunched together, wrinkles creasing as confusion fell over him. Lamely lifting her arm, Lochlyn motioned to the run-of-the-mill dark wooded bedside drawers. On top of the nightstand was a table lamp and some lodge brochure. A tissue box was tucked between the lamp and the mattress. There was an old cord phone hung off the other side as well.

Even though it otherwise looked exactly like the other four rooms, something was sticking out of the corner of the drawer here. Someone had stashed something inside in a rush. Lochlyn stood eerily still as she watched him kneel in front of the furniture piece.

Oliver went to grab the handle but paused and reached for a tissue first. As he glanced Lochlyn's way, Oliver shrugged his shoulder. "Rule number three of sleuthing. Never leave prints behind."

Good point. How many doors had they already left prints on? Actually, their DNA would already be all over this lodge. It felt odd that it only now was it a concern.

Still, Lochlyn didn't voice her doubts and allowed him to continue. Oliver used the tissue to grab hold of the drawer and pull it open. Whatever had been sticking out slid fully inside, blocking her view of what it was.

Oliver's head fell to the side, his brow arching as a 'huh' escaped his lips. The suspense was killing her as she moved closer. Peering over his shoulder, Lochlyn was dying to see what he found. Reaching his hand inside, he lifted out a white material.

Her blood ran cold at the sight of the pink rubber snout. "Please tell me that's not what I think it is."

Examining the item in his hand, Oliver's usual grin was nowhere to be seen. "If you think it's a creepy white pig mask, then fine. I won't tell you."

Swatting his shoulder, Lochlyn shot him a look that said now was not the time for jokes. "Don't joke. This takes inspired by the movie to an entirely new level of psycho. Whoever is behind this must be a big *Scream* fan. Between a mask and a phone call, I mean."

Looking around, Oliver climbed to his feet and reached for the purse hanging on her shoulder. Instinctively, she took a step back. He was quick to pull back as the mask dangled between his fingers. "Here, hold the bag open. We should take the mask to show the others when we regroup. I don't know about you, but I do not feel like carrying this around for the next hour. Chances are, one of us will put it down and accidentally leave it behind somewhere."

His thinking was solid. They should have thought of taking something bigger than her small purse to carry clues around in, but that didn't change the fact that it was all they had on them.

Nodding, Lochlyn slipped the strap off her shoulder and opened it for him to put the mask inside. Once done, she zipped it closed and lifted it back onto her shoulder.

"I don't suppose there's anything else in there, like a receipt or tag that says, *'this belongs to the masked pig man terrorizing us'* on it."

Peering back into the drawer, Oliver shook his head. "Sorry to disappoint, but there's nothing else except what you'd expect to find in here. Bible, little hotel notepad, some hotel keychain, a pen, and the menu for room service."

Her shoulders drooped with disappointment. She'd been hoping for anything to give them a lead on the mask. For all they knew, this was part of Kitty's original game as a prop. Maybe whoever had lured them back here had found it and decided to use it? They could have stashed it back in here after in a rush. There was no way of knowing if they'd stumbled across a legitimate clue until they could talk to Kitty.

That made her wonder if the person she'd seen in the library had been for the game or if the killer had already stolen the mask by then.

Something dawned on her then. One of those items didn't match what was usually left in the hotel room. "Wait, did you say keychain? Is it for Moose Hollow?"

Oliver dug around, pulling the item out of the drawer for her to see. Peering closer, Lochlyn immediately recognized the white and red striped lighthouse. From the way Oliver's body went ridged, she had a feeling he recognized it too.

"Isn't that Olive's Lakeside Cove keychain?"

An angry expression fell over Oliver's features as his fingers curled around the item. "It would seem like it, but it's just as likely it was left behind by another guest. I mean, Lakeside Cove isn't that far from here."

It was possible, but Lochlyn had a gut feeling it wasn't. It was too big of a coincidence they just happened to find the same keychain Olive was showing off earlier with the mask.

"Yeah, I'm sure you're right," she said instead, flashing him a small smile.

But none of this added up in her head. Olive was with them when they saw the pig man outside. She'd been sitting right beside her in the truck.

Olive had been in the library with her though. How easy would it have been to simply take off the mask and tuck it in her purse before Lochlyn stumbled upon her? Pretty easily, Lochlyn noted.

Olive couldn't have moved Camden's body on her own though. For one thing, Olive had been there with them the entire time. There wasn't a time she wasn't standing with her brother. Shouldn't that be enough to prove her innocence?

An awkward silence fell over them as the weight of this discovery sat like weight in her gut. She had once theorized Gab had been working with Kitty to pull all this off, but what if she was only half right? What if it was Olive pulling the strings?

They wouldn't know for certain until they questioned her about it. "Should we ping them over the walkie to tell them we found something?"

Oliver opened his mouth to answer, but the words froze on his lips when they heard the floorboard creak in the attached bathroom.

Both turned their attention to the closed door with eyes wide. Her fingers gripped his shoulder and squeezed his sweater vest. Lochlyn didn't realize she was shaking until he placed his warm hand over hers.

Her attention darted to him. She wouldn't be surprised if he could see the fear shining in her green eyes.

Oliver raised a single finger to his lips and slowly raised himself up to his feet. He slipped the keychain into his pocket as he angled himself between her and the doorway.

Reaching over, he grabbed the desktop lamp and yanked it from its spot. Lochlyn wasn't sure how good of a weapon choice it was, but it was better than nothing. Which was what she currently had.

Holding it like a bat, Oliver crept forward. She stayed one step behind him, ready to bolt at a moment's notice. The room was silent besides the sound of the pitter patter of rain hitting the window.

Standing a foot away from the closed door, Lochlyn knew there was no going back once they opened it. If they were going to run, it had to be now. She wanted to ask him if he was sure about this, but the words were stuck in her throat.

Would she doom them by speaking out loud? Would it be the distraction the source of the creak needed to attack and leave them for dead? She didn't dare risk finding out.

Lochlyn watched with bated breath as Oliver extended his hand and reached for the doorknob. Straining, Lochlyn tried to listen for any signs of a presence on the other side. But there was no heavy breathing, no more creaking, not even a whistle of wind outside. It was as if the fates were waiting to see what happened next too.

His fingers curled around the metal bulb and twisted. Nudging it open with his foot, Oliver adjusted his grip on the lamp, anticipating an attack. Lochlyn squeezed her eyes shut and her fingers clutched Oliver even harder as she turned her head. She couldn't look.

In front of her, Oliver released a sharp, audible intake of breath. He clearly saw something inside the room, but Lochlyn wasn't sure she wanted to see it too.

"Pumpkin," he gasped.

Even through the darkness, Lochlyn recognized those dark maroon shoes tossed over the side of the claw-footed tub with the someone's feet still attached. They didn't have to see her face to know it was Pumpkin.

Oliver hesitantly stepped into the dark bathroom. Lochlyn froze where she stood and attempted to tighten her grip on his sweater vest, as if that would keep him in place. She suddenly hated how her fingers shook, or was that her entire body? Lochlyn couldn't tell.

He turned his head, his eyes meeting hers. "I'm just going to check to see if she's okay. Maybe she slipped and hit her head. That could be what we heard," he hurriedly asserted, attempting to convince her to release his clothing from her viper-tight grip.

Still shaking, she uncurled her fingers and lowered her hand. Lochlyn nodded shakenly as she pulled his jacket tighter around her body. She knew she had to let him go. It wouldn't be a good look for her if she clung to him like a sobbing child while Pumpkin laid hurt two feet away.

He hesitated, searching her face for something she couldn't understand. Was he making sure she wasn't about to bolt and leave him to fend for himself? Lochlyn wouldn't blame him for doubting her. She certainly was acting like a reliable form of backup.

"I'm fine," she reassured. "Check on her. I-I'll turn the light on and check the rest of the room."

Lochlyn wished her body believed her words. Her heart was pounding against her rib cage. Lochlyn was a mess, but still, she didn't move from her spot.

Nodding, Oliver inched forward. As brave as he was trying to be, Lochlyn noticed how white his knuckles were as he tightened his grip on the lamp. He crept through the darkness from the doorway to the tub where Pumpkin lay.

Stepping behind him, Lochlyn ran her hand along the cold tiled wall until it bumped into the light switch. As the light illuminated the small room, it took her eyes a moment to adjust to the sudden brightness.

Still, her attention didn't leave the tub as Oliver sat on the edge and leaned over, pressing two of his fingers to Pumpkin's neck. The lingering silence was deafening as Lochlyn waited to hear if she was alive or not.

With a quick scan of the room, she didn't see any sign of a fight. There was no blood. The shampoo and soap bottles weren't disturbed either, although the shower curtain was pulled open and slightly ripped from its clips, no doubt pulled free when Pumpkin fell back. But that was the only thing out of place.

"She's alive, but her pulse is weak. It looks like she hit her head when she fell," Oliver called out.

"How bad is it?"

Oliver blocked Lochlyn's view of Pumpkin as he shifted her body around. Being this close, Lochlyn could now see a line of red ooze on the inside of Pumpkin's head.

There was something not right with the look of the blood though. It appeared too goopy, too dark. Not like Lochlyn had been around a lot of bleeding people, but she was pretty sure it didn't typically look like this.

"Call the others on the walkie. Tell them we found her and we're going to head back to the lounge." Oliver's instruction broke through her thoughts.

Nodding, Lochlyn jolted into motion and pulled it free from her belt loop. "Come in, guys. Come in. We found Pumpkin, but she's unconscious. I repeat, Pumpkin's alive. We're going to bring her back to the lounge. Over."

Tense, Lochlyn let her eyes again search the room as she waited for a reply. Something glimmering caught her eye. A shine flashed from behind the claw-foot tub. As if hypnotized, Lochlyn knelt by the tub and reached her hand into the small space.

"What is it?"

Her face scrunched as she strained to reach whatever had caught her attention. It was hard to grab something she couldn't see. "I'm not sure. It might be nothing," *ah there it was*, Lochlyn thought as she pulled it free.

"Or it could be an …. Huh," Lochlyn said, puzzled as she held it up and inspected the dangly piece of jewelry. "An earring? Is Pumpkin wearing the other one?"

Oliver's face creased as a flicker of annoyance passed over his features while he inspected Pumpkin. "Uh, no. She's not wearing any earrings. Have the others answered back yet?"

Lochlyn could have sworn Pumpkin was wearing earrings earlier, but maybe she was misremembering? It was possible.

"I don't recognize it. Do you?"

Passing it over, Lochlyn watched as he ran his thumb over it. Oliver inspected it closer while she scanned the room again.

How could someone have dropped it all the way back here? If it wasn't Pumpkin's, was it from a previous guest like the keychain? Maybe someone was lounging in the tub, and it fell off the side. It was possible, but it wasn't coated in any dust, suggesting it had fallen or been dropped very recently back here.

All of a sudden Lochlyn remembered Gab was still missing. Could it be hers? Could they both have been trapped in here? Or was Pumpkin right earlier when she accused Gab of helping Kitty put all of this in motion? Did Gab attack Pumpkin to shut her up? Gab's earring could have fallen off in the struggle.

How would Gab have gotten out of here without going past them though? There wasn't another doorway in or out. No window to the outside either. Her eyes lifted to the wall above the toilet and she felt her body tense.

"Oliver, someone else was in here," Lochlyn whispered. "Look, the vent's open."

Raising to her feet, Lochlyn didn't take her eyes off the gaping hole in the wall. Whoever had been in there hadn't had time to, or wasn't able to, close it behind themselves. It was a tight and likely time-consuming squeeze after all.

"Help me up," Lochlyn said suddenly.

Oliver's face scrunched before he sighed and carefully set Pumpkin's upper body back into the tub and pulled himself to his feet. He extended a hand, letting Lochlyn use him to keep steady as she climbed onto the top of the toilet seat.

Her knees wobbled for a moment, but Oliver kept her from falling. Stretching up onto her tippy toes, she peered inside the vent. "It's big enough for a small person to squeeze through. They must have heard us, panicked, and left through here."

"Okay, but how tiny are we talking?"

"Maybe someone small like Gab," Lochlyn replied. "Who, might I add, also knows this lodge better than anyone else?"

She and Oliver shared a look, coming to the same conclusion.

Did that mean they finally had a solid lead on a suspect?

Chapter 17

Gab, last name unknown, was the wild card.

Lochlyn, nor presumably anyone else, knew anything other than she worked for the lodge and was friends with Kitty.

Someone who wasn't invested in tonight would have gone home when the storm started, but Gab had volunteered to stick around when she really had no reason to.

So, who was she really and how was she connected to all of this? Kitty had mentioned earlier that they'd done an internship here at the lodge together, but their friendship came off as more than what one would expect from a relative's employee.

Was Kitty really the master mind behind the events of tonight? But why? What was her motive?

At the time, a murder mystery hadn't been in the literal sense. It was supposed to be a game, but that idea had twisted and gone wrong when a very real murder occurred before the game even started.

Or had that been the plan all along?

Had Kitty brought them here under false pretenses? What if they were taking part in her own twisted game? But it was more of a hunting party than a dinner. Gab could be her fall guy, her knife to wield, so to speak. It was Gab who had access to both Camden's food and Pumpkin.

While she did the actual killing, Kitty plotted and directed her to who to target next. Camden saw a heated moment between her, Pumpkin, and Boomer and before he could tell anyone he was killed at dinner. Pumpkin outright accused Kitty before she and Gab went missing.

What if Kitty intended on picking them off one at a time? If that was the case, then the rest of them just handed Boomer over to her on a silver platter.

Obviously, Gab and Kitty had the best knowledge of the lodge since it belonged to her uncle and Gab worked here.

They were here first, giving them plenty of time to sabotage the four-wheelers. Kitty *conveniently* picked the weekend it was supposed to be an epic downpour, which left no way to leave by car or even foot thanks to the psycho on the quad.

And she was sitting directly beside Camden, giving her the best opportunity of slipping the bag of nuts into his food. An allergy only Kitty knew about.

All the clues led to her with a perfectly wrapped bow on top.

Pumpkin had likely been right on the nose in assuming Gab was the one to follow them on the quad. And, Gab would have known about the employee phones just as Kitty would have.

Except it was almost too perfectly convenient. It also didn't explain Olive's keychain being found with the mask or the fact Twiggy had allegedly been the one in possession of the bag of nuts according to Oliver.

Lochlyn leaned against the wall. She pulled the haunting pig mask out of her purse, staring hard at it. Her lips pursed as she pondered. It was obviously a clue, right? Or was it a prop to throw them off her trail?

That would explain Olive's keychain. Perhaps she was intended to be the killer in their game, and it had been put there as a clue. In the chaos of tonight's events though no one had thought to retrieve it.

But that didn't sit right.

Afterall, Lochlyn had seen someone outside by the storage shed. She was relatively sure of it, or was she? Oliver was right. It was raining hard out there. Maybe it was nothing but her own imagination running wild like they said?

Even though it was dark out, Lochlyn was convinced it was clearly a silhouette. Objects didn't move in the way the figure darted off. But people did. Kitty, Olive, and Twiggy had all been with the rest of them at the time in the lounge, but Gab wasn't. It was totally possible she'd been out there.

"If we go back and accuse them, we must be a hundred and ten percent sure about this. We must have solid proof and we don't," Oliver said reluctantly. "Thinking Kity was involved is just another theory."

He had a point there.

Just because Gab was likely the killer, it didn't mean she was working with Kitty or Olive. She could be doing this all on her own for an unknown reason, or someone else could have paid her off just as plausibly.

Oliver was right. Theories alone weren't going to solve this mess, but it was a start.

Glancing over to Oliver, Lochlyn wondered if he possibly suspected her. She was the newest to join the group, while they have all known each other for years. That was one downside to sticking to their characters.

It didn't look good for her that this was happening now. If she wanted to keep her name clear *and* stay alive, Lochlyn would have to figure out the truth.

That, and if it came down to believing it could be his twin or accusing her of being the mastermind behind this, Lochlyn had no doubt which direction his finger would point.

Inhaling deeply, Lochlyn straightened and slipped the mask back into her purse. "So, we'll find concrete proof. We need to wake Pumpkin up and ask her what happened. We don't bring our suspicions to the group until we're sure."

The way Oliver was watching her now made her squirm. It felt like he was seeing right through her mask of bravery to how scared she really was. Thankfully, he didn't call her out.

Instead, he dipped his chin and turned to the unconscious Pumpkin on the bed. Oliver had lifted her from the tub and brought her into the other room so she was more comfortable. Unfortunately, Pumpkin had yet to open her eyes.

"I don't suppose you have smelling salts in that purse of yours, do you?" he asked over his shoulder.

"Sorry, that wasn't on my check list of things to bring to dinner."

Nodding, he turned and leaned over the unconscious form of Pumpkin. She would look like she was sleeping peacefully if not for the streak of dark gooey blood running down the side of her face.

"Come on, Pumpkin," Oliver coaxed as he patted her cheek with a fair amount of force. "We need you to wake up now. Come on."

Much to Lochlyn's relief, the girl's eyes opened slightly. Her hazel eyes were disoriented as she looked around the room before finally settling somewhat on Oliver.

Panic seized her as she suddenly pushed herself back against the headboard. "Get away from me!"

Oliver sat back, his hands raised to show he meant her no harm. "Whoa, hey, you're safe. We're not going to hurt you."

Her frightened eyes flickered behind him, landing on a worried Lochlyn. Instead of relief, her expression changed to dread and sadness of all things. It felt like Pumpkin was disappointed to see them together, but why would she? It didn't make any sense, particularly right now.

Taking a cautious step forward, Lochlyn attempted to ease her worry. "Oliver's right. We're not going to hurt you. We found you in the bathroom. It looks like you fell and hit your head. Do you remember what happened?"

Pumpkin raised a trembling hand to her head and she winced as her fingers touched her wound. As she pulled her hand away, her eyes widened at the sight of the red coating the tips of her fingers.

Lochlyn could see the alarm in Pumpkin's eyes as the memories hit. Her fear appeared to grip tight as her hands shook. Nudging Oliver, Lochlyn motioned for him to switch spots with her. His features scrunched again, conflicted over doing as she instructed.

After a moment, he seemed to change his mind, nodded, and stood from his spot on the bed. He was choosing to trust her and for that Lochlyn was grateful.

Slipping into the vacant spot he'd just occupied, Lochlyn slowly reached forward and took Pumpkin's hand. The other girl flinched from the touch but didn't pull away. "No one else is going to hurt you, Pumpkin. You're safe," Lochlyn promised, though she hoped this night didn't make a liar out of her.

Pumpkin's body started to relax, though her eyes still showed she was guarded. Promises were just words. They didn't mean anything until a person's actions proved them true.

"No one is safe as long as we're here," Pumpkin whispered, as her attention briefly flickered back to Oliver with accusation.

It had happened too quickly for Lochlyn to figure out what it meant. "If you're talking about Gab, don't worry. Once we get back to the lounge and regroup, we can come up with a plan to beat her at her own game."

A bitter laugh slipped through Pumpkin's lips. "If you truly believe it'll be that easy, you're an idiot. You can't trust anyone to have your back in this place. Everyone has an ulterior motive. Even Prince Charming over there."

Her words hit a sore spot within Lochlyn, and she fought the desire to look over her shoulder to see Oliver's face. Pumpkin's words, cruel as they were, did ring true. How can you trust anyone when no one was who they said they were? She couldn't. Not even Oliver with the charming smile and comforting presence.

If it came out that Olive was involved with this mess, Lochlyn had no doubt in her mind that Oliver would do anything to protect her. Loyalty between siblings wasn't something easily dismissed.

"I never said I trusted anyone here," Lochlyn asserted somewhat defensively. "But I'm pretty sure no one else wants to die tonight. So, you'll have to trust us enough to get back to the lounge. Or you can be stubborn and go by yourself. We won't force you to stay with us."

The choice was simple. Pumpkin could trust them, or she could let fear take over and risk being caught alone up here by Pig Man.

A sour expression settled on Pumpkin's face as she turned away, her glance landing on the mattress as she crossed her arms. Her decision was made. She was going to risk staying behind out of spite and distrust.

Lochlyn didn't move, giving Pumpkin a chance to change her mind. Just as she was about to give up, Pumpkin let out a heavy sigh and rolled her eyes.

"Well, I guess going off on my own didn't really work out so well for me last time."

Oliver stepped forward then. "What happened after you left the dining room? Do you remember?"

Pumpkin hesitated, watching Oliver with something like disdain. She wasn't a fan of his, Lochlyn had gathered by now. "Gab caught up with me and told me that what I said was uncalled for. She's a bit of a cheerleader for Kitty. She kept praising how much hard work Kitty put into making this weekend fun. She told me to get over whatever jealousy I felt and get back to the others. Then she left me in the library alone."

Lochlyn's head snapped up, confusion filling her. "Wait, you guys were in the library? How did you end up in here?"

Most importantly, if Gab had left her there alone, where was she now?

Pumpkin pulled at her neck, wincing as she rolled her shoulders to ease some pain. "That's where it's fuzzy. I remember hearing the library doors open again and thought she came back. I started telling her I'd head back in a few minutes, when all of a sudden, I caught the reflection of the masked freak standing directly behind me. Then all I remember is pain, until I woke up in here with *him* looming over me."

That explained her panic upon seeing Lochlyn and Oliver. Not that she could blame her for feeling that way. It would freak Lochlyn out too if she woke up with people looming over her.

Peering over her shoulder, Lochlyn's eyes caught hold of Oliver's as a silent conversation passed between them. Pumpkin's story had blown their Gab theory out of the water. There was still the chance she'd turned around with the mask and attacked Pumpkin, but why go through the trouble?

If Pumpkin was telling the truth, it meant Gab wasn't around when Pumpkin was attacked.

It also meant Gab was still missing. Whether she was the Pig Man in disguise, or another victim was still to be seen. They couldn't rule out either option until they found her.

"We need to keep looking. She could be trapped in one of the rooms like Pumpkin was and no one is looking for her," Lochlyn said, her concern spiking as she stood.

Oliver reached for her hand, pulling her a step closer to him. "We can let Boomer and Kitty look for her. We should get Pumpkin back to the lounge. Don't worry. They'll find her."

His fingers squeezed hers to comfort her. Deep down, Lochlyn knew he was right. Pumpkin could have a concussion and it wasn't a good idea to push her more than they needed to.

"Okay," she sighed.

Raising the walkie to her mouth, she held down the button on the side. "Kitty, Boomer, come in. Over."

The line crackled with static for a moment before their answer came over. "What's up? Is Pumpkin awake? Over."

Looking over her shoulder, Lochlyn noticed how Pumpkin's entire body had gone tense at the sound of Kitty's voice. Odd.

"Uh, yeah. She's awake, but we're going to take her back to the lounge and regroup. Look, Gab wasn't with her when she was attacked. She was on her way back to us, I think. Have you guys seen any sign of her yet? Over," Lochlyn said over the line.

The silence stretched, lingering to a point it concerned Lochlyn that maybe they had found her, and it wasn't good. Her mind immediately went to the pig mask currently tucked away in her bag.

Sharing a glance with Oliver, Lochlyn didn't know how to voice her concerns. What if the guy had intercepted Gab when she left the library before he attacked Pumpkin? What if the caller before didn't mention her because Gab didn't need saving? She was already dead.

Taking the walkie, Oliver held it to his mouth. "Have you guys seen her or not? Over."

Silence went by as they waited for Boomer and Kitty's reply. Lochlyn shot Oliver another look as the seconds went by. What good were having the walkies if no one answered? Even Pumpkin appeared to be on edge waiting to hear a response.

A full minute had gone by before they heard the crackle of static again. "We found her a few minutes ago. She's a little steamed, but otherwise okay. We're heading back n-wait, what was that?"

Straightening, Lochlyn felt her breath catch as she waited to hear what was said next. She could feel her anxiety rising as the static buzzed.

Raising it up to her mouth, Lochlyn held the button down. "What's going on? Over."

No response.

Chapter 18

"Kitty? Boomer, come in," Lochlyn tried again. "What's going on? Can you repeat? Over."

The static coming through the line felt like it was taunting them. Before she could try again, Pumpkin came up beside her, and placed her hand over the walkie. Lochlyn's eyes immediately shot up to meet Pumpkin's, questioning her action.

"If they're hiding from someone, you might be putting them in danger by talking over the line. Let's just head back to the lounge and hopefully meet everyone there. Kitty said they were going to head back, right?" Pumpkin tried to reason with her, but they both knew the chance of Kitty and Boomer being there was going to be slim to none. "Maybe their walkie died or broke. Come on."

Lochlyn wanted to argue and suggest they look for them instead, but as if it was a sign not to, Oliver's alarm rang. It was time to head back anyway.

"I guess that answers that," Oliver piped in. "We've got to get back so they don't think something happened to us. Like Pumpkin said, Kitty and Boomer are on their way to the lounge too."

All Lochlyn could do was tell herself there was a slight chance they were being truthful. Boomer and Kitty could very well be on their way back to the lounge with Gab and a busted walkie. It was a simple explanation.

Even if Lochlyn was correct and something had happened, Pumpkin was still right that yelling over the walkie was only going to make things worse.

Lowering the walkie, Lochlyn signaled that she agreed. "Let's get moving then."

Much to her surprise, Oliver reached over and took her hand back in his. Their fingers laced together as he gave a squeeze. "Pumpkin's probably on the right track. It's just a busted walkie. No need to worry."

How could they be so sure about this? Pig Man was terrorizing them, yet they were acting like *Lochlyn* was being irrational. It didn't make sense.

Too stunned to argue, Lochlyn forced her lips to curve and gave Oliver a grateful smile. Her doubts were screaming at her to listen, but frankly she didn't want to. She didn't want the little voice whispering not to trust these people to taint her actions. Oliver was trying to comfort her, that was all.

Leading the way, Oliver paused long enough for his eyes to dart from each end of the hall before he pulled her towards him. "Come on, stay close," he whispered as his hand tightened around hers. Lochlyn tried to ignore how it felt more like a leash than a comfort.

Pumpkin shut the door behind them as she brought up the rear. As Oliver kept Lochlyn close behind him, she tried to focus on their surroundings instead of his scent invading her senses.

He was so close Lochlyn could feel the warmth from his body against her. It did help to know he wanted to keep her close and protect her. He was acting as her lifeline as they crept into the darkness. Glancing over her shoulder, she noticed Pumpkin glaring with disgust at their entwined hands.

Given Pumpkin's Velma inspired outfit, it made Lochlyn wonder if this was how that character felt every time she was paired off with Fred and Daphne, who were clearly into each other.

The thought caused a lump in her throat. Lochlyn did her best to ignore the way her stomach fluttered thinking Oliver might be into her.

'*Get a grip,*' Lochlyn scolded herself.

Now was absolutely not the time for this. So what if she found him attractive or that his support literally made her stomach do flips?

"You okay there, Ivorie?" he whispered over his shoulder. "You look a little flustered."

Swallowing, Lochlyn refused to meet his eyes. It would only make this moment worse.

"I-I'm fine," she squeaked out.

Damn hormones.

The faint sound of his chuckling confirmed that Oliver was *well* aware of the thoughts racing through her head. Pumpkin's exaggerated eye roll did not help.

"Oh, I wish the guy had killed me. It would have been more exciting than watching you two attempt to flirt," she whispered, her glare shooting between them.

Scowling, Lochlyn continued to walk until a sudden thump came from the room next to them.

Lochlyn reached for the doorknob when the sound of static came over the walkie. It crackled for a moment before Olive's voice came over.

"What's taking you guys so long? Is everything okay? Over."

Lochlyn's eyes drifted from the door and lingered over her shoulder for a moment. Turning back to the door, she figured it wouldn't hurt to check one last room. The others would understand, right?

As if in a trance, Lochlyn curled her fingers around the door handle and started to twist it open.

Pumpkin took the walkie from Lochlyn's belt loop and raised it to her mouth as she held the button down. "We're on our way there now. Your brother is just charming the new girl. It's quite disgusting, actually."

Lochlyn opened her mouth to tell Pumpkin to cut it out, when lightning flashed and illuminated the hallway. Her blood ran cold when she saw the shadow of a face flicker in the slit of the door opening.

Lightning flashed again, but the face was gone from the opening as if it had never been there. Her feet stumbled backwards away from the doorway. Lochlyn might have tripped if Oliver wasn't holding onto her.

"Whoa, are you okay?" he asked with concern.

Nodding, her body trembled as she tugged him to keep moving "We need to go. Now."

Leading the way, Lochlyn refused to let them see how wide and full of shock her eyes had become as they left.

Thunder boomed next and Lochlyn swore she heard the click of a shutting door. It was too late to see if it was the door they'd left behind though.

"Did you hear that?"

Oliver, Lochlyn, and Pumpkin paused as they stopped in front of the emergency stairs. They didn't dare take the elevator during the storm. Nothing good would come from getting stuck in there. They'd definitely be the next victims.

"Hear the thunder?" Oliver asked.

Shaking her head, Lochlyn peered over her shoulder as if expecting to see someone following them. "No, it sounded like a door closed."

Oliver squeezed her fingers with a sense of reassurance. "Look, we're all on edge. Someone's been messing with us all night. The wind is pretty bad out there. It wouldn't surprise me if it shut the door on its own."

Another unlikely coincidence, but feeling self-conscious, Lochlyn didn't argue the point.

Except she was almost certain she'd seen that haunting white pig mask looking back at her when the lightning struck. Perhaps it was just her mind playing tricks on her because it was what she wanted to see? Everything was scarier in the dark. Like how a broom with a coat draped over it was suddenly a stalker standing in the corner of the room. Lochlyn just needed to get a hold of herself.

Twiggy's earlier taunt of being the girl who cried wolf came back to her mind and solidified her decision not to mention the face she might have seen in the doorway.

"I'm sure you're right," Lochlyn agreed, though her gut was telling her he was wrong.

Satisfied with her answer, Oliver squeezed her hand again before pulling the door to the stairs open.

Lochlyn followed, giving the hall one last scan. Pumpkin was right behind her. Still, she couldn't shake off the feeling of being watched.

Was it all in her head? Lochlyn could have sworn she saw a face in that doorway, but it could have easily been the shadows playing a trick on her again.

Oliver had to be right about the wind. He *was* right, she told herself. It was entirely possible that's what shut the door.

With a glance over to Pumpkin, she could see the other girl wasn't as easily convinced that everything was okay.

The walkie malfunction was entirely possible too, but all of these incidents occurring within five minutes of each other felt like one coincidence too many.

Still, Lochlyn followed Oliver's lead as they descended the stairs. The lounge was three floors down, she remembered sourly. Her feet were crying out with every step, not used to wearing heels let alone wet ones for this long. Not to mention running up and down stairs in them.

By the time they'd made it down two flights of stairs, Lochlyn was starting to fall behind. It didn't take Oliver long to notice given their hands were still entwined.

It wasn't until her heel shifted out from under her foot and she nearly fell forward that she realized she'd zoned out. Her hand whipped out from his to catch herself, her fingers curling around the hand railings on either side of her.

He slowed to a stop, peering over his shoulder with worry in his chocolate eyes. "Are you okay? Did you want to stop for a second and catch your breath?"

Panting, Locklyn shook her head. "I just need to-" she paused as she yanked off one of her shoes. "take these stupid things off."

Oliver, and even Pumpkin, chuckled as she tossed the other one aside with a huff. "I take it you're not a heel kind of girl then?"

Running a hand through the red locks of her wig, she shook her head. "You could say that, but I'd deny it. Heiress and all. Gotta keep some secrets to myself."

His laughter was a welcomed sound. It calmed her nerves, which was definitely something she needed at the moment.

"Heels are not for everyone," Pumpkin added. "Though I was born to shine in them."

Adjusting the shorts of her romper, Lochlyn rolled her eyes before she flashed Oliver a satisfied smile. "Shall we continue?"

Holding her chin up high, Lochlyn adjusted his white jacket on her shoulders and moved past him, now a good two inches shorter than she'd been a second ago.

The pads of her feet smacked against the cold steps, but she paid no mind to the echoing noise. Lochlyn would walk barefoot through the lodge with confidence. Pumpkin might be fine wearing her own heels, but Lochlyn was not one of those girls who had walked in them before she could even crawl.

Twiggy's earlier comment about how she looked the part but didn't have the confidence of an heiress ran through her head again, but at this point, Lochlyn didn't quite care.

If they had to run on a moment's notice, she'd rather do it barefoot than risk breaking her neck in those ridiculous shoes.

Chapter 19

Arriving back to the lounge, Pumpkin led the way inside. Just as Lochlyn was about to follow, Oliver's hand wrapped around her upper arm and pulled her back. "Hey, before we go in there. I just can we keep the keychain between us for now? At this point, we have a solid lead with Gab and there isn't a reason to point the light on Olive. She isn't behind all of this."

Lochlyn had to shut her mouth before her jaw dropped. This request should have been expected. Oliver was simply looking out for his sister, and she wanted to allow him the ability to do so, but what if he was wrong? What if ignoring the keychain did more harm than good?

No doubt seeing the conflict across her face, Oliver was quick to add. "I'll ask her about it myself, but the others don't need to get involved, okay? Please, just don't send an angry mob after the wrong person."

Biting her lip, Lochlyn's response was right on the tip of her tongue. She wanted to tell him not to worry, that she would keep the reveal of the keychain to herself, but the 'what ifs' kept the words locked in her throat.

"I don't know, Oliver. What if-"

Her words ended as a sudden shout for help came from inside the lounge. Oliver shot her a look before he jolted into motion. Lochlyn was right behind him, but suddenly stopped at the sight that welcomed them.

Twiggy was laid out flat on the floor unconscious, Pumpkin kneeling beside him. A gasp slipped through Lochlyn's lips before she brushed past Oliver and dropped to his side.

"I found him like this," Pumpkin explained.

Pressing two fingers to his neck, Lochlyn was relieved to feel his heartbeat. A puff of air parted his lips, and hit the dark curls now fallen onto his face. "He's alive. Just knocked out. There's a bump on the back of his head," Locklyn informed her companions.

Scanning the area around her, Lochlyn noticed a literal bloody candlestick discarded a few feet away. Whoever hit him must have dropped it in a rush and taken off.

"Where's my sister?"

Lifting her head, Lochlyn's gaze scanned the room. Her heart sank as she realized what Oliver was talking about. There was no sign of Olive anywhere. She was gone.

Her study of the room continued, trying to take in as much detail as possible. There was broken glass near the drink cart, the loveseat was turned over, and the rug was askew. All of it showed clear signs that there'd been a struggle.

"Do you think she-"

Oliver's narrowed glare landed on her, silencing her theory immediately. "She did not knock Twiggy out and make a run for it."

Lochlyn raised her hands up, blood coating her fingers from checking Twiggy's head wound. "I believe you, but that doesn't tell us what *did* happen."

Lochlyn shrugged off Oliver's jacket and used it as a pillow to support Twiggy's head after she carefully pushed him onto his back. Her stomach churned at the sight of Twiggy's blood staining the white material.

"Is it wise to move him around like that?"

Lochlyn didn't spare Pumpkin a glance as her focus remained on the boy between them. "Just help me get him awake and up."

Lochlyn finally tore her gaze from Twiggy when Pumpkin didn't move. She was in shock and wasn't going to be of any help to her. Pumpkin's eyes were wide, her body frozen as she stared at the bloody candlestick.

Looking over her shoulder, she sent Oliver a pleading gaze. If they were going to figure out what happened, she needed his help in waking Twiggy. "Please, Oliver," she begged.

Oliver didn't immediately move, but eventually he nodded and took Pumpkin's place on Twiggy's other side.

Together, they lifted his upper body and dragged him to the couch. It took two tries before they were able to get him up there thanks to Pumpkin's lack of help. Lochlyn knelt on the cushion behind Twiggy, allowing him to lean back against her.

Patting Twiggy's cheek, she continued to urge him to wake up. Oliver took the chance to check the rest of the room for his missing twin. She could hear him calling for Olive and the fear in his voice tugged at her heart strings.

Pumpkin quietly turned the loveseat up right before she lowered herself into it. Lochlyn's focus returned to Twiggy. She might have feared he was no longer breathing if not for the slow rise and fall of his chest.

The longer he stayed unconscious, the more panic she felt. She couldn't explain why, but the thought of no longer sharing a round of banter with Twiggy broke her heart.

As much as he got under her skin, she enjoyed the challenges Twiggy threw her way. He kept her on her toes. It'd be a shame to no longer have that in her life. Even if it was only over the internet.

"Come on, jerk. You've got to wake up. Please, come on," Lochlyn pleaded as she brushed the dark curls from Twiggy's eyes. "Please, you need to open your eyes."

Her breath caught in her throat when she noticed the left corner of his mouth twitch upward. "Did you just call me a jerk?"

His eyes fluttered open and his glassy gaze tried to focus on her face. Relief flowed through her as she took in his icy blue eyes. Those same blue eyes had unnerved her earlier, but now Lochlyn was happy to see them open and alert.

"You're okay," she sighed with relief and a small smile.

A half snort, half chuckle, rumbled in Twiggy's chest. "Don't tell me you were worried, heiress. I'm flattered."

And there was the Twiggy she knew and loathed. She had half the mind to smack him, but instead, Lochlyn found herself wrapping her arms around him in an embrace. It surprised them both judging by the stunned expression that replaced his cocky grin.

Twiggy's form went ridged under her arms, a wide panicked doe-eyes expression on his face as he pulled back. It would appear he was just as clueless on how to show and receive affection as she was. In true Twiggy fashion though, he awkwardly patted her arm.

"Don't go soft on me now, heiress," he teased.

His cheeks had taken on a pink hue. Lochlyn felt her heart skip, realizing she was the cause of his blush. "Don't get used to it. I'm just relieved we don't have to worry about another body going missing."

Pumpkin's throat cleared, reminding her that they weren't alone and Lochlyn immediately released him. Turning, Lochlyn saw Oliver behind them with his jaw clenched. Considering Olive was currently missing, maybe her joke had been in bad taste.

Twiggy rubbed his head and his eyes narrowed on the other man as he sat up again Lochlyn. "What happened?"

"Why don't you tell us? Where's my sister?"

His tone was accusatory, as if Oliver believed Twiggy might have done something to Olive before knocking himself out. Lochlyn sat back on her heels, watching and waiting to see how this played out. She tried to ignore the sudden coldness she felt when Twiggy moved away from her.

"We were gonna head out and look for Kitty and Boomer since they never replied again. I was against the idea, but she's more stubborn than a moose. I told her we should wait for you guys to get back with Pumpkin, but she was too antsy. She didn't want to wait anymore," Twiggy explained.

"What happened next?"

Twiggy spared her a glance before shifting his attention back toward Oliver. "We were just about to leave when we heard the dining room door open. I, uh, I remember hearing her shout to look out, but before I could turn around, I got hit. There might have been a scuffle, but everything after that is a blur."

Twiggy rubbed his sore head as he looked at each of them, trying to evaluate whether they believed him.

Lochlyn looked between the two men with suspicion, wondering if Twiggy was to be trusted. Did Oliver or Pumpkin believe him? Oliver was stoic, his expression unreadable. She couldn't make heads or tails of where Pumpkin's thoughts had turned either.

"You don't remember seeing anything else? Not a flash of clothing or a voice?" Pumpkin said, breaking her silence.

Twiggy was trying to remember, but appeared to come up blank. "No, sorry. Wait, uh, I do remember seeing boots. They looked familiar, but I-I can't describe them. I just remember thinking I've seen those boots before."

Boots.

It wasn't much of a lead, though at least it was a start. Lochlyn tried to remember what Boomer was wearing. Were they work boots or sneakers? She couldn't picture them. Gab had been wearing boots though. She remembered thinking how they stood out against her uniform.

Looking over to Oliver, her eyes dropped to his shoes, which were clean black and white checkered vans. Definitely not boots. Plus it couldn't have been him. Oliver was with her the entire time and so was Pumpkin.

"Was Boomer wearing boots?" Pumpkin inquired.

Oliver appeared to seriously consider her question, doing his best to remember. It was always a good thing to remember what a person was wearing in situations like this one. Whether to give someone a proper description of a missing person, or to identify the person in question. That was one thing she'd learned from *The Twisted* podcast.

"Uh, maybe. I can't remember," he admitted. "You can't think Boomer did this."

Lochlyn bit her immediate response of '*yes, I do*' because in the span of just a few hours, she would have accused just about all of them of some kind of crime.

"I-I don't know. It'd be easier to check him off the list if we knew what happened to him and Kitty. Gab is also still unaccounted for and I know she was wearing boots," Lochlyn offered with a less hostile approach.

She had to remind herself that these people had all known each other, basically, for years. Maybe not face to face, but that didn't really matter. They could just as easily share secrets online as they could in person. They trusted each other enough to meet for a murder mystery party.

Except, Lochlyn was the exception, and it wasn't smart to accuse each one of them of murder.

Gritting his teeth, Twiggy propped himself up. "So, let's go find them."

Lochlyn wanted to find them just as eagerly as he did, but he wasn't in any position to go charging out of here. "You could have a concussion. Scratch that, I have no doubt you do after being hit with that antique monster. You're in no condition to go anywhere."

A sour expression crossed Twiggy's face as he rubbed his neck. "I can't believe they got me with the candlestick."

"In the lounge," Oliver spoke up, his eyes lifting from the floor to meet their confused expressions. "They got you with the candlestick in the lounge."

He couldn't possibly be serious right now? Oliver was really making a *Clue* joke? His timing couldn't be worse. There was already one dead body and four people unaccounted for, and he was choosing *now* to make a bad joke?

"Really, man? A *Clue* joke?"

At least Oliver had the decency to look guilty, realizing his comment was in bad taste. "What? Too soon?"

Lochlyn had to catch her jaw as it hit her lap. Her astonishment grew when Twiggy and Pumpkin's laughter broke the silence. They were laughing and joking about this? What the actual hell was this? What was with these people making light of this horrendous night? It was strange.

Oliver's twin was missing, and someone was dead. Kitty, Gab, and Boomer could both be behind this for all they knew, but these boys had jokes to tell? Unbelievable.

Rolling her eyes, she scoffed and rose from the couch. "I can not believe you two are making a joke out of this. I'm going to look for Kitty and Boomer. Oliver, stay with Twiggy and Pumpkin. Keep them awake. Neither of them are in any condition to be wandering the halls. I'll be-"

"Don't you dare say you'll be right back," Twiggy cut her off, his tone serious again.

Waving off his warning, Lochlyn padded across the room and paused back at the double doors. "I've got the walkie and Twiggy has his. I'll keep in contact and let you guys know when I find them."

Poking her head out, Lochlyn checked both ends of the hall before slipping through the doors and closing them behind her.

Pausing, she leaned against the doors and took a moment to breathe. Her heart was racing, and her body was buzzing with panic.

Closing her eyes, Lochlyn released another breath. "You're gonna be fine. It's gonna be okay, you can do this."

Shaking out her nerves, she gave herself another moment before she was ready to get moving. Looking down at her hip, Lochlyn opened the flap to her bag and stared at the mask inside. Someone was trying to scare them, and Lochlyn was determined to find out why and stop them before another body dropped.

Time to keep sleuthing.

Chapter 20

Heading toward the Eastern stairwell where Kitty and Boomer were supposed to be, Lochlyn tried to keep her eyes peeled for any movement.

It was impossible to figure out what floor Boomer and Kitty could have been on when they suddenly went radio silent. They could have started at the top and worked their way down or vice versa.

Allegedly, Gab was with them and fine, but Lochlyn wasn't going to believe that until she saw it for herself.

Starting with the second floor, Lochlyn checked four locked doors before she finally found one that was open. It was left slightly ajar, and the flash of that face she'd seen earlier appeared in her mind. Someone could be waiting to attack as soon as she stepped inside.

Looking around the hall, Lochlyn didn't find anything she could use to defend herself. So, she chose to make her purse the weapon. With enough force, she could really hurt someone with this thing.

At least she hoped so.

The first thing that hit her upon entering was the foul, rustic smell. The room was too dark to make out what the source of the smell was though. Light, Lochlyn needed to find the damn light switch.

As her fingers ran along the side of the wall in search of a light, she paused as something warm and sticky covered her fingertips. Her face scrunched, disgusted, as Lochlyn finally found the switch and the room illuminated. But as soon as Lochlyn did, she sorely wished she hadn't.

Blood was *everywhere*.

Stepping further into the room, Lochlyn took in the horror all around her. It appeared as if someone had been hit with something repeatedly. It caused the substance to spatter across the walls, before whoever it belonged to fell into the bed, where the amount of pooled blood suggested they had bled out.

But where was the body? Lochlyn seriously doubted anyone could have walked away from this attack.

"What did you do?"

Spinning on her heels, a gasp left her lips at the sudden appearance of Pumpkin in the doorway. Her purse fell from her hands, the mask peeking out as it hit the floor.

"It wasn't me!" Lochlyn exclaimed, though her bloody hand could suggest otherwise. "I didn't do this."

Pumpkin was tense as she crossed her arms. "I didn't think you did, but that doesn't answer the question lingering on my mind. What did you do? Did you touch anything?"

Stunned, Lochlyn hadn't considered wearing gloves during her search for the others. It was such a rookie mistake. This was twice now she'd forgotten to cover her tracks.

"Oh, um, just the door and the light switch," Lochlyn said as she tried to retrace her steps to remember what she'd touched. "Is that bad?"

Pumpkin rolled her eyes, muttering 'amateur' under her breath. "Only if you're hoping whoever is behind this wants to frame you."

Lochlyn couldn't blame her for calling her an amateur. Her prints would be all over the place now, making her an easy person to frame. She should have done better this time around, but her racing heart was making it hard to think clearly.

"That leads to my next question," Pumpkin said as she stepped into the room, taking in the sight of the destroyed space. "What the hell happened in here and who did it happen to?"

Lochlyn opened her mouth, but was unsure of what to say, so she decided against it when nothing came to her. Did she want to argue Pumpkin should have stayed down in the lounge with the guys? Yes, but it wouldn't change the fact she was already here.

Pumpkin studied the room with a sharp gaze. She inspected every detail. "I don't think it was Olive. If they were trying to cover up the crime of her death, they would have done a better job of cleaning the room. Whoever did this wanted us to know it happened."

How could she be so calm about this? But also, Lochlyn pondered, why was Pumpkin so quick to assume whoever died in this room was Olive and not Gab, who was also still unaccounted for. It was just as likely Pig Man could have grabbed Gab when she left the library before he attacked Pumpkin.

Lochlyn saw Pumpkin's gaze drop to her feet and widen. She didn't need to look to know what caught her attention. Kneeling, Lochlyn hastily shoved the white mask back into her purse and tugged it onto her shoulder.

"I can't explain the mask. Oliver and I found it in the room before we found you. We were going to show everyone else, but never got the chance to," she explained.

Though, if roles were reversed and it was Pumpkin standing here with that mask in her possession, would Lochlyn believe she was innocent? No, she didn't think she would.

Pumpkin remained quiet, the silence lingering into an uncomfortable stretch. "Right, well, we can return to that Pandora's box once we figure out what happened in here."

Pumpkin was right, but a sour feeling in the pit of Lochlyn's stomach told her this wouldn't be forgotten. It wouldn't surprise her if Pumpkin tried to get as far away from her as soon as possible. Only, there was a bigger issue pressing for attention right now and it was the literal bloody room they were standing in.

Lochlyn took Pumpkin's lead and started looking for clues as well. Were Boomer and Kitty in here when they lost contact? Was this where Gab was being held? Could Olive have been in here after being taken from the lounge? Not likely given the timing, but Lochlyn wasn't counting the theory out just yet.

Kneeling to look under the bed, Lochlyn was careful not to disturb the scene too much.

Bingo.

"I've got something," Lochlyn announced as she pulled an item free from underneath the bedframe.

In her hand dangled a lanyard. Not just any lanyard though. No, it was one with the Moose Hollow Ski and Skate Lodge logo. Flipping it over, she saw a small grainy picture of Gab's face smiling back at her. Her full name was printed out on it with a barcode underneath. It was Gab's key card for work.

"Gab was in here," Lochlyn revealed as she passed the lanyard to Pumpkin. "But does that mean she was the victim or the killer? Twiggy said he remembered seeing boots dragging Olive away. Gab was wearing boots."

Pumpkin studied the lanyard with the concentration a person with a concussion shouldn't. She didn't appear as off-kilter as she had before.

"I think we should head back to the lounge. It's not safe up here," Pumpkin said suddenly.

It wouldn't necessarily be any safer downstairs, Lochlyn wanted to say. It would just put a bigger target on their backs being all in one spot. Pumpkin appeared ready to bolt from the room whether Lochlyn agreed or not.

Just then something twinkled from behind the bedside table. Squinting, Lochlyn attempted to subtly get a better look without alerting Pumpkin to what she was doing.

Holding the object between her fingers, Lochlyn immediately recognized it as the earring matching the one that she and Oliver had found earlier.

Whoever had been in the bathroom with Pumpkin had been here too. Glancing over at Pumpkin, Lochlyn studied her face for a minute. She didn't have earrings in, but Lochlyn could have sworn Pumpkin was wearing some earlier when they arrived. It was possible she'd taken them off at some point before dinner, but Lochlyn couldn't be sure.

Pumpkin's lack of serious alarm about the scene didn't sit right with Lochlyn either. No one in their right would be this collected, unless they knew a reason they could be.

Where had Pumpkin really been during that hour unaccounted for that she and Gab were missing? What was it she was doing? Lochlyn was no fool though. She knew Pumpkin wouldn't tell her anything.

Looking around one final time, Lochlyn stood and brushed off her knees as she slipped the second earring into her bag. "You're right. Let's get out of here," she said as she motioned for Pumpkin to lead the way.

Pumpkin held the door for her, allowing Lochlyn to slip by and leave first. "Actually, I left my phone in the other room earlier when I was looking through it. It's right down there. I'll meet you back at the lounge," Lochlyn quickly blurted out.

Without giving Pumpkin a chance to take in what she had said, Lochlyn was at the end of the hall and disappearing around the corner. She ducked into the first room that was unlocked and could hear Pumpkin's heels click against the wooden floorboards.

Softly shutting the door behind her, Lochlyn twisted the lock into place and even slipped the bolt into place as an extra measure. It felt excessive, but necessary. It might even be childish running from her and hiding like this, but Pumpkin was hiding something. She didn't trust that Pumpkin wouldn't hinder Lochlyn's search for clues.

Pressing her ear against the door, she listened to the clicking of Pumpkin's shoes pass by before a sudden slam of a door vibrated the room. Pumpkin was probably aggravated Lochlyn had taken off and hid.

Maybe Lochlyn should go back out and apologize? Given the circumstances of tonight, it was expected that tensions were high. But something about her story didn't add up. Her odd behavior was even more reason not to trust her. Lochlyn needed to trust her gut about this.

Instead, Lochlyn let loose a deep breath and turned to face the room. To her shock, she quickly realized this wasn't any ordinary room. Looking at the little plaque above the light switch, she found it was one of the conference rooms.

When searching the Lodge's website a few weeks ago, Lochlyn learned that they hold a lot of company conferences up here. It gave them a source of income during the off season.

Not knowing what to expect, Lochlyn pressed forward slowly and with caution. It wouldn't hurt to look around, Lochlyn thought to herself. That was why she'd taken off away from Pumpkin, wasn't it? So she could investigate more.

Walking further into the larger space, she took in the sight of the three long tables creating a C-shape. The room wasn't as empty as Lochlyn expected it to be though. There were folders spread out across one of the tables, sheets of papers poking out from inside like they were gathered up in a rush.

Upon closer inspection, Lochlyn realized they were short biographies on all of them. Picking up one of the stapled packets, she realized it one about herself. Well, kind of.

It was the Ivorie character art she'd had commissioned a few months back staring at her. Not Lochlyn. All Ivorie's likes, dislikes, quirks, there were even some notes added recently in pen.

'Paranoid, easy to startle, doesn't miss anything.'

They were observation notes, Lochlyn realized. Someone had been keeping tabs on her since her arrival. Looking at the others' sheets Lochlyn couldn't help but notice there were no observational notes about them. It was just hers. Was it because she was so new to the group or because she was the real target? It was her name that was written in blood on the wall. This all happened after *she* joined the group.

There were too many coincidences to ignore.

Setting down the papers, Lochlyn scanned the rest of the room until her attention caught on the bulletin board. The first thing she noted was the large amount of red string.

Moving around the table, Lochlyn stopped in front of the board and crossed her arms as she took in the details. It was all here, Lochlyn noted. *All of it.* She leaned against the table as she took in the sight of all their character headshots spread out across the board.

It felt like a stab to the chest as she noted the big red X's across Gab and Camden's photos. Olive's photo had a big question mark written over it. Did it mean Olive was just off the board or was she dead? Was her body hidden with Camden and Gab's, waiting to be found by them at some point? Why was she targeted next? There were so many questions.

Below their pictures, Lochlyn saw the red string moved to different events and connections. There was a notecard labeled '*Present the crime*' under Camden's photo and it was connected to another notecard that said '*Poison Surprise*' on it.

One of the cards connecting Kitty and Boomer said 'Sabotage' across it in thick red marker. The ruined four-wheelers and dead phone lines came to mind, but there was no way they could have controlled the rainstorm currently happening. Was it why they picked this exact weekend to host the event?

Under Pumpkin's photo was a notecard that read '*Houdini act*' and that was when she realized she was reading pieces of the big master plan. This was someone's murder board, a way to keep their plot straight. Her eyes jumped to the next red string connecting Oliver and Twiggy.

Misleading the target.

They were purposely throwing her off. Oliver had listened to her theories, comforted her when Lochlyn thought she was losing it, but he had also dismissed her ideas just like Twiggy had. They'd gone about it two different ways, but their objective was the same. Throw her off the trail of who was behind this chaos.

What the actual plot twist was this?

The walkie at her side crackled to life, startling her as the noise filled the silence. "Not to be that guy, but I'm just checking to make sure you're okay. Did Pumpkin find you? Over."

Her brows scrunched together, the debate of whether or not to answer him going on in her head. Was Oliver genuinely worried about her, or was he just attempting to keep tabs on her? Was the group all in on it? Was there a single person in this building she could trust? Or was she missing a big piece here? What if they were part of someone else's bigger plan? They could all be pieces on someone's board and have no idea.

Still, Lochlyn couldn't deny that the idea he was concerned for her made her insides flutter. It felt like a betrayal by her body and heart. Her head knew she needed to be cautious, but her heart held onto the hope his worry was genuine.

Lochlyn couldn't have imagined the small moments they shared, could she? The sparks of attraction and the chemistry between them. She wanted so badly to believe Oliver couldn't be that cruel to make her think there was something happening between them, only to pull the rug out from under her.

Except, he *could* be that cruel.

She'd only met these people today. Sure, they'd been talking online for the past six months, but it is easy to lie when you're already pretending to be someone else. How do you trust anyone when they aren't who they said they are? *You can't*, she noted bitterly.

Lochlyn took a picture of the board with her phone before hurrying out of the room. Not bothering to check any of the other rooms, or look for any sign of Pumpkin, she headed back for the stairwell.

"Ivie, you there? Over."

Scanning the stairs, Lochlyn raised the walkie to her mouth and hit the button. "I'm not jinxing myself, but so far, no creep in a pig mask has yanked me into any doorway never to be heard from again. Pumpkin found me, but, uh, we got separated. She should be headed back down there to you guys. Over," Lochlyn said as she peered through the doorway leading back into the second level.

Lochlyn was about to head up to the next level when the sound of door clicking shut echoed from a few floors above. Was someone on the stairs with her? Maybe it was Pumpkin, admitting defeat having not found her and on her way back to the lounge. Maybe it was Kitty, Gab, and Boomer finally on their way down after whatever had sidetracked them.

Opening her mouth to call out, Lochlyn instead stopped herself and pressed her body against the wall to stay out of sight. There was a good chance that could be the person who kidnapped Olive. Perhaps it was the person she'd seen outside.

Pig Man was still in play and his identity was still a mystery.

The longer this night went on, the more it seemed there really was another person here pulling all the strings.

Straining to hear another noise, Lochlyn didn't dare blink. A full minute went by before she heard the tap of shoes against the metal stairs. Whoever was coming down was doing their best to be just as quiet as she was. It definitely wasn't the click of heels she'd heard from Pumpkin's a few minutes before.

Looking around, Locklyn felt like a mouse stuck in a trap. No matter where she moved, they'd see or hear her. Her only chance of getting away was to head back inside the second floor and get into an unlocked room.

Lochlyn would have to bolt as soon as she opened the door since she had no doubt the person coming would immediately pick up their pace. She had to decide now whether she was going to wait and see who descended the stairs or else chance getting into a room without being seen.

Sweat rolled down the side of her face and her blood raced with panic. The shoes came to a stop as they reached the floor above her, pausing as if waiting to see what she did. Lochlyn took a deep breath, amping herself up before she flung the door open beside her and pushed herself into a sprint.

She paused at the first door, tugging on the handle. Nothing. It was locked. Right, she'd tried these doors before. There was nowhere for her to duck for cover this time and time was running out.

Screw this, she thought to herself. Not giving herself a moment to linger, Lochlyn made a run for it.

Her feet fumbled to get traction against the wooden floor, but she pushed herself to run to the opposite end of the hall. Her balance wavered as she attempted to turn the corner smoothly.

Lochlyn felt her shoulder bounce off the wall as she pushed herself to keep moving. But in the moment it took her to regain footing, the stairway to the door opened.

Lightning illuminated the hall, casting a shadow upon the figure. Standing there was a slender man, panting as he caught his breath. His face was covered with the same pale, sunken-eyed pig mask that was in her purse. Her blood drained as the realization hit. There was more than one mask.

Lochlyn didn't stick around to get a better look. Sucking in a breath, she scrambled to keep moving forward. This hallway would loop to the other side of the building and bring her to the elevator. It wasn't the best plan. In fact, it was a means of escape she was hoping to avoid, but it was the only option Lochlyn had if she wanted to get back to the lounge.

Looking over her shoulder, she noticed the pig man was not far behind her, though he wasn't exactly chasing her either. Was he taunting her? Letting her think she could get away? Well, Lochlyn wasn't going to go down that easily.

Pausing at the elevator, she frantically pushed the button. It wasn't working. Why wasn't it …. oh yeah, the key card! Kitty said it would control the elevators.

Yanking it loose from her pocket, Lochlyn repeatedly pressed the card against the screen. "Come on. Hurry up! Open. Come on. *Come on!*"

He was getting too close. Even if the door opened, he could slip right in with her, and she'd be trapped with this psycho. Looking around, Lochlyn noticed the encased axe. It was there in case of emergencies. Well, she'd certainly say this would count.

Using her elbow, Lochlyn rammed it into the glass hard enough to cause it to shatter. Her elbow throbbed, but she couldn't focus on that now. She could wallow in her pain when she was safe.

Grabbing the weapon, Lochlyn pulled it free and raised it, ready to attack. "Try me, creep! I'm ready for you!"

Ignoring the searing pain in her arm, she didn't dare take her eyes off the pig man. He had paused a few yards from her and his head fell to the side as he studied her. Gulping in air, Lochlyn shifted her footing. He was not going to take her down easily.

The elevator door opened beside her. Her body was frozen, wondering if it would be a mistake to take her eyes off him. The door started to shut, jolting her into motion as she dived inside.

Lochlyn immediately started hitting the button to shut the doors quicker. As the door closed, Lochlyn saw Pig Man standing there, and his haunting, rubber mask staring back at her.

Once the doors were closed, Lochlyn realized the elevator wasn't going to move until she selected a floor. It would make the most sense to head back to the lounge, but would the psycho be expecting that? Was he waiting for her to lead him to the others?

Pressing a button, Lochlyn settled on the other option. Picking a random floor would hopefully throw this creep off. He would likely see which floor she ultimately got off at, but it would take him time to get there and find her.

It was a game of cat and mouse, and she was determined to come out the winner.

Chapter 21

Moving quickly away from the door, Lochlyn only stopped as her back hit the wall. The man could have easily followed her inside the elevator, but he hadn't. Instead, he, at least, she had been assuming it was a 'he', just made her aware that he was letting her go.

But why?

Why do any of this? Not just to her, but to them all? No one really knew about this outing besides the group and obviously Kitty's uncle and the staff. Which included Gab. Although, they could have told their friends and family about it. It wasn't like they were purposely keeping this trip a secret.

Lochlyn had more questions than answers at this point and she didn't like it.

The elevator dinged as it stopped at her selected floor. Rolling her shoulder, she held the axe to her chest, ready to swing if something, or rather *someone*, awaited her on the other side.

The idea that Pig Man could already be standing there popped into her head. It would truly be a scene from a nightmare.

As the doors opened, a shadow invaded the safety of the elevator. Lochlyn shifted, raised the weapon in preparation to attack first. She wasn't about to be caught unsuspecting.

"Wait!" a voice shouted as their hands shot up in defense. "Wait, it's us! It's just us!"

Lowering the axe, Lochlyn filled with relief at the sight of Boomer and Kitty. Both were panting with sweat dripping down their faces. They'd clearly been running from something.

But where was Gab?

Before she could question them, Kitty pulled Boomer into the elevator and hit the button to shut the doors. It was then she noticed the blood running down Kitty's arm. There was a deep cut just under her shoulder. Lochlyn couldn't tell if Kitty had even realized it herself yet.

Boomer leaned against the side of the elevator with his hand pressed against his side. He was hurt too.

"What the hell happened to you guys? Where's Gab? I thought you said she was with you," Lochlyn blurted out like rapid fire.

Hitting the button labeled '*LOBBY*', Kitty gave herself a moment to catch a breath before answering her. "We were about to head back with Gab. When we rounded the corner, there was this creep just standing there. She chased us with a chainsaw. *A fucking chainsaw*! We almost didn't get away. She landed a good kick to Boomer's ribs. She almost got me, but I ducked, and she hit the window. I got cut up by some of the glass."

Lochlyn swallowed hard. "And Gab?"

An expression of guilt crossed over their faces. Lochlyn had her answer before the words left Kitty's mouth. "Dead. There was no saving her. We'd be dead too if we had tried."

Something stuck out to Lochlyn almost immediately. Pieces of her story didn't add up compared to what she had just gone through herself. Kitty's story was too detailed, too rehearsed. Also, she specifically referred to their assailant as a woman, though the person who had chased Lochlyn wasn't clearly defined in their oversized jumpsuit.

"You're sure it was a woman?" Lochlyn inquired. "Was, um, was she wearing anything? Boots? A mask? Gloves? Anything you can remember?"

The subservient look shared between Boomer and Kitty felt off. Lochlyn tightened her grip around the handle of the axe and shifted her weight from one foot to the other.

Her mind went back to the room she and Pumpkin had found. She'd assumed someone had been hit with something, but that kind of spatter could have come from a chainsaw attack too. Given how large the lodge was and the storm brewing outside, it was entirely possible no one would have heard the attack either.

"Uh, no. No mask. I didn't get a good look at her feet. We were kind of running for our lives."

Kitty was being too defensive.

Swallowing, Lochlyn nodded numbly as she tried to let all this new information sink in. It was clear they were lying to her, but she couldn't call them on it while they were locked in the elevator together. Even with her axe, Boomer was twice her size, and could quickly disarm her.

He was definitely on edge as he leaned against the wall. His eyes kept flickering from Lochlyn to the weapon in her hand. Boomer was nervous too. Of her. The irony was not lost on her, and she didn't blame him for it.

The sight of an axe could put a normal person on edge, let alone when a psycho was on the loose and adrenaline was running high. It probably didn't help that her hands were still coated in dried blood.

"What's with the axe? Where's Oliver?"

Her eyes shifted between them, debating how much to share. They were obviously lying about something, but it didn't make them guilty of murder. Everything so far had pointed to a male assailant except for the size of the open vent and the earrings.

Perhaps there were two masked psychos running around? That would also explain the multiple pig masks.

And maybe Lochlyn was currently stuck in an elevator with them.

"He's fine," Lochlyn offered. "He's back with Twiggy. Pumpkin should be with them too. Twiggy got hit pretty badly over the head while we were split up, and Olive was taken. I came to find you guys. Speaking of, I should probably let them know we're on our way back."

Lochlyn reached for the walkie hanging on her hip. Kitty's hand slapped Lochlyn's hand away. Panic flowed through Lochlyn, her eyes wide with fear. If she could just hit the button, she could scream for help. It might be too late for her, but the others could be alerted and prepare to fight.

"Don't," Kitty warned. "That psycho has our walkie. She'll hear you over the line and know exactly where we all are."

Hesitating, Lochlyn nodded in understanding and released hold of the device. It did make sense. Even if they were lying about it being a woman who attacked them, it explained how the wacko located her after she'd talked with Oliver.

"Okay, I won't."

The elevator dinged again before the door opened to the main floor. The three exited and made their way back to Oliver, Pumpkin, and Twiggy.

Lochlyn fell back, putting some space between her and the duo in front. Something was off about their story. Was Gab really dead, or had they given her another opportunity to wander around the lodge in a pig mask to terrorize them? Lochlyn would have to figure out what was really happening. If they were behind all of this?

Lochlyn was a dead girl walking.

Chapter 22

Upon returning to the lounge, Lochlyn realized right away that something was amiss. Pumpkin wasn't with Oliver and Twiggy. After a brief inquiry, Oliver said she hadn't returned after going after Lochlyn earlier. She was still somewhere out there alone.

Perhaps she was still upstairs looking for her? Maybe, but Lochlyn noticed the feeling of a heavy rock in her stomach. The feeling that something else bad had happened couldn't be ignored.

But that wasn't the only issue at hand. There were two liars sitting across the room recounting their tale of escape to Oliver and Twiggy.

One thing Lochlyn had previously learned was that stories tend to change the more a person tells them. Different details were remembered, or key details were changed, if they weren't true to begin with.

Kitty's story remained *exactly* the same. Not one detail was different, and it sounded just as rehearsed as before.

Sitting on the couch, Twiggy held an ice pack to the back of his head and beside him Boomer had another one against his ribs. As far as injuries went, they'd gotten fairly lucky. Neither battle wound was fatal.

And then there was Kitty, who was almost bursting with adrenaline. It actually came off as excitement. It almost appeared she was loving every moment of this chaos. It was *off*, to say the least. Everything about this felt wrong.

Her attention caught at the sound of her name being called. Judging by the way they were all looking at her, Lochlyn realized they must have called it a few times already. She was too lost in her thoughts to hear them.

"I'm sorry. I spaced," she admitted. "What was the question?"

Oliver straightened, uncrossing his arms as he pushed off the desk he was leaning against. "You were up there for almost a half hour. Did you find anything? See anyone? I thought Pumpkin found you."

Lochlyn wanted to tell him about the murder scene she and Pumpkin had stumbled into, the conference room, and the masked psycho, but the words got caught in her throat. Last time she claimed to have seen someone watching them, they said she was paranoid.

More importantly, given what she saw in that room, it seemed likely that Gab was also dead, and Lochlyn wasn't even sure if she could trust any of them.

They could all be in on this nightmare for all she knew, and Pumpkin, Gab, and Camden had been the unfortunate casualties.

Clearing her throat, Lochlyn shook her head. "No, I didn't find anything. As for Pumpkin, she headed back without me because I went and checked another room before I ran into them."

Oliver's gaze narrowed, flickering to the bag at her side briefly. "You're sure about that?"

It was a challenge if Lochlyn had ever heard one. Oliver was the one who'd said to keep quiet about the mask they'd found. Not to mention the keychain that she was almost certain belonged to his twin, who was currently missing. Why would he be the one questioning her now.

If he wasn't talking about the bag, he was insinuating something more sinister concerning Pumpkin. She clearly saw Oliver and Boomer glancing at the axe beside her.

Lochlyn hated the way those bits of observations hurt her. What did she care if he thought ill of her? They were still basically strangers and tensions were high. Except, Lochlyn did care what

Oliver thought of her. He'd asked her to trust him and keep quiet about Olive's keychain, but now it felt like he was interrogating her.

His sister was missing, she had to remind herself. Oliver could joke with Twiggy all he wanted, but she could see the worry behind his brown eyes. He was terrified about his sister's fate. How could she blame him for acting strangely?

Still, this wasn't the time to turn on each other. With Pig Man on the loose, they needed to stick together. But how could they when they were all obviously keeping secrets from each other?

Squaring her shoulders, Lochlyn averted her eyes. "I'm sure."

Boomer piped in then. "Then what's with the axe?"

Thunder rumbled in the sky at that exact moment and Lochlyn immediately had her next excuse ready. "I thought I heard someone following me. I panicked and grabbed the axe from the emergency box and got on the elevator. Considering everything that's happened tonight, do you blame me for being on edge?"

He didn't call her out on her lie.

"Did you have a run in with red paint?" Kitty questioned, her gaze dropping to the red on Lochlyn's hands and knees.

Lochlyn opened her mouth, but nothing came out. How could she explain that away without mentioning the room? Should she tell them about it? Mentioning how Pig Man chased her would poke holes into Kitty and Boomer's story and it might push them into a corner.

Lochlyn didn't want to be in striking distance if that happened.

"Uh, yeah," she muttered. "It was pretty dark up there. One of the rooms was getting a renovation, I think. The new paint must not have dried yet"

Twiggy was watching her with a suspicious stare. "Seems weird to me Kitty's uncle didn't mention renovations to, you know, *Kitty*."

Swallowing, Lochlyn shifted with unease and her answers lacked the confidence they did before. They would see right through her if she wasn't careful.

"Tell that to the room covered in wet paint. When Pumpkin comes back, she can tell you if you don't believe me."

Another lie. Too defensive.

Looking outside again, Lochlyn noted the weather had gotten worse. How much longer would this storm rage on before lightening up? Even if it did, how long would the flooded roads keep them stranded here?

They might have had a better chance of pushing Boomer's truck out of the mud if it was still all eight of them. But now? They'd be lucky to get it to even budge.

A light shined through the foggy rain. Lochlyn's eyes widened as she inched closer until her nose was basically pressed flat against the glass. "There's someone out there," she announced.

Lochlyn didn't dare take her eyes away from the moving light. She could feel the others all squeezed in around her. "Look, there's a light moving out there. It looks like a flashlight."

A gasp escaped Kitty's lips, and Lochlyn knew that this time someone else saw what she did. She wasn't being ridiculous or paranoid this time.

"Someone's out there," Kitty confirmed. "What the hell? No one's supposed to be messing with the lifts."

She said it as if everything else had gone according to plan tonight except for this, Lochlyn noted.

"Do you think it's the same person as earlier?" Lochlyn asked, her eyes flickering between the other four.

Boomer tossed down his ice pack. "I'm over this. I'm going out there."

He didn't pause long enough to hear any complaints. Stopping at the desk, Boomer searched the drawers before pulling out a letter opener. Tucking it into his boot, he continued to prepare.

Lochlyn said nothing as she watched Kitty step in his way and touch his chest. "Whoa, hey. Bad idea. You can't go out there. You'd be going there blind with that storm. Think this through."

Boomer appeared to hesitate and considered her warning. Instead of giving in, his eyes shot toward Lochlyn. "You coming, Newbie?"

Stunned, Lochlyn didn't know what to say at first. Why was he inviting her and not Oliver or Twiggy? Kitty was looking between them like they were insane. Lochlyn wasn't sure if it was the stress of the night, or the confidence she'd gained tonight, but she was in.

Lochlyn grabbed the handle of the axe and stood. "I'm coming. Anyone else?"

Twiggy looked at the others then threw his arms up in frustration. "Well, if we're just throwing the rules out the window why not? Marching in half-cocked always works for the idiots in the movies."

A snort came from Oliver. "I think it's way too late for that notion. The rules went out the window a long time ago."

Her eyes shifted to Kitty, who was now having a hushed conversation with Boomer. He then raised a brow, questioning whether Kitty would join or not.

Sighing, she nodded and reluctantly gave in. "I guess I'm coming too."

Lochlyn started turning toward Oliver, only to find him standing beside her. The sudden closeness surprised her before a small smile formed when he held up a pair of pink *Crocs*. They must have been Olive's.

He gave her a small smile, but his eyes still held some guilt. Maybe for his earlier accusation? Or something else. She didn't know.

"I think you'll need these if you're gonna be running outside in the rain," he suggested with a pointed glance to her bare feet. "Also, uh, sorry about what I said. I'm just worried about Olive. With Pumpkin missing again and Gab knocked off the board, I'm just scared for her."

"I don't even wanna know how you found these," she said with a small chuckle as she accepted the shoes. "And I get it. I'd be more concerned if you weren't worried about her. For what it counts, I hope we find her and she's okay. For all we know, she's the one out there."

He shrugged his shoulder, refusing to meet her gaze. "Olive is pretty tough when she wants to be, but I'll feel better when I have her in front of me."

Lochlyn slipped the shoes on and thanked whatever force might be listening that they fit. They were a little loose, but not enough to be annoying. At least she wouldn't have to walk through the mud barefoot.

Kitty retrieved flashlights from one of the desk drawers and passed them out. "My uncle keeps these handy everywhere in case of power outages."

Accepting one, Lochlyn checked to make sure it worked before slipping it into her purse. With no time to bother finding the ponchos, the group of five headed for the main doors and braced for the cold rainy weather.

Chapter 23

The five remaining members headed around the building and through the field moving toward the storage shed. Boomer led the way with Kitty beside him as their flashlights guided them.

Lochlyn shivered and rubbed her arms as she pushed forward. She could feel her red wig hair sticking to her skin and the skirt of her romper dragging behind her as it got stuck in the mud. She wasn't entirely sure why she hadn't tugged the damn wig off yet, but it wasn't something she could think about now.

To her surprise, Oliver wrapped the side of his suit jacket around her shoulders, encasing her in as much warmth as he could. He must have taken it back after she used it to cushion Twiggy's head earlier.

Her eyes widened by the gesture, but she dipped her chin showing her thanks. It was too cold to do anything else.

He flashed her a grin and wink.

At least this time she could hide that she was blushing given the redness the cold created on her cheeks. Peering over her shoulder, she noticed Twiggy shrink into his own coat with a grumbling frown.

Was he jealous?

Lochlyn scoffed at her own thought. With everything else going on tonight, she was sure jealousy was not on anyone's mind right now. Not that he would be anyways. He'd been nothing but rude to her since arriving here today, as if he was determined to get under her skin and rile her up.

The rain was falling so densely that it was hard to keep her eyes open. If it wasn't for Oliver's arm around her, Lochlyn probably would have fallen behind. Another gust of wind hit them and the chilly breeze attacked her exposed skin like tiny needles.

"It's probably one of the staff checking for supplies in case the power goes out," Oliver said down to her.

He might have been shouting over the wind, but she could barely hear him. With a quick scan, she knew the others hadn't as they continued onward.

Refocusing on Oliver, Lochlyn wasn't sure what to say. It could be the staff, but Pig Man was still out there somewhere. It didn't seem smart to let their guard down just yet.

Still, there was also the chance Olive was hiding out here from her captor. Or it could be Pumpkin digging around. There were too many possibilities and none of them made her feel any safer.

"I want you to be right," she said back, but her voice was lost in the wind. "Though, I want it to be Olive for your sake too."

Silence fell over them as they approached the storage shed. They could see the doors swing open with a bang as they hit against the sides.

Oliver and Lochlyn halted to a stop beside Kitty and Boomer. Twiggy appeared on her other side a moment later.

"Those were locked. I'm sure of it," Kitty shouted over the rain. "I locked them myself after Boomer, Gab, and I left earlier."

Shivering, Lochlyn knew they'd come too far to head back now. But they couldn't just stand there too afraid to investigate. Someone needed to take the first step.

Releasing a shaky breath, Lochlyn slipped free from the safety and warmth of Oliver's embrace. "I'm going to see what's inside." Or rather, *who* was inside?

No one immediately moved to follow. Not that Lochlyn blamed them.

She had almost reached the banging door when a hand grabbed her wrist and pulled her to a stop. Lochlyn had half a mind to snap at whoever it was when she noticed it was Twiggy. Her lips parted with surprise.

His eyes were locked on the shed before them, but his hand was still firmly wrapped around hers. "Whoever had the light might still be in there. We can't count on it being Olive or Pumpkin. You shouldn't go in there unarmed," he said as he leaned in closely.

The faint smell of tobacco mixed with musk hit her nostrils. Oddly enough, Lochlyn found it to be an appealing aroma. It was different than the sweet cologne Oliver had on.

Lochlyn lifted the axe and rested it on her shoulder with a pointed look. "I'm not unarmed, but I appreciate the concern."

Boomer then appeared in her peripheral and grabbed ahold of a shovel leaning against the shed wall. He stood close to Kitty, angling his body in a way that put him between her and any danger that may come.

Oliver stood uncomfortably by them, as if he felt out of place. Lochlyn could understand that feeling. It would be so much easier to say she imagined the light and run back to the lodge. But it wasn't any safer in there than it was out here.

Shoving her nerves down, Lochlyn released another breath and nodded, telling herself she could do this. Reaching for the door again, she pulled it open before she could talk herself out of it.

Twiggy held up his flashlight, making it easier for them to peer inside.

Thankfully, nothing immediately jumped out. Stepping inside, the aroma of gasoline and more musk hit them full on. Lochlyn noted that the remaining four wheelers lined up to the right.

Kitty had been telling the truth that one was missing. Though they had all seen the pig man straddling the unaccounted vehicle, so it was likely still out there wherever he stashed it.

As they all fully entered the storage shed, the white noise of the rain immediately faded to a deafening silence. It was almost worse like this. It was more ominous.

It felt like a scene in a movie where the unsuspecting group of teenagers walked straight into a trap and realized the villain was waiting to unleash his attack from the shadows.

"What's that over there?" Twiggy whispered.

Following the beam from his flashlight, she noticed what had caught his attention. It was a pile of wet clothes. Cautiously stepping closer, Lochlyn knelt and reached for the soiled garments. Upon further inspection, she found a men's shirt, but it was dark and too wet to check for any other details.

Lochlyn inched forward to search the surrounding area and then reached for something else. It was a shoe. Not just any shoe though, she noted as she held it up into the light.

"That's Olive's," Oliver spoke up, voicing what she'd been thinking.

It was the same beige heel she'd noticed Olive wearing earlier today. It had a unique flower embroidered design on its left side. Lochlyn remembered thinking it went nicely with her olive-green pants and the blood red shirt.

"What's it doing way out here?" Kitty voiced the question they were all wondering.

Continuing her search, Lochlyn thought she spotted another article of clothing, but before she could inspect further, a shadow suddenly loomed over her.

"Shit," Twiggy cursed. "Ivie, move!"

Her body shook uncontrollably as she noticed the mud-covered brown work boots. They still had a newness to them, she somehow managed to notice. Lochlyn felt paralyzed with fear as she lifted her gaze. Her lips parted and her jaw dropped. A silent scream was stuck in her throat as she took in the sight above her.

It was a pig mask with sunken dark eyes, snout, and a permanent chilling smile. Its pale coloring reminded her of the *Michael Meyers* mask, but it wasn't quite the same. It was more fleshlier.

An arm suddenly snaked around her middle and yanked her backwards. Her body was twisted as she was thrown to the ground with weight from someone's body covering her.

All she could see was a flash of movement as Boomer stepped in front of her. His reflexes were clearly much quicker than hers, as he caught hold of the bat the masked man started to swing at her.

Peering over her shoulder, she noticed Twiggy was laying over her, sucking in breath with panic in his eyes as he watched the power struggle between Pig Man and Boomer. Thankfully, he'd been able to react to save her when she froze.

Kitty and Oliver swarmed around them and pulled at their arms. "We can't stay here!" Kitty said as she helped Lochlyn to her feet. "Come on!"

Lochlyn's body mindlessly followed Kitty as she couldn't move her stare from Boomer. Her body jolted when she saw Pig Man land a swing. The crack from the impact startled her as Boomer hit the ground with a hard *thud*.

Kitty and she clung to each other as they watched in horror while Boomer took another hit to his back. "NO! Boomer, *no!*" Kitty screamed, tears running down her face. Lochlyn had to tighten her hold around Kitty to keep her from getting in between Boomer and the pig man.

"Get them out of here!" Oliver called to Twiggy as he grasped at something nearby.

Lochlyn should help him. She had an actual weapon. Wait, where *was* her axe? She'd put it down when she went to see what they'd found. Her eyes darted to the ground, searching through the dark, but it was gone.

Twiggy again tugged on their arms and pulled them toward the doorway. Lochlyn couldn't tear her eyes away from the fight behind them. She watched as Oliver, shovel in hand, went up behind Pig Man and smacked him over the head.

Oliver's honey brown hair fell wildly into his face, dripping with rain and sweat as his chest heaved. There was a strange, almost sadistic glint in his eyes, as he stood there.

Pig Man was barely phased by the attack. If anything, Oliver had drawn his attention away from Boomer to himself. His eyes widened as that realization occurred to him.

"Shit," Oliver cursed, his eyes frantically looking for an escape as he took a step back.

Pig Man straightened and turned. As he did, Lochlyn noticed something shining at his side. Her heart nearly stopped as she realized what it was.

"Oliver, move!" she screamed, pulling free from Twiggy and Kitty's grips. "Get away from them!"

Without a thought for her own safety, Lochlyn grabbed the flashlight at her side and whipped it at the assailant. It hit the target with a '*thump*' before falling to the ground.

Oliver took advantage of the distraction and ducked past him, grabbing Boomer's arm. They watched as he dragged him toward the doors. They weren't moving fast enough though. Pig Man was coming out of his daze.

Lochlyn dove forward, grabbing ahold of Boomer's other arm. Together, the two yanked him to his feet. Not wasting a moment, the trio hurried to the doorway where Kitty and Twiggy anxiously waited.

They were almost out.

Their freedom was steps away. Lochlyn's body protested, already tired from the earlier run, but she pushed on. Oliver and Boomer got through the opening first, panting as they slowed. Next Kitty and Twiggy grabbed either side of the door and waited for Lochlyn to pass so they could slam the doors shut behind her.

Her shoe hit the invisible line where shadow met the light when suddenly death wrapped around her ankle and yanked the relief away from her. Her body fell forward, slapping against the muddy hard ground. The air felt like it was sucked out of her lungs.

Looking back, she saw Pig Man on the ground behind her. His hand was wrapped around her leg and determination blazed in the eyes under his mask.

He started to drag her back, pulling a dagger free from his boot. He raised it above him, the metal shining as it awaited its next victim.

No. She refused. Lochlyn would not die here tonight. Not like this.

Releasing a scream of frustration, she kicked back her other foot. With a satisfying crunch, her shoe made contact with the face under the mask. Reaching forward, Lochlyn tried to drag herself away as she felt his grip loosen.

A pair of hands swooped under her arms and pulled her with a hard tug. Looking up, she saw Oliver above her. He gritted his teeth as he dragged her out of the darkness of the shed.

Once they were clear, Boomer and Twiggy slammed the doors shut and Kitty wrapped the chain around the handles before slapping the lock into place.

Oliver and Lochlyn collapsed into the mud, both trying to regain their breath as the rain continued to pour down on them. His arms had moved around her and held her to his chest. She felt herself clinging to him as well, relief flowing through her now that they were safe.

"I've got you," he whispered into her wet hair, pressing a kiss to her head. "You're safe."

As if to remind them that they weren't safe yet, the blade of the axe jutted through the wood of the shed door. They all jolted into action, knowing they needed to get back to the lodge before the masked man got free.

Climbing to their feet, Oliver grabbed onto Lochlyn's hand and pulled her along. Twiggy, Kitty, and Boomer scampered to follow. They weren't even sure they were going in the right direction.

At this point, they were moving on the instinct to get as far away from the storage shed as possible.

At that moment, nothing else mattered.

Chapter 24

Going back to the lounge wasn't an option. Pig Man had already gotten in once and obviously knew exactly how to find them. It wasn't safe.

Once inside, Kitty led them down to the kitchen. Boomer was wheezing, no doubt nursing a broken rib after the attack. There was nothing they could do to fix it, but the least they could do was find him some ice.

Lochlyn shivered, though she wasn't sure whether it was from the cold or from being drenched. This freak seemed determined to target *her*, but why? What had she done to him?

The image of a crushed car with a cold, still body beside it on the ground came to mind. The faint sound of someone calling for help echoed through the darkness. Squeezing her eyes shut, Lochlyn banished the image from her mind.

"You okay over there, heiress?"

Of course it was Twiggy who'd noticed she was acting off. Nothing seemed to miss his attention. Not when it came to her anyway. The fact he'd saved her aside, Twiggy had been suspicious of her all night.

Rubbing her arm, Lochlyn forced herself to give him a small smile of reassurance. "Just peachy. You guys?"

It gave her a moment to study them all. Everyone was soaked to the bone, but that was the least of their worries. Boomer was leaning against one of the counters, sans shirt, as Kitty held an ice pack to his ribs. It was easy to get distracted from the rows of muscles running down his stomach, but she didn't appear phased.

She was rightfully more concerned about his wellbeing than checking out his physique. Her dark hair was plastered to her face, her once perfect outfit soaked and stained with mud. Her face was splotchy with redness from crying and her hands shook as she checked for his other injuries.

Suddenly Lochlyn noticed that Boomer's earlier injury was non-existent. The only marks on him were caused by his fight with the masked freak in the storage shed.

What the hell?

Boomer placed a hand over Kitty's and leaned in to whisper something into her ear. Was he reassuring her that he was fine?

Telling her that it was going to be okay? Or was it something else? Whatever it was, Kitty almost appeared to be ... disgusted?

Lochlyn couldn't forget what she'd seen in that conference room or how Kitty and Boomer had lied about being attacked earlier.

But how could she explain the latest attack? They were both present and utterly terrified just like she and the others were.

Kitty suddenly straightened, her body tense. "I'm gonna go grab some supplies. They're just down the hall."

Before anyone could point out how bad of an idea that was, Kitty was already out the door with it shutting loudly behind her. As if she'd slammed it shut. Odd.

Anger wasn't the emotion Lochlyn would have expected from Kitty. Perhaps whatever Boomer had said to her wasn't to comfort her after all.

Perhaps he was telling her to get a grip? That would explain the disgust she saw written across her face.

"You're thinking hard over here," Oliver said softly as he appeared at her side. "What's bouncing around in that brain of yours?"

Glancing over, she saw that his once slicked back hair was loose and curly. It gave him more of a boyish look than the British gentleman he'd been pretending to be earlier.

His soaked jacket hung next to the oven to dry it off. His off-white dress shirt puffed out around his arms with a brown sweater vest buttoned around his middle. The rain only added to his old-fashioned appearance, but that wasn't a complaint. He was a living, breathing, 90's Brendan Fraser.

He reminded her of the men from the books she secretly loved to read between mysteries. The tales of forbidden passion, pirates, and magic. A blush burned her cheeks as she scolded herself for thinking of such things now. It was *absolutely* not the time or place for that.

Clearing her throat, she gathered herself together. "I'm just trying to process everything."

"And how's that going for you?" he pushed. "Any new theories?"

Was he teasing her? Was he genuinely curious? She couldn't tell, but she didn't appreciate the pushing or prodding. It almost felt like he was looking forward to hearing what she had to say next. Like this was a game.

He was acting like a little kid who knew the big secret and was waiting impatiently for someone to figure it out.

Wait.

Giving the group another once over, Lochlyn noticed no one appeared on edge. Not like how she felt anyway. Kitty was the only one who seemed to be on the verge of a breakdown. Twiggy was sitting on a countertop, snacking away on a bag of chips. His dark hair was dripping wet, but he didn't seem to care. He almost looked …. bored.

Boomer was leaning against the counter with the ice pack against his stomach, his gaze shifting to the doorway Kitty had left through. A concern crease had formed between his dark eyebrows.

"Ivorie?"

Startled, Lochlyn's eyes shot to Oliver's face. His features showed genuine concern but she wasn't so sure it was there for the right reason.

Swallowing her fear, she attempted to clear her face of emotions. "Did you notice the freak in the mask was wearing Camden's boots? I almost didn't recognize them since we really only briefly saw him. Why do you think he would take Cam's boots? Unless   unless he didn't. Maybe he was always wearing them."

Something close to frustration crossed Oliver's face then and Lochlyn knew she'd noticed a particular detail she wasn't supposed to.

Straightening, Lochlyn pushed off the counter she was leaning against and took a step back. "Oh, my god."

Oliver raised his hands, as if hoping to calm a startled animal. "Ivorie, we can explain."

We.

They were all in on it.

Shaking her head, she took another two steps backwards. She didn't need to look over her shoulder to know she was close to the door. Though Lochlyn didn't dare to fully take her eyes off the three others in the room, they slightly flickered to the door to make sure Kitty wasn't returning.

If she did, Lochlyn would be trapped in here with all four of them.

She ran her fingers down the length of the counter before brushing against something. With a brief glance, Lochlyn noticed a cutting board.

One of the staff must have left it behind in the rush to get out before the storm hit. To her luck and surprise, they'd also left one of the small steak knives resting on top of it.

Reaching over, Lochlyn grabbed onto the handle and held it out in front of her. "Stay back. All of you."

Twiggy set aside his bag of chips and watched her intently. A sadistic smile spread across his face, as if this was amusing. Boomer straightened and set the ice pack down slowly. His dark eyes snapped into focus on Lochlyn as he turned his attention toward her.

"Whoa, hey, Ivorie. It's okay," Boomer said. "Put the knife down and we can talk. We can explain all of this. I swear."

A bitter laugh erupted from her throat. "You *promise*? You've done nothing but lie to me since getting here. Starting with the fact that *none* of you are actually strangers. Ending with you all have been playing with me this entire time."

It occurred to Lochlyn that it might have been so easy for them to deceive her. They were strangers. She wouldn't know the difference between how they were acting and how they would react in a real situation.

Oliver took a cautious step forward, to which Lochlyn took another backwards. "Look, I can explain everything, Lochlyn. You must trust-"

A hurt expression passed over her face as her eyes shifted to Oliver. "*You* convinced me to trust you, but *you* are in on whatever the hell this all is. No, I know what this is. This is sick!"

The knife shook horribly in her hands, but she didn't dare lower it. Oliver edged another step forward and Lochlyn jolted as her back hit the wall.

In her second of hesitation, Oliver jumped forward and grabbed ahold of her hands. A panicked cry escaped her lips as they wrestled over the weapon.

Dread filled her as he successfully knocked it from her hands. Using his momentum, Oliver turned her back to his chest and locked her into an embrace. "No, no, *noo*! No, I don't want to die! Please," Lochlyn cried, struggling with all she had.

His arms only tightened around her. "I'm not going to hurt you. I just want to explain what's going on. Please, just hear us out."

"Let me go! Let go!" she screamed. "All you've done is lie to me! All of you! I don't want to hear another damn word from your mouth. Let me go!"

As luck would have it, the lights suddenly went out. Using the distraction, Lochlyn got her elbow loose and jammed it into Oliver's side. He cursed as his arms fell from around her. He hunched over with a groan.

Turning, Lochlyn reached for the door handle. She only paused when she heard her name shouted. *Her* name. Not *Ivorie's*. She thought she'd heard Oliver mutter it earlier, but assumed it had to be a mistake since he shouldn't have known it. None of them should have.

"Lochlyn! Don't go out there!" Twiggy suddenly shouted. "If you go out there   " His threat was left unfinished as a scream filled the halls of the dark lodge. Lochlyn pulled the door open and took off running.

Chapter 25

In a horror movie, the cast of characters usually makes the decision to run toward the calls for help. It is typically a ruse created by the murderer to draw out the remaining survivors.

How many times had Lochlyn laughed at that very mistake? She had always prided herself in thinking she'd never make any of the common missteps the characters always did.

Except, when put in a real horror movie type situation, she did just that.

She trusted the wrong person, said she'd be right back, went off by herself, and now she was going *towards* the screaming. How many mistakes could Lochlyn make before it was *her* curtain call?

The pounding of footsteps behind her told her she wasn't alone. The others were following. Whether that was a good thing was still to be determined. "It's coming from the pool!" Kitty suddenly shouted from up ahead. "Around the corner. Go left!"

Was Lochlyn running into another trap? She could ignore Kitty's directions, go right, and find a new place to hide. Would they pursue her or continue on to find the source of the screaming? Should she sacrifice another life to save her own? Her head told her it was the smarter move, but her feet turned left as she approached the turn.

Skidding to a stop, Lochlyn nearly missed the door labeled **POOL**. The door had a glass window, revealing the inside to passersby. The inside looked enormous and fun. There was a water slide in the form of a mountain with a small rock wall blocking off a splashpad area for the younger kids.

Lochlyn couldn't see much else, but from her memory of being here earlier, she knew there was a jacuzzi in there too. Had it really only been hours since she and Oliver were in there, dipping their feet into the water as they chatted? It felt like a lifetime ago.

A moment went by before she was joined by the others. Any chance of escaping was gone. Lochlyn had made her choice and if it was the wrong one, she'd have to live with it or die because of it.

"There! Look by the life vest wall," Twiggy instructed. "Is that Daisy?"

Before she could question who Daisy was, Oliver went rigid beside her. "What? Where?"

From the terror flashing across his face, Lochlyn could tell it was his sister.

Following Twiggy's gaze, Lochlyn saw two still forms on the wet floor, a woman and a man. They were both wearing bathing suits, but that was the only detail she could make out from here.

Neither was moving as they lay feet apart.

Oliver didn't hesitate to tug on the door handle, his other hand pounding on the door. "It's locked. Daisy, get up! Daisy! Sam, where are the damn keys?"

All eyes turned to Kitty, or Sam as Oliver had called her, assuming she had the master keys. "I don't have the keys. I-I left them in my room after introductions."

Oliver started hitting the door even harder with his shoulder when it became clear that trying the handle was pointless. Boomer pushed between Lochlyn and Twiggy and grabbed Oliver's other shoulder.

Oliver looked ready to protest, but Boomer just shook his head. "On three. One, two-"

"Three!" they said in unison.

It cracked open from the impact and the two nearly fell inside. Oliver fumbled but didn't let it slow him down as he hurried across the length of the pool. A burst of concern shot through Lochlyn at the thought he might slip and end up in the pool, but she shook that feeling off. After what he pulled today, he deserved to end up in the water.

"Daisy!" he shouted. "Daisy, hey! Day!"

There was real panic in his voice as he slid to his twin's side. The others stopped short, watching as he turned over the girl Lochlyn had known as Olive in his arms.

Tears stung her eyes as she watched Oliver cradle his sister's limp body, shaking her with pleas to wake up.

"Come on, wake up. This isn't funny, Day. Wake up!" he pleaded, real tears running down his cheeks. "Wake up, Daisy."

Covering her mouth, Lochlyn watched in horror as he broke down. Her eyes fell from their faces as she took in the awkward way Olive's leg was bent and the wounds to her abdominal area. Her fingernails were bleeding, probably either from fighting or trying to claw herself away from something.

Olive, or rather *Daisy*, had fought for her life.

Lochlyn looked over to the second body and her blood ran cold. The familiar curly hair and lean form were enough to tell her who this was.

"Camden?"

If any of them heard her mutter his name, they didn't react. Twiggy was the first to move, dropping to the other body's side.

Lochlyn watched numbly as he pressed two fingers to Camden's neck.

"He's alive," Twiggy announced. "Just unconscious."

He's alive. Camden was *alive*.

How?

Suddenly, everything felt too loud and hot. Oliver's sobs, Twiggy's orders as he instructed the other two to help him, her heartbeat pounding in her ears. Taking a step back, Lochlyn felt feverish as the room around her started to spin.

"Lochlyn, stop!" Kitty shouted, but it was muted by her heartbeat.

Taking another step back, her foot met air and she suddenly fell backwards. A gasp slipped through her lips, a silent cry releasing as the room tipped.

SPLASH.

As water surrounded her, the rest of the world went silent. Lochlyn could hear their muffled calls, but she let herself fall deeper into the abyss. Her lungs began to burn, pleading for air. What if she didn't listen? What if she just stayed down here?

No, that would mean they won. That would mean all the running and struggling to survive would be for nothing. She was not going to give up now.

Lochlyn Jones was a survivor.

Pulling off her heavy red wig, Lochlyn felt the weight lift from her shoulders as she was filled with new determination. If she was going to beat this chaotic game, she was going to do it as herself, not as someone else.

Lochlyn pushed off the bottom of the pool and gasped for air as she broke through the surface. Her purple hair hung limply around her face, and the weight from the wig fell off her shoulders. It was a relief. Lochlyn felt more like herself already.

A hand reached out toward her.

Following the length of the arm, she saw it was Kitty. Should she accept the help? Shaking her head, Lochlyn swam toward the side of the pool and lifted herself up. If Kitty was put off by the rejection, she didn't show it.

Looking over, her heart tightened at the sight of a sobbing Oliver rocking his twin's body in his arms. Shifting her attention, Lochlyn noticed Twiggy and Boomer helping a dazed Camden to his feet.

He was dripping wet and there was a line of blood running down his face. Otherwise, he looked fine. There was no sign of having had an allergic reaction, or you know, *dying*.

Lochlyn could feel a headache coming. "How are you alive? W-we watched you die?"

Kitty dropped a towel into her lap as she passed by. "We'll tell you everything, but right now we need to get out of here. I think we're in some real danger."

And they weren't before?

Chapter 26

Kitty led the way back to the kitchen. Lochlyn walked behind Twiggy as Camden leaned on him for support. Peering over her shoulder, she saw Oliver silently carrying his twin. He'd protested leaving Daisy's body behind and, to their horror, Kitty said they could put her in the large freezer until they could get help.

Boomer brought up the group's rear, his eyes searching the shadows for any sign of unwelcome company.

They were all on edge, which was a stark difference from how the others had acted earlier in the night. The fear in their eyes was real, as was the shake in their hands.

Kitty locked the door behind them, and Lochlyn felt her heart tighten with panic. Had she just willingly been locked in with a group of psychos? Was that her next, and possibly last, mistake? How many chances would she be given with this group before her luck ran out?

Lochlyn kept her distance as she leaned against the counter closest to the doorway. To her surprise, they gave her space and settled in. Twiggy went to find another ice pack for Camden's head while Boomer assisted Oliver with Daisy's   body.

A sharp gasp met her ears and her attention snapped to the large walk-in freezer. Boomer was standing in the doorway with a horrified expression. In his stiff arms was a frozen form.

No, not just a frozen form. It was a person.

It was Pumpkin.

There was a dark ring of bruising around her neck. She'd been strangled by something. Her eyes were closed and her body was stiff from being in the freezer.

Lochlyn turned as bile rose up her throat and emptied into the sink. Another rush of vomit spewed out before she could stop it. Her arms shook as she gripped the side of the counter to keep her steady, her chest heaving as sweat poured down her face.

"What the actual fuck is happening right now?" Twiggy exclaimed as he crossed the room to help steady Boomer.

Boomer who had paled three shades as he stiffly stood there with Pumpkin's body pressed against him. "Just get her off me, man."

"This is not what we signed up for, Sam," Twiggy continued to rant. He was spiraling. "Not at all."

Lochlyn didn't dare turn to watch Twiggy, Oliver, and Boomer prop Pumpkin back up inside along with Olive's body. This was too much for anyone to handle. With the addition of Oliver's sister, that made four, scratch that, three bodies now. Camden was no longer on that growing list.

Kitty spun on her heels, glaring towards Camden. "Explain. *Now*. You two were supposed to stay hidden, not go for a swim."

Nodding, Camden's eyes seemed distant as he accepted the bag of peas from Twiggy and held it to his head. He appeared to be in shock. They all were. "We were just goofing off. Daisy got covered in that motor oil from the busted four-wheelers out in the storage shed."

"So, you two decided to go clean up in the hot tub? Unbelievable," Kitty scoffed.

Something pieced together in Lochlyn's head as his words sunk in. "You were the one who attacked us! You and Ol-Daisy, you were in there changing."

Kitty's eyes widened before her glare narrowed again on Camden. "Tell me you guys weren't hooking up."

The blush burned across his cheeks as he averted his eyes. That was all the answer they needed. They'd broken another sacred horror movie rule.

Twiggy groaned and rolled his eyes as he dropped his head into his hands. "You idiot."

The sound of the freezer door slamming shut alerted them of Oliver and Boomer's return. Oliver's expression brought the saying *'if looks could kill'* to a whole new level. He suddenly charged forward, no doubt to strangle Camden.

"What the fuck happened, Peter? *What happened*?" he snarled as he grabbed hold of his neck and shook him.

Twiggy and Boomer immediately jumped in between them. "Whoa! Not cool! Let him go, man!" Twiggy shouted as he shoved him off.

Boomer managed to pull Oliver away and held him back while he strained to get free. Camden coughed as he tried to regain his breath. "I'm sorry! I'm so sorry!"

"Everyone needs to cool off. *NOW*. We're not going to figure this out if you strangle him to death," Kitty intervened, wincing when she realized her poor choice in words. "Peter, talk."

Clearing his throat, he gave Oliver a wary glance before nodding. "We were cleaning up in the pool. We were only in there a few minutes before the lights went out. I went to turn them back on. Last thing I remember is hearing her tell me to watch out. Next thing I remember is waking up and seeing you guys."

"Why leave you alive and only kill her?"

Oliver had a good point, Lochlyn noted. It could have been easy to kill her and knock himself out. He could be lying about all of this. Considering that earlier Lochlyn had been convinced he was dead, she wasn't sure what to believe at this point.

"How are you not dead?" Lochlyn questioned. "I saw you take your last breath. We all did! Is this another lie now? I mean, it'd be easy to fake a few cuts and smear on some fake blood."

Her mind immediately went back to when she and Oliver found Pumpkin in the tub. Her blood had looked so wrong because it was fake. She probably opened the vent herself and planted her own earrings.

Releasing a breath, Kitty shared a loaded glance with the others before turning her attention to Lochlyn. "Maybe we should start at the beginning."

Lochlyn gave her a pointed look that said '*you think?*'

"Every time we get a new member to the group, we set up a top-tier murder mystery game. It's like an initiation thing. We all had to go through it. It's a two-part thing. It gives the latest player a chance to show their chops at planning and executing their game, and it lets us see if the newbie has what it takes to actually survive and win," Kitty explained, crossing her arms as she leaned against the counter.

So, there *was* a game in play this weekend. Just not one she'd been privy to. That explained the bulletin board in the conference room. It wasn't just the pig man keeping tabs on her. It was everyone through their storyboard. It was why Lochlyn felt like the target this entire time. Because she was.

"So, this has all been some game? Camden's allergy stunt? Pumpkin's kidnapping? My name written on the wall? The bloody room? That masked freak chasing me in the hall? All of it?" Lochlyn felt betrayal on an entirely new kind of level.

With a glance across the room, Lochlyn saw the guilt written clear on their faces. They had played her for a fool the entire day. Most of it made sense now, but not everything. Like what about Pumpkin and Daisy's very real bodies currently cooling in the freezer?

"Wait, when did you get chased in the hall?" Twiggy suddenly asked.

Boomer shot a look of disbelief his way. "*That's* what caught your attention? Not the bloody room part?"

Swallowing, Lochlyn debated explaining further, but she cleared her throat and continued. "When I went to look for Kitty and Boomer, I was on the second floor, and I tried a couple of doors before I found an open one. That's when Pumpkin found me. The room was covered in blood. It looked like a crime scene."

Concerned glances went around the room and Lochlyn got the terrifying impression maybe that part hadn't been a plot point for their game. "What? When you said you'd seen Gab get attacked with a chainsaw, I thought they were connected."

Kitty shook her head. "No, it wasn't. Gab, or actually Nik, wasn't with us. Even though she didn't show up for her part we didn't want to go off script. So we improvised to explain why she was missing."

Gab didn't just not show up though. Someone had actually murdered her in that room and her body was still missing.

"When Pumpkin and I split back up, I ended up in a conference room. Or your command central, I guess," Lochlyn admitted.

Realization dawned on Kitty's face. "You found the storyboard."

Nodding, Lochlyn continued. "Yeah, only I didn't know that's what it was when I saw it. I thought someone was just keeping a timeline or something. I didn't know what to make of it, that's why I was hesitant to mention it."

"Day and I were hiding in the closet. We heard you checking the other doors and hid in case you came in," Peter filled in.

Lochlyn felt validated knowing her sense of being watched wasn't paranoia afterall. "Did you chase me in the hall wearing that pig mask?"

The confused expression on his face unsettled her. "No, we radioed Kitty and told her you were getting too close."

Her attention turned to Boomer and Kitty then. "That's why you found me and had that bullshit story about being chased by the woman with a chainsaw. To throw me off because it wasn't on the storyboard."

Kitty nodded solemnly. "Yeah."

Lochlyn tried to make sense of everything she'd just been told. "Only, you two didn't know I'd just been chased by a guy in a mask, did you? He chased me on to the elevator. You swear that wasn't you?"

Peter shook his head. "Swear. We were packing up the conference room and moving it to another spot in case you brought them back to it. That's part of why we went out to the shed. We were stashing everything in there."

Lochlyn's attention turned to Oliver. "The mask we found. You knew it belonged to one of them. Was Olive's keychain a prop or was it there by accident? Was that why you didn't want to tell everyone about it? That if she dropped it by accident it would mess with the plot."

She half expected Oliver to ignore her, too lost in his own grief to pay attention.

To her surprise, he looked up. "The mask we found was a prop. It was part of the narrative we wanted to tell. The keychain and the vent weren't though."

"So, let me just get this straight," Twiggy piped up. "We've got three very real murder victims, a very real masked psycho trapped in here with us, and we really are stuck here until the storm passes? Do I have that right?"

No one bothered answering. They all knew no one wanted to admit it out loud. If they were now to be believed, then everything pointed to one chilling conclusion.

There was a real murderer among them. Something else occurred to her. Lochlyn still didn't know half of their real names.

This night of mayhem and murder was far from solved. The real game had merely just begun. It brought about one more question.

How could she trust anyone in this room?

Chapter 27

After some heated debate, the group decided to head back to their rooms and change into dry clothes. Safety was the biggest issue, given separating meant no one would answer their calls for help should they need it. But walking around in wet clothes could easily slow them down.

Eventually, it was decided they'd go to their rooms in pairs. Twiggy had immediately offered to go with Cam-*Peter*. That was going to take time getting used to. But, she now knew his name was really Peter. It was one of the only truths she'd been told today.

Much to Lochlyn's surprise, Boomer offered to go with Oliver, who wasn't happy about it. Relief hit her hard though. A part of her was, if she was being honest, content with not being paired with him. Her mind was still trying to process all the revelations.

The last thing Lochlyn wanted was to be left alone with Oliv-*Casper*. She scolded herself again for forgetting. His name was Casper and his twin's name was Daisy.

Given the circumstances, the others had decided it was time to come clean. They had all been friends for years and knew each others' real-world names. The group had started online like she'd been told, but over time they got to know each other. Only Lochlyn was left in the dark, and danger was lurking in the shadows.

Boomer's real name was Marco, Oliver's was Casper, Twiggy's was Xander, and Kitty's was Sam. Olive's name had been Daisy, Pumpkin was Ava, but Gab was the most complicated one. Lochlyn knew her online as Nik, but they'd needed an inside man out of sight, so Gab's personia had been created for the sake of the game.

Nik's actual name was Sully.

What came as a surprise to her was they were all well aware of who *she* was. They knew her name was Lochlyn and that she was from a small town called Woodhaven. They knew she'd almost failed geometry class sophomore year and that she'd run her school's props department.

"You're quiet over there," Sam said softly, almost cautiously as if she was worried Lochlyn would bite her head off. "Are you okay?"

This vibe was so different from the girl she'd met hours ago who appeared so put together, so confident, and fully aware of how intimidating she was.

Had her attitude suddenly shifted because of the guilt she felt? Did she feel bad for lying to Lochlyn like they did? Bitterly, Lochlyn doubted it. They'd come up with this entire disaster of a night to scare her.

Terrorizing her was more like it.

"No," Lochlyn grumbled as she searched through her duffle bag for something to change into.

Lochlyn had assumed she'd be in *'Ivorie mode'* for most, if not all, of the weekend. Finding something comfortable that wasn't sleepwear at first felt impossible, but eventually Lochlyn had decided on a pair of sweats.

The off-white pants puffed out around her legs and hung low on her hips. Grabbing the sage green shirt, she pulled it on over her head with a frustrated huff. It was more fitting than she was comfortable with, only falling to her belly button and leaving a strip of skin exposed. But it would have to do. Her purple locks of hair were starting to dry, curling as they just barely brushed her chin.

"You were never in any harm, you know," Kit-*Sam* spoke up. "No one was supposed to actually get hurt this weekend."

Peering over her shoulder, Lochlyn saw the haunted look in Sam's green eyes. She was clearly still in shock. Daisy, Ava, and Sully were her friends. They weren't supposed to die tonight.

No one was.

They had all trusted Sam to strand them here for the weekend to play a mystery game. Now they really were stuck here and the danger was very real.

The urge to be mean died on Lochlyn's tongue. It wasn't who she was, or wanted to be; kicking someone when they're down.

"I guess you had no way of knowing someone would crash the party," Lochlyn said as she pulled her matching off-white jacket on. "Is there anything else that's been off plan?"

Sam's eyes hardened for a split second before they flickered with panic, as if she hadn't considered that question until this moment.

Clearing her throat, Sam pulled her hair free from her new T-shirt. "Actually, Sully was on the four-wheeler outside and she put your name on the wall during lunch. She and Pumpkin staged Pumpkin's attack, but after that Sully disappeared. Definitely not part of the script. She was supposed to be with us after you found Pumpkin."

"So Sully did it all herself?" Lochlyn asked. "Or did you all help her pull everything off?"

Sam nodded solemnly. "The phone call was Peter. He was supposed to put clues around the lodge while we sat in the lounge. When we split up, he was supposed to take Xander and they-"

Lochlyn's head snapped up. "He was supposed to take Xander?"

"Yeah. Xand is a pro with special effects. Guess it's a perk to being great with technology. He was going to mess with the lights and continue with the phone calls. Give you the whole '*Scream*' experience."

"So, why did Peter switch it up and take Daisy?"

Sam shrugged her shoulder. "My guess is they wanted to fool around and convinced Xand to let them switch places."

Big mistake, Lochlyn noted.

"What about the person I saw outside of the bay window?" Lochlyn asked.

A shade of green tinged Sam's skin as she pushed down whatever nausea she was feeling and finished changing. "If you saw someone, it wasn't part of the game."

Sam still didn't believe she'd seen someone.

"But why would someone want to terrorize us?" Lochlyn cried. That was the million-dollar question, wasn't it?

But Lochlyn knew Sam's didn't have an answer. None of them would. If they did, they weren't sharing it with the group.

Lochlyn was reminded of her own secrets, her own demons hiding the shadows of her closet. She wasn't about to load that onto any of them. She shouldn't have had to, but someone was targeting them for real and it could be because of something in their pasts.

"Your guess is as good as ours," Sam answered as she grabbed her shoes. There was a new sense of bitterness in her tone and a sharpness in her glare as their eyes met for a moment. "We should go and meet up with the boys again. Are you ready to go?"

Nodding, Lochlyn swallowed her fears and pushed her body to move. She could hide in here all night, but it wouldn't guarantee survival. At least there was safety in numbers.

That, or she was circling back to the very group of people trying to kill her.

Chapter 28

The six of them met up back in the dining room. Lochlyn scanned the space with a knot tying in her stomach as she saw sight of her name still written across the wall.

Before, Lochlyn assumed it was blood until Xander had taken it upon himself to test it, but now she had the suspicion it was more likely the same fake substance Pumpkin had used on herself.

Her gaze dropped to the floor, noting the mess still scattered around where Peter had 'died'. She still hadn't worked up the nerve to ask how they pulled that off, but Lochlyn wasn't sure she cared.

It wasn't the only thing he'd faked either, Lochlyn realized. His southern accent was noticeably missing too. It just showed her how truly naive she was about this entire event.

Distracted by her own thoughts, Lochlyn didn't hear Casper's approach until he was right beside her. "For what it's worth, I'm sorry. It was supposed to be harmless fun. We've all had to go through it after we joined."

Lochlyn didn't bother to look up from the salad left behind on the floor. "That doesn't make it right."

Silence followed. She wondered if it was because he knew Lochlyn was right or because he just didn't have another excuse.

All night they'd been telling her she was paranoid. All night she was under the impression someone was after her and she might not make it home. Lochlyn was forced to consider that her mother would have had to bury another loved one. Another child.

Now that terrifying reality could seriously come true, and Lochlyn had no idea who, if anyone, she could trust to help her stay safe.

"When Day and I joined, they planned out a *Shining* themed game for us. Twins factor and all. It was the most terrifying weekend of our lives. I sucker punched Marco, and Day was in tears, but once the adrenaline wore off, we laughed about it."

Was he seriously trying to convince her to forgive them? That what any of them did to her today was alright? Alls fair in fake terror and murder? He had to be kidding himself.

Casper must have noted the bitter expression across her face because a flash of guilt appeared on his own. "Right, not the time or place. I'm just trying to say we're not a terrible group of people. We just love the game. Maybe a little more than some would consider healthy.”

Except it never felt like just a game to her. All it was for her was nail-biting terror that made her question everything and everyone. Lochlyn was just exhausted at this point. Physically and mentally.

Casper released a heavy sigh of defeat upon seeing he was getting nowhere. Part of her wished he’d just go sit with the others and leave her alone, but there was some part of her that wanted him to stay. It was the piece of her that felt attracted to him all night, no doubt.

Lochlyn should nail that piece of her heart in a box and bury it six feet deep inside of her.

Unfortunately, her mouth had other plans. “Were you just playing me the entire time?”

What did Lochlyn mean by that? Was she even sure? Wasn't it already clear that’s exactly what they were doing all day? But there had been moments when sparks flew between her and Casper.

Had she imagined them or was that part of the game? Was it all one sided and in her head? Was it his character, Oliver, or was he was acting like himself in those moments? Could her feelings for him be real if she didn't know who Casper really was? There was no way to know for sure.

Casper swallowed. "Not the entire time."

Before she could say anything, he excused himself and returned to the group. Giving herself a moment to recover, Lochlyn crossed her arms and followed behind.

Sam was sitting at the dining room table with a notebook in front of her. She must have grabbed it when she'd changed. Lochlyn hadn't seen her take it from her room, but then again, she'd been doing her best to avoid making eye contact.

Taking the seat to Sam's left, Lochlyn peered over her shoulder and saw a detailed timeline written out. "We must assume this Pig Man, as you called him, knows enough about the original plan. I mean, he stuck close enough to it to keep himself from standing out."

He'd been wearing the same mask they all had planned on wearing at some point this weekend. One of them was currently tucked away in Lochlyn's room in her purse along with the pair of earrings and Daisy's keychain she'd found.

Lochlyn thought back to the room she'd discovered with all their plans spread out. If she had stumbled across it so easily, maybe their creepy friend had too?

"The room with the storyboard in it and the files on us all," Lochlyn spoke up. "Did you keep that room locked up when no one was in there?"

Sam glared towards Peter. "It was supposed to always be locked. Even when someone was in there. You were never supposed to stumble across it. We never considered anyone else might be around to either."

At least he had the decency to look apologetic. "We were preoccupied."

Hooking up, is what he meant, or at least too preoccupied with each other to remember to lock the door behind them. "Dude, seriously?" Xander scolded.

Lochlyn heard a subtle growl behind her and could practically feel the rage simmering from Casper. Peering over her shoulder, she noted his murderous glare that was locked in on Peter.

Against her better judgement, Lochlyn reached behind her and entwined her fingers with his. She watched as his eyes widened with surprise before shifting down to her.

Turning back to Sam, Lochlyn didn't want to see whatever thoughts were racing behind his chocolate eyes. Still, she didn't move her hand away either.

The others noticed, judging by the scoff she heard from Xander. So, his bitterness wasn't all for show when it came to her and Casper's interactions then.

Interesting, but also confusing.

What really threw her was the flare of anger across Sam's expression. It was there and gone before she could understand it though. Marco and Camden didn't react. They appeared to be more concerned with everything else going on. Which, fair. There were more pressing matters at hand than comforting Casper.

"What about the missing four-wheeler?" Lochlyn inquired. "Do you know where Sully stashed it? Are the other ones really sabotaged? Could we use them to get back to town?"

Sam's body became tense as she and Marco glanced at each other. "They're really busted. We thought Sully switched out the tires for ruined ones to make it look more legit," Marco explained.

Sam nodded and continued. "We had three spots picked out in case Sully needed to hide it quickly. We wanted genuine reactions if for some reason we stumbled across it, so Sully didn't tell us where she put it."

Marco crossed his arms as his eyebrows pinched together with thought. "There's no telling if this guy knows about it or not. He could have found it and taken it somewhere else for all we know."

That would explain how Pig Man was getting around. If he managed to find where Sully had parked, it was safe to assume he'd take it. The storm would have been perfect cover for the four-wheeler's rumbling engine.

Finding it was their only chance of getting down the mountain. The roads might be flooded, but the four-wheeler could go off road. If they could figure out where it was being kept, they could head into town for help. It was just a matter of finding the vehicle before Pig Man found them.

"Let's check the three agreed upon places. If we find it, two of us can head into town for help," Lochlyn suggested. "The others can find a place to camp out until we come back with the sheriff."

No one voiced any complaints.

"Where should we look?" Xander asked

All eyes turned to Sam. It was her uncle's ski resort. If anyone knew the layout it would be her.

Grabbing a map of the resort they kept at the check-in desk, she used a pen and circled three different spots. "These are the spots Sully and I chose to potentially hide the four-wheeler. The locked garage out in the parking lot. They usually don't let anyone park in there except for my uncle. Then there's a shed for ski and sled rentals on the East side of the building. It's not big, but it'd be out of sight. The only other spot to really hide it would be back here by the kitchens. There's a door that leads outside to the dumpster and trash compactor."

Silence fell over the group. Three locations to check and not a lot of time left to do it. It was only a matter of time before Pig Man made his next move. Lochlyn didn't want to be sitting here waiting for that to happen.

"We'd cover more ground if we-"

Xander groaned. "I swear to god if you suggest we split up again, I will riot."

Blushing, her hand slipping from Casper's as she crossed her arms in front of her. "You know we're not actually in a horror movie, right? I know we're using the tropes to our advantage, but they're not guaranteed to save us either. Besides, it's not like we haven't done it already."

"And it's already two times too many," he shot back. "I mean, look at Daisy and Peter. They broke the biggest survival rule of all and they were attacked first."

Marco cleared his throat. "Ava and Sully were first. They both split off from the group."

Ava was alone because Lochlyn had run off to hide, she thought to herself, but they didn't know that. It wasn't going to help anyone by admitting it either. So, for now, she kept her guilty thoughts to herself.

Lochlyn's eyes shifted to Casper as her hand twitched with desire to take his hand back. To him, it didn't matter who was attacked first. It didn't change the fact that his sister was dead.

Xander seemed to at least realize his error in wording and quickly corrected himself. "Sorry, not the point, man."

Before an argument broke out, Lochlyn spoke up. "Look, the longer we sit here and argue, the longer this creep has to find us again."

At least Xander didn't argue with her about that. He knew she was right. They all did.

Sam broke the silence first. "So, it's decided. We break off into teams and each take one of these spots. We still have walkies. If we change the channel they're on, we should be safe to talk if need be. Marco and I can take the kitchen exit. Xand and Peter can take the rental shack. Cas and Lochlyn will take the garage. Sound good?"

A few meek nods later, the plan was set. As much as Lochlyn was angry with Casper for lying to her, she was relieved to be partnered with him again. Her feelings aside, Lochlyn knew it was best to keep Casper and Xander away from each other. They seemed to get along as well as water and oil. Plus, C asper and Peter together could be even worse.

As they went over the map for a final time, the sinking feeling in the pit of Lochlyn's stomach reappeared. What if Xander was right and they were pushing their luck splitting up again? It wasn't the best plan, but it was the best they could do for right now.

It just had to be good enough to get them out of this death trap of a lodge.

Chapter 29

Before heading outside this time, Lochlyn and Casper both retrieved raincoats and an umbrella. Her coat wouldn't block out the cold harshness of the storm, but it would at least keep her clothes dry.

Heading outside, the two did their best to stay underneath the umbrella. Casper held it between them while she pointed the flashlight in the direction they were headed. Huddled close together, Lochlyn couldn't ignore the scent that was so purely him as it invaded her senses. Mint mixed with smokey wood.

Glancing over, Lochlyn noticed the tense lines of his face that hadn't been there before. His jaw was clenched and his knuckles were white from his tight grip around the handle.

Casper was angry, grieving, upset, and she couldn't blame him.

His sister, his twin, had been taken from him tonight and he had to prioritize trying to survive over allowing himself to grieve. His other half was missing and Lochlyn couldn't begin to imagine how he must be feeling. It was so easy to get lost in the darkness of your own thoughts.

Lochlyn should know.

"I'm sorry," she blurted out. "About Daisy. Your sister. No one deserved that."

He didn't immediately say anything. Seconds ticked by before she saw the way he swallowed. "No, she didn't. But dammit, she's always been too emotional. If Daisy had stuck to the plan, she would have never been vulnerable like that."

Surprise filled her eyes too quickly before Lochlyn could mask her expression. Whatever response she had been expecting, that wasn't it. "We don't know that. Pig Man knew where they were. He didn't just happen upon Daisy and Peter. Just like he knew we were all in the lounge. It's like he can see our every move."

Just then, something clicked.

Lochlyn and Casper shared a look, their eyebrows raised to their hair lines. "The Security Office," they said in unison.

It would explain how this guy would know what floor she was on, and that Daisy and Peter had gone off script and ended up in the pool. He would have known exactly where to find Ava and Sully. It felt like he was watching them because he *was*.

Slowing to a stop, Casper held the umbrella over Lochlyn as she pulled the walkie free from her belt loop. Raising it up, she held the button and spoke. "You guys. Be careful of the cameras. He could be in the Security Office watching us all. That's how he found Peter and Daisy in the pool. He's watching the cameras. Over."

The time that followed without a response stretched to the point she was worried for the others. When seconds turned into minutes, Lochlyn was about to suggest they abandon their search for the four-wheeler and head back to find them.

"Warning received," a voice crackled over the walkie.

Their relief was short-lived when Lochlyn realized she didn't recognize the voice. With a glance at Casper, she could tell he didn't either. "Who is that?"

"Peter? Is that you guys? Over."

Only static answered.

Fear gripped her heart and panic set in as silence continued. Her eyes shot up accusatorily. "If this is part of your game, I swear to God, Cas, I will-"

Casper shook his head and raised his free hand. "This isn't part of the game. I swear. I don't know who that was."

As much as she wanted to believe him, Lochlyn knew she would be an idiot to do so blindly after everything they put her through tonight.

The walkie crackled again. "You should have listened to Xander. Tsk tsk. You're two steps behind, Monster. Better fix that before six becomes five."

Lochlyn's face paled. That nick name, she thought with unease. How can Pig Man *possibly* know it? There was no way. Only one person had ever called her that and they were   they were gone. Dead.

"You're looking a little green there, Loch."

Casper's voice sounded far away, but Lochlyn couldn't bounce back. Flashes of her past played out in her mind.

That name.

Hearing it again sent her heart into the pit of her stomach as bile rose through her throat. No one had ever called her that besides one person, and they were dead.

Thunder erupted across the sky, causing her to jolt out of her skin. She let out a strangled yelp and her hands trembled as her knees threatened to give out. An arm snaked around her, nearly startling her, even though she knew it was only Casper.

"Whoa, hey. What's going on with you? Lochlyn? Hey, can you hear me?"

Her eyes shot to meet his concerned gaze. Her lips were quivering as her green eyes widened with panic, but she managed to nod. Though, if she was being honest, Lochlyn wasn't so sure she even believed herself.

"I'm fine. Let's keep moving," she lied.

It was obvious she was very much not fine, but he didn't protest. Straightening, Lochlyn hooked the walkie back through the belt loop on her hip. "This creep is playing games with us. If he can see us, he knows where we are right now. Plus, if he can't, he stole one of the walkies earlier, right? All he'd have to do is scan the channels until he heard us. He knows we're out here and doesn't want us to be. But we should still check out the garage. Does that sound alright to you?"

Nodding, Casper didn't even try to argue. "I'm right behind you."

Swallowing her fear, Lochlyn nodded and turned to keep going. She just hoped she didn't live to regret that decision. The others would be fine, they had to be.

Walking onward, Casper kept his questions to himself for all over two minutes before they burst from his lips. "So, what started the fear of thunderstorms?"

Lochlyn had half a mind to ignore his question, but she knew he wouldn't drop it if. "I, um, I got into a car accident during one.

My brother didn't make it. He was only a few years older than I was. Our parents were fighting one night, and it was pretty bad. Hunter grabbed his keys and offered to drive me to Blockbuster. We used to do scary movie marathons during storms."

A small smile twitched upward on the left side of his mouth. "He sounds like a cool guy."

Lochlyn nodded, a sad smile on her face. "He was. Hunter was the best guy around. Everyone at school loved him. He was the captain of the hockey team and had perfect grades. He could make friends anywhere we went. I always used to be jealous of that. Hunt never had to try like I did. People were just drawn to him and wanted to be his friend."

Taking a shaking breath, Lochlyn continued. "It was storming badly that night. We had no business being out on the roads. No one did. As we were driving, we saw someone on the side of the road. They were having car trouble. Hunt was gonna keep driving. He said it sucked, but it was too dangerous to stop. I begged him to help the guy. It just felt wrong to keep going. So, Hunt being who he was, stopped and went out to help. He told me to stay in the car."

Casper was watching her intently now, hanging onto her every word. "What happened then?"

"It was so dark out and the storm made it impossible to see anything beyond a couple feet in front of you. He was out there for a few minutes helping the guy with his car. I was starting to get antsy waiting there. That was when I saw the headlights. Someone was coming from the other direction with their high beams on. It was a sharp turn and there was a blind spot. Now when thunder booms, all I can hear is the sound of tires squealing and that awful crunch of metal on metal."

Horror fell over Casper's face. Avoiding his eyes, Lochlyn couldn't stomach the idea of what he'd say. It was her fault they stopped and helped that guy. She'd unintentionally put her brother in harm's way. Hunter wouldn't have been pinned between the cars screaming in pain after the other one lost traction.

The memory flashed in her mind as sharply as lightning. Lochlyn had seen the pain and fear in her brother's expression when the sky lit up. The moment haunted her to this day.

They came to a stop in front of the locked garage. Lochlyn swallowed again and wiped her tears before Casper could see them. "He lived for two more days in the hospital before succumbing to his injuries and passing. Now whenever it thunders, I just hear the accident. I see his face when the lightning strikes. It plays on repeat in my head. My mom says it'll stop some day, but it's been a few years and it's still just as bad as it was then."

It was all her fault. Her brother was trying to cheer her up by driving them to Blockbuster that night. He'd only stopped because *she* begged him to. Her brother was dead because of *her* and her father had been quick to point that out before leaving her life for good.

After Hunter's death, her parents had fought more and more often until finally her dad just left them. Her mom always said she didn't blame Lochlyn, but deep down, she knew there was a piece inside of her mother that always would.

Her mother compared her to Hunter all the time. Why couldn't she be more outgoing like he had been? Why can't she make friends as easily as he could? Why can't Lochlyn just be more *normal* like he was? It was why her mother had agreed to let her come out here. This was her chance to make friends like Hunter had. To be more outgoing.

A bitterness nested in the pit of her stomach. Would her mother even mourn her if she didn't come back? Or would she be relieved that she wouldn't have to face Hunter's killer another day?

Tears burned her eyes at the thought. "Do you have the keys Sam gave you?"

Nodding, Casper dug them out from his pocket. He passed the handle of the umbrella over before turning toward the chain. Lochlyn watched as he crouched low and made quick work of opening the metal lock. It fell with a clang, and he pulled the door open as he stood.

Lochlyn raised the flashlight, illuminating the inside of the garage, and gasped at the sight that awaited them.

Chapter 30

Inside the garage hung a body.

It was Sully.

A part of Lochlyn had been hoping the bloody room had been staged like Pumpkin's attack and that Sully was out here somewhere hiding or halfway down the mountain caked in mud and rain. That hope was gone as soon as the light shined on her ghost-like face.

Lochlyn covered her mouth, tears rimming her eyes. Shadows played on Sully's form as it was suspended. There was a deep, jagged slash across the front of her body. She'd been torn open like an animal, and Lochlyn hoped to whoever was listening that she hadn't been alive to feel it happening.

Casper swallowed the lump in his throat as he moved forward. "She's been in here a while, I think."

Lochlyn's body felt frozen where she stood. It was like the rain had stuck her shoes to the cement. Who would do this?

Casper stepped in front of her, obscuring the sight of the bloodied girl. He reached forward and curled his fingers around Lochlyn's arms. Her eyes lifted when he gave her body a small shake.

"Hey, look at me. We need to get back to the others. The four-wheeler's not here. Can you move?"

Could she move? Technically, yes. Nothing was broken. Her shoes weren't really stuck to the cement. So, yes, her body could technically move. Mentally, though? Mentally, Lochlyn was frozen in place and her legs refused to budge.

"I-I don't, um, I can't," she stuttered. "She's dead, Casper. Gab ... Nik ... Sully, whatever her name was, she's *dead*. If she's dead, who's been terrorizing us all night?"

The question went unanswered.

Pity flashed across his features and her own disgust hit hard. This wasn't who she wanted to be. The sniveling, hysterical, coward waiting to be saved. That wasn't the girl who had regained confidence. This wasn't who picked up that axe and challenged Pig Man to try her.

Burying her fear, her jaw tightened as her fists clenched at her sides. "You're right. We should go find the others."

Lochlyn didn't spare the garage another glance as she turned back for the lodge. She couldn't let herself look back. If she did, her bravado might crumble and she'd be a puddle of sobbing goo again. This needed to end. Now.

Not only for her sake, but for Ava, for Daisy, and for Sully.

Lochlyn couldn't even look back to see if Casper was following. The rain soaked through her coat and painted her hair against her skin as she pushed forward. She didn't stop to let him catch up with the umbrella. She couldn't risk a spare moment to think about what she was going to do next.

Instead of heading for the main entrance, Lochlyn headed to the right side of the building. That was where she hoped they would find Xander and Peter searching the rental shed.

Footsteps splashed behind her as Casper pushed himself to keep up. "Lochlyn, wait! Hold on!"

Lochlyn spun around on her heels so sharply that her hair sliced through the air as it hit her face. "Wait for what? Huh? Someone else is dead, Casper. This guy is playing mind games with us, with me, and he made it clear splitting up was a bad idea. We need to find the others."

Casper cautiously continued closer. "I'm not saying we don't. All I'm saying is we need to be smart. Charging in without a plan is guaranteed to blow up in our faces."

Why must he make a good point?

"What do you suggest we do then?"

He took another step forward, holding the umbrella between them. "Keep our eyes open and stick together."

Hesitation crossed her face. "Why should I trust you to have my back?"

Oliver reached up, intending to touch her cheek. Initially, Lochlyn leaned away from his hand, but when he tried again, she allowed him to brush his thumb across her skin. "Because even though you have no reason to trust me, I'm still going to be here with you. I wish I could take back every lie, but I can't. All I can do is prove to you from here on that you can trust me. You have my word, Lochlyn. I will get you away from this lodge. You will not die up here tonight."

Her lips parted but no sound came out. What could she say to that? If Lochlyn told him she forgave him, they both knew it would be a lie. A small piece of her wanted to believe his empty promises though.

If she wanted to survive this nightmarish ordeal, it would have to be by her own hand. She couldn't rely on anyone else to save her.

"Casper, I-"

He shook his head, silencing whatever words were about to come. His hand slipped behind her neck and threaded his fingers through her hair. Before she could process what exactly Oliver thought he was doing, he pulled her closer.

Her hands touched his chest and the umbrella fell to the side as his other hand embraced her frame. To her surprise, Lochlyn realized she was not stopping him.

Her stomach turned into fluttering butterflies, a feeling she was becoming familiar with when it came to Casper. This was not how Lochlyn envisioned this night going. Not just in this moment, but the entirety of it. The game, the murders, and the fact someone really seemed to be hunting them.

So why was the only question now crossing her mind was whether she wanted him to close the distance and kiss her?

Her eyes fell to his lips which were slightly parted as he waited to see how Lochlyn would respond. It wasn't the first time today she'd wondered how it would feel to be kissed by those lips.

The longer they stood there the closer together they grew. Was she leaning into his embrace or was he into hers? Her eyes flickered back to meet his and Lochlyn knew she was doomed.

Lochlyn felt herself melt as he watched her with those chocolate irises. Her body relaxed and her hands slipped upward to wrap around his neck.

Just as his lips pressed against hers, something crashed behind them. Lochlyn's hand dropped from around him and spun toward the noise. It came from the side of the building.

Her heart was hammering against her ribs, but she wasn't sure if it was a result of the near kiss with Casper or from being startled. Not bothering to wait, Lochlyn took off in the direction the crash had come from.

From the splashing of footsteps behind her, she knew Casper was following. Her shoes slipped several times against the wet ground, but Lochlyn didn't let it stop her pursuit.

Rounding the side of the building, she nearly fell as she fumbled to a full stop. Casper bumped into her as he caught himself as well.

Just yards away Lochlyn could make out the small stand used for the ski and sled rentals. That wasn't what had made her stop short though. It was the sight of red splattered against the wood of the rental stand. "Oh, no," she gasped.

Xander and Peter were supposed to be searching for the four-wheeler in this spot. Her stomach plummeted as bile again rose. Pushing down the nausea, Lochlyn took off toward the stand. "Xander? Peter? Are you guys over there?" she called out.

Nothing.

Dread filled her as they approached. She couldn't see any sign of them having been over here, but that didn't settle her nerves. Slowing to a stop, Lochlyn saw that the stand was locked up for the season. The only way in was through the side door, which should have been locked just like the front opening.

The lock sat opened in the mud.

Reaching for the side door, Lochlyn intended to pull it open when Casper put an arm out in front of her. Lochlyn had half a mind to chew him a new one for his need to be her protector when he motioned to the bottom of the door.

She looked at the sliver of space between the door and the floor of the stand. It felt like the air had been stolen from her lungs as she strained to suck in a breath. Her mind tried to process what was peeking through the opening.

Blood, and a lot of it.

Red oozed through the opening, mixing with the mud on the other side. Something shined, catching her attention, to the left. Moving closer, she ignored Casper's whispered caution as she knelt down.

Picking up a looped black rope, Lochlyn realized what she had seen. The charm hanging at the bottom of the loop. It was .... Was that a *Big Foot* pendant? The back of her memory itched with recognition. She'd seen this before, but where?

The piece was a round coin with indents scratched around the circumference. The silhouette of *Big Foot* was in the center. There was no mistaking it. It was the very same necklace she'd noticed Xander twisting between his fingers earlier. Without thinking, Lochlyn shoved it in her pocket.

The nausea returned in full force as dots connected in her head. The world around her suddenly turned to a white noise as she somehow climbed to her feet. Reaching for the door, Casper didn't try to stop her as Lochlyn curled her fingers around the knob and twisted. As she pulled it toward her, something inside the shack shifted.

Familiar green eyes stared up at her as a body hit the ground with a squelching smack. It took her a moment to process that the screaming she heard was coming from herself.

It was Peter.

Chapter 31

The wind howled around her. The rain was suddenly enormously loud in her ears. She barely felt Casper push past her as he hurried to kneel beside a blue-lipped Peter. He was shouting something, but Lochlyn couldn't make out what and whether it was directed toward her.

"He's still alive," Casper's voice finally broke through the fog in her brain. "He's bleeding pretty badly, but he's alive."

Her body shook and she was trapped where she stood as she watched Casper tug off his coat. He used it to press against Peter's stomach, applying pressure to an open wound.

Peter's skin was so pale that his lips were nearly blue. If he wasn't dead yet, he was holding on only by the skin of his teeth. It unnerved her how much it appeared like he was sleeping. How could he look so peaceful after such a brutal attack?

Had it only been hours since they'd been in this very same position with Peter? Only, last time it hadn't been real. At least, not to all of them.

To her, it'd been very real. Before, Lochlyn had jumped into action and tried to help save him. Now, she couldn't move an inch. What was wrong with her?

"Lochlyn!" Casper shouted, his voice vibrating through her.

Startled, she jumped up. "We need to get him inside. Grab his other side!" he instructed.

Casper wanted her to help him. Peter needed her to get her shit together. He would surely die if she didn't move now.

Lochlyn nodded and pushed herself to move. Crouching, she carefully lifted Peter's arm around her neck. A whimper of pain escaped his lips as they carefully stood and held him between them. It was the only sign he was still alive.

He was heavier than expected, though she wasn't sure why she thought he'd be lighter. Peter was in no shape to carry any of his own weight. Sharing a look with Casper over Peter's head, it was clear he was as worried as she was.

Maybe more so seeing as Peter had been his actual friend.

Casper had already lost his sister tonight. He'd lost two friends as well. It felt cruel to put him through this now. How could he be so calm and steady?

The walk around the front of the building seemed to take forever. Lochlyn tried not to notice how much red coated the ground as they stumbled forward.

The rain was making the grass slippery and her borrowed shoes slid all over. The muscle in Casper's jaw ticked as he kept moving. He wasn't going to let them slow down.

Peter couldn't afford the wasted seconds.

Once close enough, Lochlyn reached for the door handle and yanked it open. The three stumbled in, dripping wet as they trekked in the mud. Only, theirs weren't the only muddy prints inside the front entrance. Another pair kept going inward toward the dining room.

She might have written it off as their footprints from earlier, but they'd gone straight to the kitchen a floor below. No one had gone into the other room.

Before she could ponder any longer, pounding footsteps caught her attention from the other direction. Panic seized her before she realized it was Sam.

Alone.

"I spotted you from the second floor. What happened?" Sam asked as she came forward and took Lochlyn's spot.

Together, the trio carried their friend towards the lobby to lay him out on the pool table. Lochlyn led the way holding the door for them before looking back for any sign of their other missing friend.

"Where's Marco?"

Her question went unanswered as Oliver started to answer Sam. "We came up empty at the garage, so we backtracked and went to see if they'd found anything. Peter, he was …. someone put him in the rental stand."

Lochlyn's eyes dropped to her hands and widened at the red stains. Peter had lost so much blood. It was a miracle he wasn't dead already. Oh, God, what is they weren't quick enough? What if he died because they hadn't moved faster?

Lochlyn had frozen when he'd fallen out of the stand. If he died because they hadn't reacted soon enough, it was all her fault. There was already so much death here tonight. Ava, Daisy, Sully …. Lochlyn couldn't stomach losing anyone else.

Sam suddenly moved in front of her and dug her nails into Lochlyn's arms as she gave her a shake. "Lochlyn, focus. Where is Xander? Is he still out there?"

The weight of his necklace sat heavily in her pocket. She was about to tell Sam about it when Lochlyn realized Sam had avoided answering her own question. "Where's Marco?" Lochlyn asked again.

Sam's eyes flashed with an emotion Lochlyn wasn't quick enough to decipher as her hands fell to her sides. "We were attacked on our way back from the kitchen. I barely got away with my life."

She was lying. Lochlyn knew it. Sam tucked a strand of hair behind her ear. It was her tell. Sam was *lying*.

The other girl was watching her carefully, no doubt trying to read whether she believed her lie or not. Lochlyn nodded cautiously, choosing her next words carefully. "I'm sorry. I know you guys were close. No, um, we couldn't find Xander. He wasn't out there."

The necklace felt like it was burning a hole in her side, but she kept it to herself. Why would Sam lie about being attacked? What was there for her to hide at this point?

Lochlyn's eyes flickered past her to where Casper was hovering over Peter. Was he still hiding something from her too? Was Xander or Marco waiting in the shadows to sink their knife into Lochlyn while she was distracted?

Scary movie rule number six; if there's no body, they're not dead. Even then, there's always that shock factor when the villain rises back up for one last attack.

"Where are you going?"

Startled, Lochlyn realized she'd started stepping backwards. Was her body trying to warn her to get the hell out of there? Should she stay and trust them to be on the same side this time? Would that be the stupid move? Her mind was racing with a thousand thoughts. Everything was happening too fast to focus. Lochlyn couldn't figure out what to do.

What did the girls in the movies do? What would a confident Lochlyn do?

She would take a breath and analyze the situation. She would get the hell out of here before becoming the next victim. She wouldn't let herself panic and would think things through. She would fight back.

She would survive.

"I-I don't   um, I was, um, shit," Lochlyn stuttered before turning on her heel and bolting out of the room.

She could barely make out the sound of her name being called as she raced down the hallway. She didn't dare slow down and give herself time to doubt her decision to run.

Yanking open the emergency stairs doorway, Lochlyn hurried inside and took the stairs two at a time. Where was she even going? She didn't know. It didn't matter just as long as it was away from them.

The walkie crackled to life at her side and Sam's voice echoed through the staircase. "Lochlyn, I know you're scared. I know, believe me, but you need to come back right now. Going off by yourself is not the move you want to make. I know you have no right to trust us, but we're on your side. *I'm* on your side. If you believe anything, believe that."

No, she wouldn't be doing that.

Lochlyn had just made it to the third floor when thunder rumbled outside. The rain sounded so much louder up here. It must be the echo. Breathing hard, she managed to get another floor up as the lights flickered before everything suddenly went dark.

Darkness surrounded her.

Lochlyn felt like she was dropped into an abyss. She couldn't even see her hands in front of her. A moment later the emergency lights came on, casting everything in a red hue. Lochlyn's heart thumped against her ribs. Her hands shook at her side as her back hit the wall.

Sinking to the floor, Lochlyn pulled her knees to her chest. Maybe if she made herself as small as possible, they wouldn't be able to find her here in the dark.

The storm must have knocked out the power, that was all. It was just the storm, and she was safe in here. Ha, who was she kidding? Lochlyn wouldn't be safe again until she was miles away from here.

What would her mom think if she never made it home? Would she be relieved not to have her sulking around the house anymore? She could stop asking why Lochlyn survived and not Hunter.

No.

Her mother loved her. Losing one child had nearly ruined her, but Lochlyn had to believe that her mother would care if she never made it back. She wouldn't have to find out because Lochlyn was going to make it through tonight. She was going to see her mother again. Giving up now wasn't an option.

Tears burned her eyes as Lochlyn refused to let them fall. This was pathetic. Lochlyn couldn't be curled up here counting herself out. If she didn't believe she could make it out of this alive, who else would?

Shoving down her fear, she wiped away the traitorous tears and accepted her new-found determination to survive. Using the wall for support, Lochlyn began to rise.

First things first, she needed to change out of her beige raincoat. It made her stick out like a sore thumb. Not that her purple hair didn't already do that.

Her room would be the first stop.

Taking a deep breath, Lochlyn nodded to herself and continued up the stairs. Once she arrived on her floor, Lochlyn slipped through the doorway into the hall as quietly as possible.

If Pig Man was watching her on the camera, there would be no hiding from him. All she could do was not draw more attention to herself with the echo of the door opening and shutting. She also had to be quick because she knew this would be the first place Casper and Sam would look for her.

Hurrying to her room, she made quick work of unlocking the door and moved inside. Coming to a sudden halt, Lochlyn immediately noted the disaster her room had become. It hadn't looked like this when she'd left it almost an hour ago.

Someone had been in here recently, but why? What were they looking for? What did they think she had? Was this why Sam had been coming from upstairs? Had she ransacked her room while Locklyn and Casper were outside? Had it been Marco or Xander who were now unaccounted for?

Tugging off her wet coat, Lochlyn almost tossed it aside when she remembered Xander's necklace buried in her pocket. She wasn't sure what compelled her not to leave it behind, but she dug it free from the pocket before dropping the coat onto the bed.

Stuffing it into her duffle, Lochlyn found a dark over-sized *Lakeside Cove* T-shirt she'd packed to sleep in and some dark red leggings. It wouldn't keep her warm out there, but it would have to do.

Changing as quickly as she could manage, Lochlyn grabbed an elastic hair band and pulled her short hair up into a haphazard bun. Pieces of purple strands stuck out in odd ends with some of the shorter locks falling free.

Pulling a hat loose from her bag, she pulled it over her hair. *The Barnes* logo would stick out given it was literally a red target, but hopefully the rain would hide it enough.

Satisfied enough with her outfit, Lochlyn quickly changed into her sneakers and left the room otherwise undisturbed.

Checking both ends of the hall, she shut the door behind her with a soft click and headed back toward the stairs. Lightning lit up the hall, causing Lochlyn to cringe but she didn't let it slow her down.

The chances of Sam and Casper looking for her were high. She needed to get out of here before they found her.

As she was passing the windows, something in the distance caught her eye. The ski lift was running. Confusion hit as she remembered that the lifts were totally out of bounds. Sam said even she hadn't been given the keys to get them started. Her uncle didn't want to risk any accidents.

Yet it was running now.

Lochlyn wouldn't be surprised if it had been another lie out of Sam's mouth.

If she could get over there, maybe Lochlyn could take it up the mountain and head back down towards town? She could go around the flooded roads, or at the very least, get away from this cursed ski lodge and its occupants.

It wasn't the best plan, but it was better than just wandering the halls hoping not to get caught by the others.

So caught up watching the ski lift, Lochlyn didn't hear the door to her right open until it was too late. A hand snatched onto her arm and yanked her into the room before she could even get a noise out. Her back hit the door as it shut. Another hand covered her mouth as the room spun.

Lochlyn's eyes were wide with fear as she followed the hand to its owner. Even in the darkness, she could make out striking blue eyes staring back at her with a desperation she hadn't seen before.

Xander raised his free hand to his lips, motioning for her to be silent. His black hair hung limply, dripping wet as his face hovered inches away from her own. He was still soaked from being outside, but otherwise he appeared to be okay.

"I'm going to uncover your mouth and you're *not* going to scream. Nod if you agree," Xander whispered, his gaze locked on her intently.

Did she trust him? Would that be foolish? Searching in his eyes, Lochlyn thought she saw real fear inside of them. She wanted to believe there was no faking that. These people were no amateurs, though. That much was crystal clear. Surely, it wouldn't be too hard for them to fake a look of pure and terrifying fear.

They'd already fooled her more than once tonight. How many times was she going to fall for their lies before it finally sunk in? No one in this group could be trusted.

Xander must have seen her hesitation for what it was: conflict over whether to trust him again and risk getting burned. He sighed heavily and his shoulders dropped. His hand did not move from her mouth though, Lochlyn noted bitterly. He wasn't going to risk her screaming for help and drawing attention to them.

"I know you have no reason to trust me, heiress, but   " Xander paused as he debated the correct way to go about this. "I'm not the villain in this game. I'd say I swear, but my word isn't worth much to you at this point, is it?"

Lochlyn didn't move. If she was going to trust him, he had to give her a reason to. As Xander just pointed out, his word alone wasn't going to cut it. Her brow raised, challenging him to trust her in return.

Rolling his eyes, Xander nodded and dropped his hand from her mouth. A moment passed between them and then another, but she didn't start screaming. It wouldn't do her any good anyway.

Without knowing where the others were, there was no telling if they'd even hear her in time to stop him from hurting her. That is, if they weren't on his side to begin with.

He stood entirely too close. His scent of tobacco, mint bubblegum, and musk from the wet clothes invaded her nostrils. It was so different than Casper, so alluring, but she quickly shook those thoughts out of her mind. Her attraction to these boys were going to get her killed.

"You can take a step back now. I'm not going to scream," Lochlyn stated, motioning for him to take a step back as she tugged off her hat. "You smell like a wet dog, by the way."

His perfectly cruel lips twitched upward. "Being out in this storm will do that."

Right, he and Peter had been out at the ski and sled rental stand. The image of Peter falling out of it, bleeding and barely breathing, replayed through her mind. A shiver went down her spine.

Her eyes snapped toward Xander, immediately taking in his calm composer and the lack of blood. Then again, he'd been out in the rain and was already wearing dark clothes. Maybe it helped the blood stains blend in or wash off.

Had they scuffled over something? Was that how his necklace ended up in the mud? Would he tell her the truth if she was to ask him? Would she be able to tell if he lied either way?

At the beginning of this horrific day, Lochlyn would like to have said yes, but now? Now, she wasn't so sure.

"What the hell happened outside?" Lochlyn finally blurted out.

His smirk instantly soured, his adam's apple moving as he swallowed. "What do you think happened?"

Taking a step away from the door, Lochlyn made sure to keep a wide berth as she circled around Xander. She didn't dare turn her back to him. Plus, if she was stupid enough to come straight out and accuse him, she very well might never make it out of this room.

His eyes followed her like a predator stalking its prey. "What? You've been all too happy to share every single theory you've got, every accusation you've convinced yourself of, all night. Why so quiet now?"

"I don't have any more theories. I just want to go home," Lochlyn meekly squeaked out, mad at her own vulnerability.

Her heart squeezed as the truth of her words hit her hard. Lochlyn would make up with her mom, go to college, and really try to make actual friends, if she could only make it home.

It took whatever energy Lochlyn had left to hold in the flood of tears she could feel coming. She yet again felt like there was lump in her throat and that her stomach was tied into knots. It was an unfortunate, familiar, feeling by now.

With a quick scan of the room, Lochlyn tried to find something she could use. In getting herself free from the door, she'd accidentally gotten herself further into the room. Xander now stood between her and her freedom. They both knew it.

"I already told you. I'm not the bad guy, Lochlyn. You don't need to fight me. I'm on your side here."

Where had she heard that before, Lochlyn thought bitterly.

Reaching slowly behind, her fingers curled around the lamp on the table beside her and swung as quickly as she could.

Unfortunately, he managed to dodge her attack. The two struggled over the lamp before Xander pried it out of her hands and tossed it aside. As it crashed onto the floor, Lochlyn saw the blood dramatically drain from his face.

"Someone's bound to have heard that. They'll know you're up here," Xander panicked. "Shit. Shit, shit, this is not good."

He crossed the room to the window and his entire body went rigid. Lochlyn's attention darted between his back and the door. Now was her chance to run and leave him in her dust, but her mental paralysis was back. Her feet took her toward the window and beside him.

"What is it? What's out there?"

Xander suddenly turned to face her, his hands latching forcefully onto her arms with a sense of panic. "I know you have no reason to trust me, but if we're going to get out of here you need to work with me. Can we at least agree on that?"

Why she ever would agree to that?

Lochlyn hesitated. The desire to flat out say no was tempting, but deep-down she knew he was right. She would have a better chance of getting out of here with his help. Xander had been here before. He knew the layout better than she did. He could be the key to making it out of here alive. As long as she trusted him to not double-cross her again.

Lochlyn nodded.

Relief crossed his face, but it didn't last long as his attention snapped to the closed door. Out in the hall Lochlyn could just make out what sounded like footsteps coming down the carpeted pathway. Was it Sam or Casper? It could even be Marco. She wasn't going to write him off the board yet. Not until they found his body.

Were they coming to find her benevolently or capture and kill her? Was Xander in on it or was he being genuine about helping? As badly as she wanted to believe what Casper had said outside, how could she? How many lies could she forgive? How many times could she trust him before that naive sense of hope cost Lochlyn her life?

Lochlyn supposed she was about to find out.

Chapter 32

The footsteps appeared to be getting closer. Xander motioned for her to stay quiet as he pulled her around the side of the bed. His eyes never moved from the doorway.

"Get over there and stay down. Don't make a sound," he whispered, motioning down to the mattress.

Moving as silently as she could, Lochlyn did as he said. Her eyes followed him through the darkness as he grabbed something from his pocket. It opened with a cool swish and the moonlight peeking through the window glinted off the metal.

Xander had a pocketknife.

A ripple of fear shook through her. Xander could have killed her at any time, but he didn't. He let her attack him and still pushed for her to trust him. That had to count for something, right?

Xander moved behind the door, motioning for her to stay put. Crouching, Lochlyn stayed low enough she wouldn't be immediately seen but still in a position to get up and take off running if things went south.

Shadows moved beneath the door. It felt like her heart froze, but somehow it was still beating like a hammer against her ribs.

The door swung open as lightning illuminated the room. There was a silhouette looming in the doorway, and as the room lit up Lochlyn realized it was Sam.

Sam stood there panting, covered in blood, with panic in her eyes. Her hair was damp with sweat and her hands shook as she crossed the threshold.

"Xander, wait!" Lochlyn called out before her logical thinking could stop her.

Xander froze mid strike, his position given away from her shouting. He immediately shot her with a pointed glare before lowering his blade.

Sam stumbled back a step. "What the hell, Xand?"

Lochlyn stood from her hiding spot as Sam rushed to shut the door behind her. As Sam twisted the lock into place, several questions sprouted in her mind.

Where was Casper? Was that Peter's blood on her or someone elses'? Had she abandoned them like she did Marco? What was she running from? *Was* Sam running, or was she searching for her? Had Lochlyn just made a huge mistake?

"I could ask you the same thing, Sami," Xander said tensely as he took a few steps back to join Lochlyn's side.

She took notice of the fact that he didn't pocket his knife.

"Someone attacked us downstairs after Lochlyn ran off. I barely made it out. He's not far behind me. We have to get out of here," Sam whispered with a tremor in her voice.

Lochlyn had already seen this act though. She'd been in the elevator with Sam and Marco when they'd been 'attacked' by some lady with a chainsaw. Sam's acting might have improved since that moment, but how could she be trusted when she was telling the same damn story?

"Where's Casper?"

A sense of tension loomed among them so thick it could be cut like butter. Lochlyn and Zander shared a look of unease before their attention turned to Sam.

Sadness and grief filled her dark eyes as she cried. "The guy caught us by surprise. Casper didn't move quick enough. He told me to run. He was trying to buy me as much time as he could."

A sense of anger burned through her. "Was Casper hurt badly or did you just run like a coward and leave him there to die like you did with Marco? Did you even try to help him?"

The sharpness in her tone surprised even her, but Lochlyn didn't try to push it back down. These people claimed to be experts in murder mysteries and horror movies. They talked a big game with this stupid event, but in the real situation they were just a bunch of cowards.

Correction. *Sam* was, if her story was to be believed.

"They were struggling over the knife when I ran. There wasn't time to go back and check for a pulse," Sam pleaded sourly. "These are *my* friends being murdered. Do you think I want to watch them die?"

A scoff slipped through her lips at the utter ridiculousness of these people. Casper was one of their so-called friends. So were Xander, Daisy, Marco, Ava, Sully, and Peter.

Lochlyn might have been the newbie to the group, but they had been Sam's friends for years. Yet, in the face of danger, Sam turned and ran. It was suddenly every man for themself.

Except, even amid his grieving, Casper had still stayed by her side. He didn't run when they found Sully's body or when they found Peter. He immediately went to help his friend from bleeding out and insisted on saving him.

He deserved to have someone go back for him too.

Without saying a word, Lochlyn pushed through the duo and went for the door. Twisting the knob, she remembered it was locked as Sam slammed her hand against it.

Lochlyn gritted her teeth and her eyes narrowed when Sam didn't move. "Get out of my way. You both can stay here and be cowards, but I'm going after him. Casper wouldn't have left you to die."

Sam didn't budge. "I can't let you do that. I already told you, Lochlyn. The guy was right behind me."

Lochlyn's eyes flickered to Xander, noting how he appeared ready to bolt. His frame shifted and his eyes focused sharply as he caught the same slip Lochlyn had. He nudged his black frames up on his nose and tightened his grip on the pocketknife at his side.

"How can he be right behind you if he was struggling with Casper when you ran off?" Lochlyn asked angrily.

Sam's back straightened as her mistake sunk in. Suddenly Xander was there shoving Sam back from the door. He held his knife up and his eyes darted wildly between Lochlyn and Sam as Lochlyn made quick work of unlocking the deadbolt.

Yanking the door open, she grabbed his arm and pulled him through the opening. Her immediate thought was to run to the stairway, but gasped as she fell back in a sudden attempt to stop.

Standing there at the end of the hall was the same Pig Man from earlier. Shadows were cast eerily against his haunting mask. Her eyes dropped to his side, taking in the chilling sight of liquid dripping from the dagger.

"Get up, get up, come on. This way," Xander fumbled, tugging on her arm as he all but yanked her to her feet.

Lochlyn suddenly wished she hadn't left her axe in the storage shed. It certainly would have come in handy. But there was no use dwelling on that now, Lochlyn scolded herself, as she pushed to keep up with Xander.

As the two rounded the corner of the hall. Lochlyn made the mistake of looking back at the last moment. She saw Pig Man stop in front of the doorway they'd come from.

A blood curdling scream followed, and Lochlyn momentarily squeezed her eyes shut. She almost missed Xander stopping at the elevator and pulling out his key card to activate it.

He was hitting the card against it incessantly, but Lochlyn knew they were sitting ducks out here. The elevator was the least reliable exit strategy. It never came quickly enough and took forever for the doors to close once it did.

"We can't wait for it, Xander," she whispered, though her eyes never left the hall they'd come from.

Xander gritted his teeth, slamming his fists against the doors. "Damnit!"

Lochlyn scanned the rest of the hall before stopping at the window at the very end. '**EMERGENCY EXIT**' was printed out above the window. There must be a fire escape on this side of the building. Grabbing Xander's hand, Lochlyn tugged him along.

"Over there," she directed. "Come on. Hurry!"

Barely giving herself enough time to stop, Lochlyn pressed her hands against the window to soften the impact. Xander reached up and switched the lock. They yanked the window open with every ounce of strength they could muster.

Lochlyn already had one leg out the window when she looked back down the hall. As she ducked her head through, her eyes made contact with Pig Man. Fresh blood was splattered across his once blank mask.

"Oh, shit,"

Lochlyn nearly tumbled over to get her other leg out. Xander hurled his body through after her. "Keep moving. Go! Don't stop." he ordered, shoving the pocketknife into her hand as he motioned for her to continue.

Not wasting a moment to argue, Lochlyn nodded and rushed to the other end and started to climb downward. It was only when she made it to the next landing that she realized Xander wasn't right behind her.

Looking up, she could see him through the grated landing. He'd stayed behind to shut the window after them. From the look of it, it appeared he was struggling to close it. Lochlyn was about to climb back up to help him when she saw the glint of Pig Man's dagger.

"Watch out!" Lochlyn screamed, but her warning came too late.

A scream ripped through her lungs as she watched the dagger sink into Xander's thigh. Pig Man yanked it out and moved to stab again, but Xander pushed himself away from the window as he slammed it shut and stumbled back with a pain filled cry.

Lochlyn was halfway up the ladder when he shook his head frantically. "Don't! I'm right behind you. Go!"

Lochlyn moved up another step, ready to tell him off for ordering her to leave him behind. She'd literally just called Sam a coward for doing the same thing.

He was at the opening before she reached the top and she quickly dropped out of the way so he could get down. Looking up, Lochlyn saw Pig Man getting the window open again. When Xander was off the ladder, she wrapped his arm around her shoulders and the two rushed to the next ladder down.

Pig Man was on the top landing as they descended to another level. There was only one more and then they'd have to jump. There wouldn't be enough time to get the ladder lowered.

Her eyes searched the ground as they fumbled down the metal rungs. Xander was losing blood too fast. He wouldn't be able to land a jump from this height. Lochlyn wasn't even sure she could either without snapping her ankles, and she wasn't the one dealing with a stab wound.

"The dumpster," Xander panted. "Jump into it. Don't wait for me. Just run."

Lochlyn saw the dumpster he was talking about. They must have been right above the kitchens. It was going to be a pain to climb out of, but at least the bags of trash would cushion their fall. It was going to be even harder for Xander to pull himself out with a bleeding leg.

"Xander," she started.

He immediately shook his head. "Don't. I'm not worth the risk. I'll buy you time to get to the ski lift and get out of here. GO."

Before Lochlyn could argue, he shoved her off the fire escape. A scream had barely escaped her lungs before she crashed into the bags of trash. It felt like the air had been knocked out of her, but there was no time to regain it.

With a grunt, Lochlyn struggled to get to the edge and hoist herself up. She had one leg over the side of it when another body fell next to her into the dumpster.

For a moment, she waited to see if Xander would emerge. "Come on, Xander. Come on."

Looking upward, she saw Pig Man descending another level. He would be joining them in here any second now.

Just when Lochlyn was about to dive back in for Xander, his head emerged with a gasp. Relief filled her as she reached for him. "Take my hand. Come on, hurry!"

His eyes settled on her as he accepted her outstretched hand, allowing her to pull him over to the edge. "You weren't supposed to wait for me," Xander scolded, though there was some definite relief in his blue eyes.

The two climbed out of the foul-smelling bin. She hit the ground with no issue, but as Xander hopped down, his injured leg buckled. A curse slipped through his lips, but Lochlyn was quick to wrap his arm around her again.

Peering upward, she saw Pig Man leaning over the second landing, his head tilted as he watched them. He wasn't pursuing them.

"Why isn't he coming after us?"

Xander grunted as he hobbled forward, pulling her with him. "Let's not stick around to find out or tempt him to change his mind."

There wasn't anywhere for them to go but back inside and that wasn't an option. A thought tugged at her. Casper was still inside too. He could still be alive and the thought of leaving him in there didn't sit well with her, but the game of cat and mouse would only continue if they went back in.

The only way to help Casper, and anyone else who was alive, would be to get out of here and find help. The only problem with that was there wasn't a safe way back down the mountain.

An idea suddenly hit her. What if they didn't go down? What if they went up instead? "There was a Ranger's Station on the map of the mountain online, wasn't there? If we can get up the mountain, we can find it and call for help," Lochlyn suggested as they stumbled down the length of the building.

For some reason Pig Man had decided not to keep following them, which worried her more than anything else. He could have easily done so, especially since Xander was in no condition to make a run for it.

Xander glanced over, the exhaustion clear on his face. "How do you suggest we get to the lift? I'm not exactly in any condition for a hike."

Stopping, Lochlyn glanced back to make sure their masked creep hadn't changed his mind before ripping a strip off from her shirt.

Kneeling in front of him, Lochlyn started to wrap it around the open wound. "It won't stop the bleeding, but it'll at least slow it down. We can find you a big stick once we're off the lift."

For once, Xander didn't point out any fault in her plan. If she looked closer at his face, Lochlyn might have even seen a blush on his cheeks. She was going to blame that on the loss of blood though.

"As for how to get to the lift from here, would that do?"

Feet away, behind some bushes was the missing four-wheeler. It wasn't even hidden well, and had clearly been left here in a rush.

How could Sam and Marco have missed it in their search? Unless they never made it out here? There was also the possibility that it had been a lie all along too. Either way it still didn't tell her what happened to Marco or where he was now.

Oblivious to her turn in thinking, a weak grin twitched up on Xander's lips. "Yeah, I think that would do it."

As they climbed onto the machine, Lochlyn was pleased to find the keys waiting in the ignition. Twisting it, the engine purred to life. She'd never driven one of these before, but her cousins had her whole life. She'd seen how they did it and hoped she would figure it out quickly.

"Ready?" Lochlyn asked over her shoulder.

Xander wrapped his arms around her and pressed his chest against her back. It was such an intimate position, but now was not the time or place to focus on. "Have you ever driven one of these before?" he asked.

Twisting the handle, the engine revved. "Nope! Hold on tight, jerk!"

His laughter was quiet in her ear. "I'll be happy when this nightmare is over."

Lochlyn turned her head enough to meet his gaze. His chin was resting on her shoulder as his eyes fought to stay open. If she didn't get him some help soon, he wasn't going to make it.

"Yeah, I'm ready to end this game."

Without another word, Lochlyn pressed her foot against the gas and they jolted from the sudden movement. The wet, freezing wind hit her head-on, but she ignored the chill as they headed for the ski lift.

The game of survival was on.

Chapter 33

The rain hadn't let up much since it started, making it hard to see which direction they were going. Thankfully, the ski lift was lit up acting as a beacon guiding them through the darkness.

Either her face had gone numb to the stinging water thrashing her, or Lochlyn had just gotten used to the feeling.

With a brief glance over her shoulder, she saw Xander's blue eyes keeping a careful watch on the surrounding woods. His skin had gotten pale, no doubt from the blood loss. Even using that scrap of shirt to tie off his leg, it was still an open wound. He wouldn't last much longer if they couldn't find a way to fully stop the bleeding.

His arms tightened around her, giving her a squeeze of reassurance. "I'm not gonna drop dead off this thing. Stop worrying about me."

His words should have been reassuring, but the ball of concern was still knotted up inside her. Until he was safe in a hospital, she wouldn't stop worrying.

Then there was the matter of Casper.

Had she left him and Peter to die? What about Marco? Pieces of Sam's story didn't make sense, but Pig Man *had* been there. He'd gone into that room, and Lochlyn had heard Sam's screams of terror.

God, this vacation had turned into such a nightmare.

Swallowing her sorrow and guilt, a new sense of determination filled her as she straightened her shoulders. Lochlyn might not have been able to save the others, but she could save herself and Xander.

Maybe if they were able to find the Ranger Station, they could send back help for the others. *If* anyone else was still alive, they would be fine. Lochlyn wasn't being a coward. No, she was just doing her best to survive this terror inducing night and help whoever else she still could.

"Hey, you didn't happen to find my necklace when you found Peter, did you?"

Well, that was unexpected.

"Um, yeah. It's back in my room in my bag. Why?"

Xander nodded, tucking that information away. "It's not just a *Big Foot* charm. It's a flash drive too. I put some stuff on it that could help us put this creep behind bars."

Lochlyn was shocked. She wasn't sure how she was supposed to response, but Xander wasn't expecting her too.

He kept talking. "There's something I need to tell you once we're not running for our lives."

As they reached the base of the ski lift, Lochlyn slowed to a stop and turned the engine off. The two of them slid off the seat and gathered their bearings. Xander's breathing was labored. Not a good sign.

"We should stop and check your leg. Maybe we can find something to-"

Her suggestion was cut off as the roar of another engine caught her attention. Looking back toward the lodge, she could see a faint pair of headlights coming their way. Apparently, Pig Man changed his mind about letting them go.

"Shit, come on," Lochlyn said as she looped her arm around him.

The two of them hobbled forward. Now that they were closer to the lift, Lochlyn could see the benches rotating over the mountain.

Looking back, she saw the other four-wheeler stop beside theirs. Apparently not all of them were sabotaged like they'd been led to believe. The headlights shut off, masking the person in darkness before Lochlyn could get a good look.

"Lochlyn, come on," Xander urged.

As the two made it to the landing another obstacle became clear. The benches were moving too fast, and there was no one to slow them down long enough for them to get on safely. "We're going to have to jump on one," Lochlyn realized as she looked down to his wounded leg.

If getting off the four-wheeler had tired him, this was going to be next to impossible. Never mind figuring out a way to get back off and onto the ground.

"I'll slow it down for you," Xander spoke up. "I can buy you time to get up there. There's a Ranger Station two miles down the west side of the mountain."

Panic set in as Lochlyn processed what he was saying.

Xander grabbed her arms and gave her a small shake. "There's no time to argue about this. We both know I'll only slow you down. The least I can do is give you a head start."

Tears rimmed her eyes as Lochlyn continued to shake her head. "That wasn't the plan."

His thumb stroked her cheek, wiping away a tear. A sad smile played on his lips as he tried to be brave for her. "Didn't you learn anything from *Scooby Doo*? The original plan never goes right. Time to improvise, heiress. Go!"

He gave her a gentle push back, as if to emphasis his point. Xander was right that there was no time to argue. Pig Man was almost upon them.

Angrily wiping her eyes, Lochlyn nodded and headed for the benches as he maneuvered himself to go into the other direction toward the controls.

Xander pulled a lever and the benches started to slow enough for her to safely hop into one. Her hands shook as she settled in. Once Lochlyn was securely on the seat, she twisted around to look at Xander.

He moved the lever forward and the lift started to pick up speed. She had to hold onto the side railings as the bench jostled her.

Her eyes widened as she noticed Pig Man approaching the control booth. "Xander!"

Despite by the wind, Xander's head snapped up indicating he might have heard her. He turned in time to dodge an attack and sparks flew as the assailant's weapon clanged against the machinery.

Lochlyn watched helplessly as Xander grabbed a nearby wrench and swung it unsuccessfully.

Pig Man was able to block the move and snatch the tool away. A strangled sob rose out of her throat as Xander was left empty handed. The glint of a familiar dagger flashed through the darkness. "Noo!" Lochlyn cried, screaming as she saw it strike downward.

She was too far away to see if Xander was hit, but his chances of avoiding the swift blade again were slim given his injured leg. Even if he did, there was no telling if Xander would survive the rest of the fight.

Tears ran down her wet face, mixing with the rain falling around her. Lochlyn's hands shook as she held onto the lift. A few minutes went by before she felt another jolt. Someone else was getting on the machine.

Lochlyn didn't have the energy to look back, knowing in her heart it wasn't going to be Xander's face grinning at her from a distance.

All she could do was get up to the top of the mountain and get to the Ranger's Station before Pig Man caught up to her.

Xander's pocketknife felt like a heavy weight in the side opening of her leggings. It bulged out across her thigh, but she paid it no mind as the mountain loomed in the distance.

If she was going to land safely at this speed, she was going to have to be careful. Given the time of year, there wouldn't be much snow, if any at all, on the ground to cushion her fall. There would only be hard dirt and mud to welcome her instead.

As she got closer to where she'd have to jump, another jostling of the lifts alerted her that something else was happening. Was he getting impatient?

This time, Lochlyn looked over her shoulder, searching the darkness for that haunting face. There. Six ski lifts back sat the menace that would be haunting her dreams for years to come. That is, if Lochlyn survived this nightmare.

Pig Man sat there calmly though he appeared to be hunched in a way to keep the cold at bay. He wasn't nearly as large as he'd been back at the hotel, but that might just be because he was so far away.

Pig Man raised his hand, giving her a slow wave. A chill ran down her spine. Turning back to her goal, Lochlyn willed the lift to move faster. The sooner it was at the top landing, the sooner she could take off running and put distance between them.

Another jostle made her turn again. Pig Man shifted and leaned forward like he was preparing to jump. Looking down, Lochlyn realized they were at a safe enough distance to drop. If they landed correctly, they should be fine.

Not wanting him to have the advantage, Lochlyn took a deep breath before letting herself drop from her lift first. Her body landed in a roll. Her ankle screamed in protest, but Lochlyn pushed to her feet and took off running.

She didn't pause to see if Pig Man followed her lead. She assumed he would once he was close enough to the ground.

Run, Lochlyn. Run like your life depends on it, she thought to herself. *Because it does.*

Lochlyn hoped she was going in the correct direction. Xander had said to the West side of the mountain, but did he mean if you're looking at it or if you're facing the lodge? She couldn't be sure and he wasn't there to ask.

Thunder rumbled in the sky like an ominous warning. Lochlyn didn't let it slow her down as she entered the woods and started her descent.

Twigs and leaves crunched under her shoes as she pushed forward. Rocks sank into the mud as she stepped on them. Lochlyn could feel the branches trying to entrap her as she rushed through them, catching on to her skin and clothes.

Her body felt like one big, exposed, cut, but all she could do was ignore the pain and keep moving. Her breath heaved and her hair was sticking to her face like a second skin. It was nearly impossible to see where she was going, but somehow, Lochlyn managed.

The sound of a body hitting the ground met her ears and Lochlyn knew that meant Pig Man was in pursuit of her. He couldn't be that far behind if she could hear his landing.

Lochlyn didn't miss a step as she pulled Xander's pocketknife free from her leggings. Thank God someone finally designed these with pockets or else she would have lost the weapon a while ago.

Refusing to make the classic mistake of looking back during a chase, Lochlyn kept her eyes forward on the path in front of her and focused on where she was going.

Hopping over a fallen log, Lochlyn stumbled for a moment, but pushed forward. Xander had said the Ranger's Station would be two miles down the mountain, but would she be able to see it from a distance? In this storm, Lochlyn didn't have much of a chance, though it wouldn't necessarily be impossible.

Would the Rangers hear her if she started screaming?

Lochlyn's heart sank at another possibility. What if there was no one waiting there to hear her screams? What if they weren't here during the off season or what if they didn't have a person covering the overnight shift? She could very well be running to an empty building.

Distracted by her thoughts, she wasn't careful enough as her foot suddenly slid out from under her. Lochlyn went down with a cry of pain, landing on her side in a puddle of mud. She tried to climb back to her feet, but her ankle protested. Lochlyn returned to the mud with another thud.

She pulled herself behind a tree and huddled in closely to make herself less visible. Looking down, Lochlyn could see her ankle was already swollen. It wasn't broken though, which meant she could keep moving. Pausing, she strained to hear any sound of movement.

Leaves squelched under footsteps somewhere nearby, but she couldn't tell how close he was. He could be just feet away for all she knew. If that was the case, her hiding was pointless. He'd already knew where she was.

Peering around the side of the tree, her body went rigid at the sight of Pig Man coming in her direction.

He hadn't spotted Lochlyn yet by some miracle given she'd already tumbled twice. She watched him walk around cautiously as his eyes scoured the darkness. He clearly realized she wasn't running anymore.

Lochlyn continued to watch in horror as Pig Man reached up and pulled the white latex off his face. An audible gasp escaped her lips before she could stop it. Slapping her hand over her mouth, Lochlyn hoped it hadn't been heard.

Her heart nearly stopped as familiar dark eyes locked in on her. Lochlyn didn't wait. She scrambled to her feet, pushing herself off into a run. Her limp was evident as she hurried, but Lochlyn didn't even notice.

Her mind was still trying to process what she'd seen. There was no way she'd seen what she thought she had, but there was no denying it. No excuse like a trick of light or a mistaken identity.

It was *Sam* under that mask.

It was *Sam* yards behind her in the woods coming after her with a dagger.

Sam was the murderer.

Chapter 34

Unfortunately, the lighter rain didn't help with the fact Lochlyn could barely see where she was going. Her entire body was sore and tired. It wanted rest, but that couldn't happen until she was away from Sam, or even until she was in custody.

Lochlyn still couldn't believe it had been Sam this entire time. It didn't make sense. How did she pull off the stunt of being in the hall and in the room at the same time? Was that Marco? Were they working together? Where was he now?

Not only that, but Kitty had been hosting these games for years with the other players. Why was this one any different? What made her go off script *this* particular time? What about *Lochlyn* made the girl snap?

Stumbling, Lochlyn managed to loose sight of Sam and tucked herself behind a large rock. Her breath was coming out beyond heavily now and her ankle was screaming. Leaning against the boulder, she again made herself as small as possible.

Running around like this was getting her nowhere. She didn't even know if she was going in the right direction. How long was two miles really? What if she already passed the Ranger's Station or if it was on the other side of the mountain entirely?

God, why did Xander have to be a hero and stay behind? If he hadn't of tried to buy them time by closing that window, he wouldn't have been hurt in the first place. They could have made it onto the lift together. He would have known where to go.

Casper would have too.

"You might as well come out, Lochlyn!" Sam shouted. "You're running in circles, and you're clearly hurt. This won't end well for you and we both know that."

Hot tears ran down her cheeks. Lochlyn squeezed her legs closer to her chest, praying that Sam would walk right past her. She didn't want Sam to be right. This was not going to be the end of her story.

"Do you even know why this is happening? Why we chose *you* out of all the other applications we received to join the party? Do you?" Her tone was mocking as she got closer to where Lochlyn was hiding. "Do you want to?"

Sam was baiting her to come out, to respond, and give herself away. She wouldn't be falling into that trap. Not defenseless, anyway.

Opening her eyes, Lochlyn searched the ground around her. Xander's pocketknife would only help her so much. It was better for face-to-face fights, and she didn't want to be that close to Sam.

Carefully, Lochlyn reached over and pulled a large broken branch to her side. The squishing leaves made her pause, hoping it didn't give away her hiding spot. Her ears strained to listen and the telltale sound of wet leaves squelching under a shoe caught her attention. A shadow loomed over her.

"There you are."

Launching herself forward, Lochlyn nearly missed getting stabbed as metal scratched against the stone she'd just been behind. Scrambling, Lochlyn army-crawled forward and fumbled to get herself up.

It took a few tries to get traction, but soon Lochlyn was up on her feet and taking off. Sam's manic laughter echoed through the trees, belittling her attempt to escape.

The longer Lochlyn ran, the less she believed she'd make it out of here. She would just be another case of '*she almost made it*' for the newspapers to talk about before everyone eventually moved on to the next story and forgot about her.

No.

Lochlyn was not going to give up. She would fight until her last breath. Sam was not going to win tonight. Xander's sacrifice would not be in vain.

She was done running away.

It was all she'd been doing tonight. It was time to stop and fight. It was the only way tonight would finally be over.

Lochlyn would be this story's lone survivor.

Slowing to a stop, Lochlyn squinted through the darkness. She could finally see it on the right. There was a cabin.

Lochlyn couldn't make out any defining details, so there was no telling if it was even the Ranger's Station, but it was better than hiding behind a tree. Sam was closing in.

Hurrying toward the cabin, Lochlyn pushed through the pain shooting up her leg until she was in front of it. To her relief, the words *Ranger Station* were burned into the wood above the doorway. But to her horror, there didn't appear to be anyone there.

"Loch-lyn!" Sam's voice sang mockingly. "Run all you want, but no one's coming to your rescue."

Limping two steps up to the doorway, Lochlyn tested the knob and found it open. It felt like someone in the universe was finally on her side.

Slipping inside, Lochlyn didn't waste any time looking around. It was set up like a normal cabin. There were a couple of desks and a map of the area on the wall. With a quick glance, Lochlyn noted that she was halfway down the mountain.

Too far to realistically keep going on foot. At least if she was trying to outrun Sam.

Continuing her search, Lochlyn found a radio that could make outgoing transmissions. Relief hit her like a ton of bricks, and she might have cried if not for the urgency of the situation. Lochlyn was about to reach for it when she heard a sudden creak outside.

Sam was right out front.

Making a quick decision, Lochlyn grabbed the radio and clipped it to her side. Ducking down, she debated hiding under the desk but that would only trap her there. It would be the first place Sam checked.

Crawling across the room, Lochlyn kept low to the floor in case she was to peer in through the window.

Lochlyn made it to the doorway before she carefully stood. Sam would be coming inside any minute, and she had to be ready to bolt once she was out of the doorway. Holding the branch tightly to her chest, she slowed her breath and mentally prepared.

The door pushed open with a groan, but Lochlyn waited until Sam's shadow slithered inside before she swung with all her might.

The branch hit its target with a satisfying crunch. Sam screamed and cursed as she fell back with blood gushing down her face.

Lochlyn didn't give her a chance to recover as she pulled Xander's pocketknife out and opened it with a swish. Stalking forward with the knife raised, Lochlyn let out a primal scream as she launched herself forward. She landed on top of Sam, straddling her waist as she attempted to strike.

Sam was quick to grab hold of her arms and gritted her bloody teeth as she strained to keep the knife from puncturing her chest.

Lochlyn let out another scream of frustration, putting all her strength into the attack. "Why? Why did you do all of this? What did I ever do to you?"

Sam's laughter startled her. "You really don't remember me, do you?"

The question caught her off guard and gave Sam an opening to knock the knife from her hands. Stunned, Lochlyn didn't have time to recover before her world suddenly flipped. Her back hit the wet ground hard as Sam rolled them over.

Metal glinted in the moonlight as she raised the dagger. Lochlyn's eyes widened as she took in the sight of it looming above her. Her reflexes kicked in and she grabbed hold of Sam's arm before she could lower it into her body.

Sam gritted her teeth, her eyes wild with excitement as she gained an inch in their struggle. "We've met once before. It was over winter break a few years back."

Lochlyn tried to rack her brain for the memory she was trying to unlock. Then it hit her. Hunter had brought his girlfriend home with him during the winter break before his accident. Lochlyn had been too shy and had only spared her a quick hello before hiding in her room.

"You dated my brother," Locklyn realized.

A bitter laugh escaped her lips. "Hell of a plot twist, right? Hunter was the love of my life, and *you* took him from me. If you hadn't been a brat, he never would have been on the road that night. He never would have felt bad enough for you to stand me up. Did you know he was supposed to be with me that night, not run down on the side of the road helping some loser!"

Horror filled her eyes as it all suddenly clicked into place. Hunter had canceled his plans that night to have a movie marathon with Lochlyn to cheer her up. Those plans must have been with Sam. Her brother had chosen Lochlyn over her, and that choice cost him his life.

Lochlyn struggled as the dagger lowered another inch. It was getting dangerously close to piercing her skin.

A mix of sweat and rain coated her skin as her panic rose. Maybe if she kept Sam talking and distracted her, Lochlyn could manage to knock the dagger away. It was worth a shot.

"What about the others? They were your friends!"

Sam scoffed, rolling her eyes. "Those idiots were not my friends. Didn't you ever read the police report? Or keep updated on the case?"

Her blood chilled at the questions. No, she hadn't done either of those things because she couldn't stomach it. It had taken years for Lochlyn just to sleep without screaming in terror.

Thunderstorms still put her into a state. Her therapist had advised against looking into any details about the case and her mother had agreed with her. The further away Lochlyn put it in her mind, all the better for her mental health.

Clearly Sam had chosen another route.

A new sense of anger flared inside of Sam as she understood what Lochlyn's silence meant. "I might as well tell you before I kill you."

Lochlyn gritted her teeth, straining to keep the dagger from inching even a millimeter further.

"Peter was the moron your brother stopped to help that night. He had just gotten his license and didn't know how to change a stupid flat tire. Ava confronted me after finding that bloody room with you. She knew it wasn't a part of the game and wanted answers. I had to silence her before she ruined the twist too early."

"What about the others?"

Excitement filled Sam's psychotic eyes. "Unfortunately, Daisy was a casualty. She saw me attack Peter and tried to save him. She wasn't even supposed to be there. It was supposed to be Xander. That tech nerd couldn't keep his nose in his own business. I hired him to snoop, and he took it upon himself to dig into *my* background. He backed up everything he found on some USB. Too smart for his own good. As for Marco, I saved him for last. *He* deserved the worst of it."

Lochlyn had an inkling about why, but she couldn't stop herself from asking. "Why?"

A sudden and familiar sadness flashed across Sam's face. Lochlyn recognized it was because she'd felt the same grief since the night of the accident. "He was the one behind the hit and run. He was going for a joy ride and lost control of his car in the storm and hit   *he* hit Hunter and kept going. His rich and powerful family covered it up to protect him, but who protected Hunter? It certainly wasn't you. You were the reason for all of this. He wouldn't have even stopped to help Peter if you hadn't have begged him."

Sam must have somehow gained access to Lochlyn's statement that night. It was the only way she could have known that.

But how did she find out about Marco part in it? That definitely wasn't in the records. That wasn't the only missing piece in this confession.

Something else didn't add up. "What about Sully?"

A twisted grin spread across Sam's face. "Oh, I can't take credit for her. That one wasn't me."

A burst of pain hit before Lochlyn could inquire further as the tip of the dagger pressed against her chest. She didn't need to see it to know Sam had drawn blood. The warm substance trickled down her side.

Sam's smile was near giddy upon seeing the red spot blooming from the new wound. "There's only room for one final girl in this game, I'm afraid."

No, no, Lochlyn couldn't die like this. "Wait, wait! You still haven't told me how Casper fit into this? Why kill him?"

The wicked grin spread across her face again so large it might have broken her lips.

"You haven't figured that part out yet? He-" **BANG.**

A sharp gasp slipped through Lochlyn's lips as blood spattered across her face. Sam's head shot back from the impact and her eyes immediately glazed over, frozen with shock. A hole had replaced the center of her forehead as the dagger fell from her grip. Her body slumped over, hitting the wet patch of mud beside them.

Lochlyn scrambled back, hyperventilating as she stared at Sam's unmoving form. Sam was dead, life gone from her eyes so violently and suddenly.

"I guess no one ever told her that the big villain shouldn't waste time revealing their master plan."

Startled, Lochlyn twisted around to see Casper standing there with a smoking revolver. Relief and confusion filled her as she took in his disheveled state. His hair was curling wildly as it dried from the rain. His shirt was wrinkled and blood stained in various spots. It had to be from Peter's wound when they carried him inside.

"Are you okay?"

Fresh tears fell from her eyes as she scrambled to her feet. As soon as Lochlyn was up, she closed the space between them and crashed into Casper. "You're alive. I-I thought she   she said you were stabbed," Lochlyn cried into his shoulder.

Pulling back slightly, she raised her shaking hands to his chest and looked for any sign of a wound. A chuckle rumbled in his chest as his hand caught hers.

Casper raised her palm to his lips and pressed a kiss to it. "I'm okay. I'm a good actor. I knew she wouldn't let me live and I was already covered in Peter's blood. So, I let her think she did enough damage and just stayed down. Sam was too caught up in the moment to notice."

That made enough sense Lochlyn supposed.

"Sam planned all of this to get revenge for my brother," Lochlyn revealed. "She-she killed everyone."

Casper nodded, his hand cupping her face as the other pushed back her purple locks from her face. "I know. I know everything. I'm so sorry you had to go through all of this."

"I have one of the Ranger's radios. We can call for help on the way back to the lodge. We-we need to get back there. Xander could still be alive. I promised to go back for him," Lochlyn said, turning to head back for the ski lift.

Her hand was entwined with Casper's and kept her anchored in place. But as she stumbled back, he stayed in place.

Confusion filled her as she looked back. "What are you doing? We have to go find him."

Casper shook his head, a solemn expression on his face. "I came up the ski lift, Lochlyn. He wasn't there."

Shaking her head, Lochlyn wasn't sure what to think. How could he not be there? He'd been hurt. He couldn't have gotten anywhere far if he even survived Sam's attack. "You must have missed him. He-he was in the control room. We have to go find him, Casper."

Again, Lochlyn tried to head back up the mountain, but his grip tightened around her hand and pulled her back. His hand cupped her face more forcefully this time.

"I'm sorry, Lochlyn, but we can't do that."

Her eyes searched his, trying to make sense of what he was saying. "Why not? Sam's dead. It's over."

His mouth lowered to her, surprising her as he caught her lips in a kiss. Lochlyn stood there stunned for a moment before she returned it. It was slow and passionate, something she'd wondered about earlier in the night before this mess had begun. His arm snaked around hers as he deepened the kiss. She wrapped her arms around his neck, pulling him closer.

The need for air became too much as Lochlyn pulled away. Resting her head against his, she opened her eyes to meet his stare. Out here in the darkness, his deep brown eyes looked more like pitch black abysses than warm chocolate pools and there was a new sense of wickedness hidden deep inside them now.

"I was hoping to do that before I had to kill you."

Chapter 35

Lochlyn's heart stopped as his words sunk in. Confusion crossed her expression before she felt a burning sharp pain in her side. Her gaze lowered between them to see Xander's fallen pocketknife sticking out of her body and Casper's hand wrapped around the hilt.

Betrayal filled her as Lochlyn raised her eyes to meet his again. "W-why?"

His grin appeared sinister as he took a step back. As his hand released the knife, Lochlyn stumbled before her knees buckled. Did she pull it out? What if Casper hit a vital organ and the knife was what kept her from bleeding out?

Did it matter?

No one was coming to help her. Everyone else was dead and Casper was standing in front of her with an almost giddy expression.

"Did you think Sam turned to a sudden murder spree all on her own? No. We met in a support group and started talking. We were both fans of mysteries and had the fun idea of starting the group. Soon we got members, and it was going great until Marco joined," Casper began to reveal. "He and Sam broke the biggest rule. They let the real world in and started hooking up. He drank too much one night and confessed his darkest secret to her. He hit a guy with his car and kept driving. He had no idea he was in bed with the dead guy's girlfriend. Small world, right?"

Lochlyn realized now that Casper's story about his and Daisy's initiation game was obviously a lie to keep her from knowing he was one of the founding members.

"Once that bag of worms was open, there was no pulling her back from the edge. Poor, grieving Sam wanted revenge, and you know what? I was all for it. It was fun watching her dive off the deep end. We decided to use the group as a way to get it. We found Ava and Peter a year ago and Xander the year before. Sully was a childhood friend of Sam's and thought she was helping her through the grieving process. Gag me, right?"

He paused, waiting for Lochlyn to laugh with him, but she wasn't laughing. None of this was remotely funny.

"All we were missing was *you*," Casper taunted, stalking forward as she tried to pull herself across the ground.

"You let her kill your sister!"

A flash of grief crossed his face, and Lochlyn knew that Daisy's death hadn't been part of the plan. Sam hadn't been lying about that. His expression turned sour as his gaze flickered to the lifeless body a few feet from them.

"That's why I didn't let her kill you. She lost that privilege the second she went off script."

He was talking about taking her life like it was merely some prize. This was still some game to him and it had been to Sam too. This was never about solving a who-dunnit. It had become a game of hunting instead. It was about being the one to kill the target.

Said target being her.

Lochlyn winced as she pulled herself back through the mud, fighting the urge to scream as her side burned. Her other hand searched the ground for anything to defend herself with. Unfortunately, all she felt was mud and grass.

"It was you who killed Sully, wasn't it?" Lochlyn asked.

The expression that slipped over his face then could only be described as honor. He was proud of what he'd done. "She confronted me before dinner because she could see Sam was losing it. Being around you was sending her into a spiral. Sully threatened to tell all of you everything if we didn't pull the plug on the game. As you can imagine, I couldn't let the fun end early."

"But why me?"

"Do you ever stop asking 'why'?" he snapped, raising the revolver in his hand as irritation started to come through his calm persona. "What can I say? You were good for the plot line, darling. I could be the hero. *Your* hero. It would have worked too if Xander hadn't stolen my moment."

Lochlyn pushed herself to sit up. "Is that all I was to you? A game?"

Casper opened his mouth, ready to answer, but paused and thought better of it. "You're stalling, trying to distract me so that I lose the game. Well, that's not going to happen."

That was all it was and had ever been. His character, Oliver, was charming, smooth talking, and safe. Oliver was fit to be the hero who helped the Final Girl get through the night or was the one to carry her cold body out as the end credits rolled.

Casper had lured her into his trap. He made her believe he genuinely cared about her, and she'd fallen for it all.

Lochlyn had fallen for a fictional character.

Even when she'd believed the games were over and the masks were stripped away, his had stayed on.

Casper had played her.

Well, Lochlyn was done being played with.

"I'm afraid the games are finished now and it's time for you to die. Another Mak James of Lakeside Cove, a forgotten name among the ones who almost got away," Casper mocked as he clicked back the safety.

Her hand curled around the hilt of Sam's dagger as she pushed herself to stand. A scream ripped through her as she lunged. She managed to tackle him to the ground, knocking his gun away.

Lochlyn plunged the dagger deep into his chest as they hit the ground. Both were panting and their eyes were equally wide as the reality of what she'd done set in.

Leaning in, Lochlyn's face hovered over his. "I don't need a hero to come and save me. I'm going to be the Final Girl of this story, asshole."

Rolling off him, she let herself collapse in the mud. Her chest rose and fell as she sucked in breath. Exhaustion had finally caught up with her.

Looking over, Lochlyn saw his chest slow and blood poured from the new wound. It trickled down the side of his face as his last breath escaped through his parted lips.

Hot tears threatened to fall over the fresh heartbreak Lochlyn was feeling, but she refused to let them out. Not for him. Casper didn't deserve any more of her tears.

With a shaking hand, Lochlyn raised the Ranger's radio to her mouth and held down the button. "S.O.S to the Ranger Station by Moose Hollow's Ski and Skate lodge. Please, hurry. Several people are dead. Repeat, S.O.S to the Ranger Station by Moose Hollow Ski and Skate lodge. Over."

The line was silent for a moment that felt like a year before the sound of static flickered over the radio. "Help is enroute. Can you tell me your name?"

"My name is Lochlyn Jones. I think I'm the only survivor."

Epilogue

The sun was rising by the time the paramedics got her down the mountain. There was an ambulance waiting with tons of cops and reporters standing a few yards away.

The medics were able to determine the knife hadn't stabbed anything vital and were able to stitch her up and wrap her ankle before bringing her down.

They were lifting another stretcher into the second ambulance. Relief bubbled up inside of her because there was only one person she hoped to find in it. She tried move, but the man wheeling her gurney pressed a hand to her shoulder.

"Please, I need to see for myself that he's okay."

The paramedics hesitated but they must have felt bad for her because they nodded and brought her over. Holding her side, Lochlyn winced as she slipped off the stretcher and limped to the other vehicle.

"Is my friend going to be okay?"

A head of dark hair lifted and blue eyes fluttered open, meeting hers. A hidden familiar grin flashed from under a breathing mask and her worries vanished.

He raised up a hand and shot her a thumbs up. Though the motion was weak, it was enough. Xander would survive.

Lochlyn could breathe more easily. "I'll see you at the hospital. Don't pull anymore stunts on the way there. Okay, jerk?"

"Y-you've got it, h-heiress."

Once she was assured, Lochlyn returned to her own stretcher and let them roll her to the other ambulance. A sour feeling settled in her gut, knowing there was a coroner's van somewhere loading up the bodies of Sam and Casper's victims.

She wondered briefly if they'd found wherever Sam had stashed Marco yet. As they lifted her inside, a reporter slipped under the police tape and hurried over before anyone could stop her.

A cop jumped in just before she could approach too closely. Her mousy brown hair was tied up in a messy bun, two strands of hair framing her face. Black chunky frames sat on her nose, reminding her of Xander's for a moment. The casualness was not what Lochlyn expected from a news reporter.

"Hi, I'm Mavis. I run a podcast called *The Twisted*. I was hoping I could interview you for a new segment." Mavis held up a tape recorder as she introduced herself.

How was it only yesterday Locklyn had been listening to that very podcast as she drove here? It seemed unreal that the very woman she idolized was now here asking for an interview. Her terror tale definitely had more than one hell of a twist in it.

Lochlyn winced, attempting to sit up. "Maybe tomorrow. Right now, I just want to call my mom and sleep a little."

Mavis nodded, accepting her answer with a look of understanding. Pulling something out from her satchel, she clicked open her pen and scribbled something on it before handing it over. "Here's my card when you want to talk. There's also a number on there for someone I think you'll find some common ground with. Her name's Elora James."

Lochlyn looked down at the little white card in her hand before slipping it into her pocket. "Uh, thank you. I think."

Mavis flashed her a genuine smile. "Welcome to the Final Girls' Club, Miss Jones."

Acknowledgements

Another mystery is in the bag, and I thank everyone who played a part in its creation. First, and always, the biggest thank you to my mom for all the love and support. I wouldn't be the writer I am if not for you.

A thank you to my friends who are my biggest supporters. Thank you, Marilyn, Gabbi, and Nicole for listening to me work out plot holes and for getting me out of the writing cave for fun movie and game nights.

Thank you, Carrie, for all the help and guidance as we navigate the editing world. You truly worked your magic with this and I'm so grateful to have you in my corner. And to Arianna for all the feedback!

And the biggest thank you of all must go to the readers and the people who've continued to support my books. These books wouldn't be possible without all of you.

Want to stay up to date with what's coming next?

Follow my instagram @authoraliciamrestucci